"[A] beautifully written and textured novel . . . [Watson] succeeds in creating his own small world. . . . Lovely, haunting." —*USA Today*

"*Orchard* is a small masterpiece. . . . Exquisitely paced and rendered in lucid, chameleon-like prose . . . It allures, it pulls you immediately into its depths and settles inside your bones for a long and haunting stay. . . . Dialogue and narrative unerringly reflect the novel's emotional and physical landscapes, places of light, shadow and uncertainty that will dwell in the reader's memory for a long time to come." —*San Francisco Chronicle*

"Larry Watson takes the less-traveled roads, through landscapes and heartscapes vaguely familiar, intensely poetic and always jangling. . . . He has established himself as one of the leading poetic realists, painting his stories across the canvas of interiors: small-town America and the human heart. . . . [*Orchard*] is filled with characters who are as flawed as their surroundings and circumstances and a landscape that is achingly painted." —San Jose *Mercury News*

"This, Larry Watson's sixth novel, is unquestionably his best. . . . Watson has got inside each character's inmost being, understanding not only how each works, but how he or she perceives the others. Everything is done with an eloquent economy." —*Chicago Sun-Times*

"Technically flawless and quietly unnerving . . . An emotional and physical landscape composed in melancholy autumnal ochers and chilly winter grays." —*Entertainment Weekly*

"A novel of beauty and power . . . Watson's short chapters are like quick brushstrokes. . . . Throughout, [his] spare prose and exploration of time-less themes, including the difference between love and possession, and the meaning of art, create the effect of a rifle shot that echoes long after firing. *Orchard* is a rewarding, memorable novel."
   —*The Charlotte Observer*

"An engrossing story . . . Watson's clear prose simply enchants. . . . Fragments of memory enhance the sweet melancholy of the novel and draw the reader into the book's rhythm. The author's sense of the land is dazzling, serving as a vibrant element for each scene." —*BookPage*

"Lovely . . . Watson's writing is perfectly calibrated, a balance of restraint and virtuosity that serves his story to the end in this luminous novel of love, grief and fidelity." —*The Arizona Republic*

"Marvelous . . . Showing a deep maturity of thought and craft, Watson surpasses himself in [*Orchard*]." —*Publishers Weekly* (starred review)

"Disturbing and introspective. It left me mulling over the complex characters long after I finished the last page. . . . *Orchard* builds to a riveting climax. . . . Watson's writing is meant to be savored." —*The Missourian*

"At the heart of this provocative, disquieting story lie passion and obsession and the choices people make because of them."
   —*The Miami Herald*

PHOTO: SUSAN WATSON

LARRY WATSON is the author of *In a Dark Time*, *Montana 1948*, *Justice*, *White Crosses*, and *Laura*. He has won the Milkweed Fiction Prize, two National Endowment for the Arts fellowships, the Mountain and Plains Booksellers Association Regional Award, and many other literary prizes. Watson is a visiting professor at Marquette University. He and his wife, Susan, live in Milwaukee.

Orchard

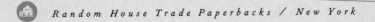

Random House Trade Paperbacks / New York

Orchard ⸸⸸⸸⸸⸸⸸⸸⸸⸸⸸⸸⸸⸸⸸⸸⸸

a novel

LARRY WATSON

⸸⸸⸸⸸⸸⸸⸸⸸⸸⸸⸸⸸⸸⸸⸸⸸⸸⸸⸸⸸⸸⸸⸸⸸⸸⸸⸸

To Susan

2004 Random House Trade Paperback Edition

Copyright © 2003 by Larry Watson
Reader's guide copyright © 2004 by Random House, Inc.

All rights reserved under International and Pan-American Copyright Conventions. Published in the United States by Random House, an imprint of The Random House Publishing Group, a division of Random House, Inc., New York, and simultaneously in Canada by Random House of Canada Limited, Toronto.

RANDOM HOUSE TRADE PAPERBACKS and colophon are trademarks of Random House, Inc.

This work was originally published in hardcover by Random House, an imprint of The Random House Publishing Group, a division of Random House, Inc., in 2003.

LIBRARY OF CONGRESS CATALOGING-IN-PUBLICATION DATA
Watson, Larry.
Orchard: a novel / Larry Watson.
p.   cm.
ISBN 0-375-75854-2
1. Triangles (Interpersonal relations)—Fiction. 2. Women immigrants—Fiction. 3. Artists' models—Fiction. 4. Married women—Fiction. 5. Farm life—Fiction. 6. Wisconsin—Fiction. 7. Artists—Fiction. I. Title.

PS3573.A853 O73 2003
813'.54—dc21   2002035654

Printed in the United States of America

Random House website address: www.atrandom.com

9 8 7 6 5 4 3 2 1

Book design by Barbara M. Bachman

Acknowledgments

Grateful acknowledgments to my wife, Susan Watson,
for her inspiration, love, and support; to my editor,
Lee Boudreaux, for her sensitivity, sharp eye, and enthusiasm;
to my agent, Ralph Vicinanza, for his wisdom and friendship.
Thanks also to Laura Ford, Elly Heuring, Amy Watson,
and Eben Weiss.

Orchard

Henry House stayed out of the orchard's open aisles and instead kept close to the apple trees as he tried to work his way unnoticed down the hill. This meant he could barely rise out of a crouch, ducking under one low gnarly branch after another. The new November snow further complicated matters. It was just enough to cover the few apples that still lay on the ground, and when Henry stepped on one it was likely to burst under his weight, causing him to skid on the slick snow and apple mush underfoot. Each time this happened, apple scent rose up to his nostrils, and in his mind he heard again his father's old reproach: Watch where you walk.

The apple trees gave out well short of the cabin, but the final eighty yards were no easier to negotiate. The scrub trees and brush thickened, the hill steepened sharply, and Henry had to dig in the edges of his boots and descend sideways to keep from hurtling headlong down the slope.

He had taken no more than three steps, however, when he lost what little foothold he had. He wasn't sure if it was another apple he'd stepped on or a pocket of wet leaves, but his foot slid out from under him, and he fell hard on his backside. In the next instant, he was sliding down the hill with the speed of a child on a sled, threatening to slam feetfirst into the very building he had hoped to creep up on.

For all the suddenness of Henry's fall, it did not feel to him, in those first seconds, so much like an accident as a fulfillment—so this is what I've been heading for.

As he bumped and skidded down the hill, he still had the presence of mind to do two things: He held his right arm—the arm that had never healed right—over his head to keep it from hitting a rock or snagging a fallen tree limb. Second, Henry managed to clap his left arm *over his mackinaw pocket and keep it closed, thereby preventing the pistol from slipping out into the snow.*

With his hands thus positioned, Henry couldn't do much to check his descent or to protect the rest of his body from banging and scraping its way down the slope. And yet with that one arm held aloft, Henry felt a little like a rodeo rider, which meant the earth itself was the bucking horse he had to ride.

Weaver had never known a model with this woman's talent for stillness. And *talent* was the word for it. For that she did not have to be taught or trained. She did not have to be reminded or cajoled. When told to pose in a particular position, she assumed it immediately and held it without protest. Without protest? Beyond that. She took to motionlessness eagerly, as if stasis were her natural state and she had been waiting for a reason to return to it.

Furthermore, her stillness had a quality as amazing to him now as when she first posed for him, though Weaver was at a loss to put a name to it. It had nothing to do with lethargy or languor. She did not relax into her pose the way some models did, leaving their bodies in order to let their minds wander. Weaver hated that, and he could tell when it happened. Energy and a degree of muscularity left the body. You wanted stillness, but not the repose of a cadaver. Even when she was in a pose— lying back on the bed, for example—that would have allowed her to relax so completely she could fall asleep, she never did. She was still, but she was *there*.

Perhaps even more remarkable was her lack of self-consciousness about her body. Weaver knew she was not immodest or vain, yet she disrobed in front of him as openly as . . . what was Weaver thinking? As his wife? Harriet had her own art: finding the odd angle or obstruction that permitted her to undress out of his sight. Back when she modeled for him, she often used the screen and stepped out draped in the sheet he provided. But this woman . . . When Weaver first told her she could undress behind the screen, she looked at him as if he were an idiot. "I'm going to be naked before you, yet I should hide myself while I get that way?"

She undressed like his daughters. That was it. She undressed as easily and efficiently as Emma and Betsy had when they were young and he'd supervised their baths. A task lay before them that required they be un-clothed, so they quickly attended to the matter. The carpenter picks up his hammer, the artist takes brush in hand. This woman shed her clothes, nakedness her craft and art.

Occasionally, Weaver's curiosity—or was it his perversity?—led him to test the limits of her talent. He devised poses difficult to hold, like this one, which required her to kneel on the bed but keep her body's jointed parts strictly aligned and perfectly angled: head in line with shoulders and hips, arms straight down at her sides, knees bent at ninety degrees. Weaver wanted all the curves in this pose to come only from the parts of her she could not control—from those magnificent breasts; that gently rounded bulge just above her pubis; the flare of her hips; the long, slight swell of each thigh—as if her eroticism were asserting itself without her consent. Weaver thought that forcing her to hold that pose—how her trapezius muscles must have knotted themselves with the effort of holding her head up, how her knees must have ached!—might break her down, might force her to ask him for relief. It did not. Weaver had also hoped, when he first conceived of the pose, not merely out of a mild malice but out of aesthetic intent as well, that it might at last reveal the secret of her. It did not.

Sonja had often wondered why all men carried their rifles in a similar manner. Had they been taught? Had they simply copied other men— their fathers, as their fathers had before them? But on that day, when she walked to the barn with Henry's Winchester cradled in the crook of her arm, she realized, given the gun's configuration, its length and weight, there were only a few ways to carry it. It was the same with babies. Sonja had heard people talk of an instinct for motherhood, and she had silently scoffed. If one wished to hold a baby, one simply lifted it, without thought or education and certainly without knowledge in the blood. Babies and rifles—their shapes furnished the necessary instruction: *Carry us this way.*

And though she would have needed instruction to tell her where on the animal to press the muzzle of the gun, her husband had provided that lesson on many occasions. He told her about the small brain that horses had, though Henry always said it with affection, and if the horse himself were present, Henry would tap with his index finger that white diamond high on the animal's forehead where the hair seemed to grow in a different direction from the surrounding russet coat. At Henry's tap, the horse always blinked, and when the lids closed over those great liquid globes, Sonja waited in vain to see tears squeezed out. Yes, if you could only cry, she thought; if you could only show remorse . . .

She stood in the barn's chaffy dark, her nostrils stinging with the smell of dung, mildew, kerosene, and sweat-soaked leather. She levered a shell into the chamber, and the horse, as if he heard the metallic slide of the Winchester as another animal's question, nickered an answer from his stall. *Over here, I'm over here.*

Perhaps if she had faced the horse head-on, if she had stood a few feet away from the stall, raised the rifle to her shoulder, and taken aim—there, at the point of that white diamond behind which the horse's brain made its horsy connections—perhaps if Sonja had acted quickly in this way, she would have been able to pull the trigger. Instead, she entered the adjoining stall, kicked her way through the loose straw, and reached the rifle over the wooden bar to aim accurately. In this narrow space, the horse gave off so much heat Sonja half-expected to see his body glow. When the gun's muzzle touched the horse's head, his ear twitched the way it would if a breeze blew down the length of the rifle barrel. His eye widened and rotated toward Sonja. A white rim showed around the eye like a sliver of crescent moon in the night sky. Then the horse stood still, as if he knew his duty was to make no move that might tremble Sonja's will or throw off her aim.

She could not stop her ears to prepare for the explosion, so instead she tried, in her mind, to move away from this moment. And once she did, her determination wavered and then left her completely. What was the use? She could pull the trigger until the rifle was empty, but it would do nothing to bring warmth back to her little boy's body or her husband's heart.

Sonja pulled her finger out of the tiny steel hoop of the trigger guard and in the corner of the stall set the rifle down, unfired but with a shell still in the chamber and the hammer still back. She walked out of the barn and sneezed twice in the sudden sunlight.

Henry carried the rifle into the kitchen, where Sonja sat at the table peeling potatoes. He held the gun toward her as if it were an offering.

"What was this doing out in the barn?" The gun was just as she had left it, cocked and ready to fire.

Sonja did not look up from her work. The peelings fell into the garbage can she held between her knees. Each potato she sliced into quarters and dropped into a pot of water.

"Did you take it out there?" he asked.

There was still enough pale autumn sunlight left to illuminate all the room's corners, but Sonja had turned on the overhead light to help her see any rotten spots on the potatoes.

"Did you hear me?" Henry said. "I asked you, did you take it out there."

"I heard you."

The rifle's bruise-dark steel looked, under the light's glare, like a machine far too complicated for this environment. In the kitchen one picked up tools of the primitive sort, instruments for cutting, spearing, scooping, and stirring. The rifle's smell, gun oil and varnish, was similarly out of place.

"Do you see this?" Henry said. "It's cocked. Do you know how easy it could go off? Somebody could get killed."

When she still did not look up at him, Henry left the kitchen. He went out the back door, and from the porch he sighted the rifle at the large sugar maple that overhung the gate leading to the small pasture. He didn't aim at any branch, scarlet leaf, or knot on the maple but simply the center of the trunk. This wasn't target practice. He didn't know whether the gun was loaded. Never before in his life had he squeezed the trigger of a gun without knowing whether the hammer would fall on a live round or an empty chamber.

The sound of the gunshot, because it had, for echo's effect, the box of the house and the emptiness of the surrounding fields, was both percussive and clanging. Though the dog was not gun-shy, it yelped and skittered sideways off the porch. It knew the difference between a shotgun's boom—a sound to which it was accustomed—and a rifle's sharp report.

Henry stepped off the porch and levered open the Winchester. The spent shell casing popped out. He worked the rifle's action again and again until all the cartridges had been ejected and were lying on the ground at his feet, their brass glinting in the soft dirt like the recently unearthed artifacts of an earlier civilization. Even after he was certain the gun was empty, Henry lifted it to his shoulder again, aimed at the maple tree, and squeezed the trigger. It was hard to believe that the same action could produce both the earlier explosion, when the air itself split open, and this small, flat, disappointed *clack*.

This time Henry did not carry the rifle into the kitchen but leaned it gently beside the back door.

She had to have heard the gunshot. And she must have startled at the noise. Yet when Henry walked back into the kitchen, she was still working on the potatoes. The peeler spit out strips of potato skin with the same speed the Winchester ejected cartridges.

"I have to be sure," he said, "that it wasn't June took it out there."

"It wasn't June," Sonja said.

Henry knew the rest would come, but he had to wait until the last potato was quartered and dropped into the pot and she had wiped her hands on her apron.

She looked squarely at him. "I was going to shoot your horse."

"I thought it was getting better for you," Henry said.

Tears glistened in her eyes, and she set her lips in resolve.

Henry pulled away the garbage can, and before she could bring her knees together, he wedged himself into the space between her legs. He put his hands on her shoulders. "Sonja? Is it getting any better?"

When she lifted her face to him, the tears ran out of the corners of her eyes and back into her hair. "I dream about him. . . ."

"Who? John? Or Buck?"

"In the dreams, he's small. Like a pet. And he's in the house. His hooves clattering all through the house . . ."

Henry dropped to his knees before her. "Do you want me to do it? Will that make it better? You say the word, and by God I'll go out there and put a bullet in Buck's brain."

During Sonja's long silence, the dog returned to the porch, his nails clicking on the wide boards. When he lay down, his flopping weight made a sound like a laundry bag of wet garments being dropped at their door.

Henry moved closer to her, forcing her legs farther apart in the process. His hands went to her waist. "Do you hear me?" he said. "Say the word."

She twined her fingers in his hair with such force he could not be sure if passion or anger tightened her grasp. She brought her face close to his.

"There is no such word," she whispered.

In 1998, forty-five years after Henry House fired a 30-30 slug into the maple tree, a tornado dipped out of the leaden August sky and skipped across the bayside waters of Lake Michigan. When it touched the soil of Door County, Wisconsin, it dug in hard and mangled and uprooted a west-to-east route across the peninsula. One of the trees irreparably damaged was that sugar maple. In the process of the tree being cut and split for firewood, the tunnel that Henry's bullet bore was improbably opened, more likely by the ax or maul and wedge than the chain saw. When the logs were brought into the house and stacked behind the woodstove, the slug slid out. A three-year-old girl, believing it was a pebble, picked it up. Even her child's hand could tell it had a warmth and softness unlike any stone.

Henry turned his back to the bar, and with both hands held his rifle overhead. He raised his voice so all the patrons of the Top Deck Tavern could hear him.

"Can I have your attention? I got a Winchester thirty-thirty here I'm willing to sell to the highest bidder."

A man at a table near the window shouted out, "What's the matter, Henry—won't your wife let you out hunting no more?"

Henry ignored him. "Those of you know me know I take care of my equipment. The man who buys this rifle will get himself a clean gun that shoots true and has never jammed."

A cigar smoker sitting a few stools away from Henry said, "If it shoots so goddamn straight, why're you selling it." He didn't pose this as a question, and his companion, the only man in the bar wearing a tie, said, "A fellow hard up for cash and in a hurry. Always a bad combination."

The bartender wiped off the bar where only a moment earlier the rifle had lain. He inspected his rag as though he expected it to show a stain of gun oil. "Suppose I bid a buck," he said confidentially to Henry, "and that's the only offer you get."

Over his shoulder Henry said, "Then you got yourself a rifle and I'm a dollar richer."

"Jesus, Henry. You could just as well give it away."

"If it comes down to it, Owen, I might do exactly that."

From the end of the bar, a man sitting alone said, "What the hell. I'll give you fifty dollars for your rifle." If it weren't for the voice—as deep and casually precise as a radio announcer's—you might have thought, as you squinted through the Top Deck's dim light, that this offer came from a boy, so slight was the figure perched on the stool.

"Maybe you're joking, mister," Henry said, "but I'm bringing this gun over to you and I expect to get paid in return."

"For Christ's sake, Henry," Owen said. "You don't want to do this. If you're strapped for cash, there's other ways."

Henry looked down at the Winchester as if he were contemplating an object that already belonged to another.

"I could help you out myself," Owen said.

"If you want to help me," Henry said, "offer me fifty-one dollars and take this gun out of my hands."

Meanwhile, the short man at the end of the bar had climbed off his stool, taken out his billfold, and was counting off fives and tens on the bar. "And that's fifty." He knocked on the small stack of bills and then spread his arms wide.

Henry walked over and extended the rifle. "Mister, you bought yourself a Winchester." He swept up the bills and without counting them stuffed them into the front pocket of his dungarees.

The rifle's new owner hefted the gun and tilted it back and forth the way a tightrope walker might hold his balancing pole.

Look here, Henry wanted to say, you buy yourself a rifle you don't want to check its weight; you want to bring it to your shoulder, peer down its sights, work its action.

Instead, this slight, wiry man dressed in a white shirt and paint-splattered khakis leaned the rifle against the bar, and then stepped back and cocked his head as if his main concern were with how the blue-black steel caught the light. When he lifted it again, he picked it up by the barrel and passed the bore under his nose. "It's been fired recently."

Maybe this fellow knew guns better than Henry thought. "I wanted to make sure it was firing properly."

"Why would you have any doubt?" He laid it back down on the bar and picked up his drink.

The man had a way of locking you in with his narrow-eyed gaze and holding you longer than you liked. Now he arched his eyebrows as if he expected Henry to blurt out a confession that would reveal his real reason for firing the rifle. *I only killed a maple tree, mister.*

"You can sight it in all you like," Henry said. "It's always going to shoot a tad high."

"What was all that talk about straight shooting? Was that just advertising?"

"It shoots straight. Just a little high."

"Whoa. Take it easy. You don't have to defend your rifle's honor. I don't give a damn if it shoots around corners. I have no interest in firing the thing."

"What do you want it for then?"

The man regarded the rifle once again in that head-cocked way. "I'm going to paint it."

He glanced down at the streaks, smears, and splatterings of white, gray, brown, black, yellow, and green paint on the man's trousers and tennis shoes, and then Henry drew a breath and asked the question, though he dreaded the answer. "What color?"

"What color? What *color*? Jesus Christ, I'm not going to paint the goddamn gun; I'm painting a picture of it."

Henry nodded in relief. "And why my rifle?"

"You mean mine." He tossed back his drink, then cracked an ice cube between his teeth just the way Henry's mother used to do back in her drinking days. "I wanted the history."

If Henry hadn't felt so embarrassed over his question about painting, he might have asked, What history? Instead he said, "Like you say: It's

your gun. You're free to paint it with red and blue polka dots, if you like."
He chose those colors because they did not appear on the man's pants.

When Henry left the Top Deck, he did not go directly home. He walked along Gull Road, past the Loch Lomond Resort and the new golf course. He remembered another walk after giving up a gun. . . . Henry's father had confiscated Henry's rifle the day before deer season opened because Henry had left it out unsheathed overnight. One afternoon Henry's friend Phil Trent came over, and by the time the boys had finished looking at the French playing cards that Phil had borrowed from his father's dresser drawer, Henry had forgotten about his gun. The faint blush of rust on the barrel did not magically appear during the night, but that sign of neglect was exactly what caught Henry's father's eye. He made Henry put the rifle in a storage locker in the cellar. On the opening day of deer season, Henry was up before dawn, and by the time the sun rose, he was out walking, weaponless, as the first shots were fired.

He could not see a single hunter, but Henry believed that with each gunshot he could name the particulars of the situation—that deep *boom*, a noise like a heavy wooden door slammed on an empty church, was a shotgun rifled for slugs and likely fired from that stand of tamarack bordering the east orchard; that sharper *krang*, a plank dropped from the scaffolding of a house under construction, issued from the stone wall separating Blander's land from Otley's; and that *blam-blam-blam* series, a screen door banging in the wind, probably came from an inexperienced hunter up on the ridge, someone shooting down at a deer running for the trees. That was the autumn of Henry's fourteenth year, and though his father returned the rifle to Henry's hands one year later, in time for deer season, Henry had always felt a vacancy in his life where that lost season should have gone.

Henry supposed he should head home, but he had trouble making himself move in that direction. The sun was low in the west, and if he stayed on this road, he would soon find himself climbing the rocky bluffs that looked down on the bay. So he had choices. He could keep walking and enjoy the view. He could return to the Top Deck—after all, he had fifty dollars in his pocket. Or he could go back to his family, to a waiting meal, though the potatoes that Sonja had boiled were surely cold by now. In another minute he'd turn around. . . . He kept thinking—as he looked out at the ashy brown-black of the tree trunks, the bone white of the rocks, the yellow-green of the grasses and leaves—of the painter's trousers. He must have been painting a scene similar to the one Henry was contemplating—how could an artist resist it?—yet there had been no streaks of blue on the man's pants. Where was the water? Where was the sky?

In the painting, the rifle barely shows. A window at the front of the house is open, and the curtains billow outward, as if the wind has found a way to reach inside the house and pull out the tattered lace. Through that window a table is visible, and leaning against the table, the rifle, only the tip of its barrel revealed. But really, one would have to stare at the painting a long time before noticing the rifle at all. It is the deer that captures the eye, the dead deer hanging head down from a tree branch. The season is obviously autumn, but perhaps the year's last warm day—hence, the open, unscreened window. Leaves, all shades of ocher, litter the yard, and the wind has swept—is sweeping, for a few leaves hover in the air—some of them into a little pile under the deer, so it appears that once the animal was split open, leaves tumbled out.

Winter still—*yes, that was both how and when Weaver first saw* her.

He had been in his gallery sorting through a series of landscapes— few of them his, and those only watercolors he had done years before— and when he came out, she was there, a brushstroke of scarlet amid all the surrounding shades of gray, dun, rust, and ash. She was sitting on a boulder, staring down at the ice-locked little bay that gave Fox Harbor its name.

As Weaver approached her—she was hatless and her red duffel coat was unbuttoned, though the northwest wind was blade-sharp and each gust tore loose a few snowflakes—she did not look his way. Yet she had to see him coming. He walked right along the edge of her field of vision, but her gaze was as frozen as the harbor and she was as motionless as the rock she sat upon. *Winter still.*

"I remember a year not so long ago," he said, "when they were ice fishing out there on Easter Sunday. In April."

When she turned to face him, Weaver almost walked away in disappointment. He wanted her for his subject, yet when he saw her full-on—the high forehead and prominent cheekbones, the square jaw, the wide-set, downturned eyes, the upper lip fuller than the lower—he thought, I'm too late; another artist has already created this work. A sculptor chiseled her from stone and set her upon stone, here on a wind-blown hill above water as still as stone. And then he gave her an expression as blank as stone . . .

But statues do not wear red coats. Nor do they pull back and plait their hair, hair the color of the bur oak leaves that hang on through the winter. And the faces of statues do not redden and chafe in the wind and the cold.

"A winter like this one," Weaver went on, "I wonder if it might just hang on. April, May—we've had snow in those months. June, July—maybe this is the year winter won't leave."

And what did she think of the man who stood before her, yammering on in so inconsequential a way? Surely she saw in him no threat. Even in his work boots, Weaver did not top five and a half feet, and in build he was thin-boned and slender. His haircut was a schoolboy's, his steel-gray thatch close-cropped. The face, however, was a man's, tanned, gaunt, and riven from days of sun and wind and nights of whiskey and tobacco. While he waited for her to finish her appraisal, Weaver burrowed in the pockets of his peacoat for his cigarettes and lighter.

He twisted away from the wind to light his cigarette, and when he came back, she was fixed once again on the frozen harbor.

Very well. Weaver would forgo any further attempts at smiling charm or weather chitchat. "Do you know who I am?" he asked.

"I know."

"Who? Who am I?"

"You're the artist." She lifted her chin in the direction of his gallery. "The painter." A tongue tap at the *th,* the vowels forward, a little lift on an odd syllable—Scandinavia? Sweden, perhaps?

"That's right," Weaver said. "And I'd like to paint you."

She did not giggle. Neither did she blush or look away or stammer a response. All good signs.

"I mean it. This is a serious proposition. Come to my cabin some-time."

"For money?"

Weaver drew deeply on his cigarette. He exhaled hard and watched to see how close to her face the wind would blow the smoke before it diffused in the frigid air.

"If that would be the only circumstance under which you would pose, then yes. For money. Certainly for money."

Was she about to answer? Over her shoulder, Weaver saw a young man and a little girl approach. They came from the direction of the Lutheran church, and they were dressed for services, he in an ill-fitting dark suit and she in a pale-green gingham dress and white shoes. Her new Easter outfit. But her dress hung below the wool coat that she had outgrown and that would need to be replaced before next winter. Weaver guessed she was about seven or eight. The color of her hair and the geometry of her jaw—she was without doubt her mother's daughter. But her father's as well. She wore the same unguarded, ready-to-smile expression as the tall, wide-shouldered man at her side.

The woman must have noticed where Weaver's gaze had gone, and she turned quickly. When she saw the man and child, she climbed down from her rock and joined them. She put one arm around her daughter, linked the other with her husband's, and together they walked away from Weaver. The husband, however, kept glancing back over his shoulder and finally tugged his arm free to wave to Weaver.

Then it came to him—this was the young fellow who had been so desperate to sell his rifle that day in the Top Deck Tavern. Weaver wondered if that desperation had anything to do with his wife's refusal to enter church. Of course it did. Desperation did not enter one room of a family's house and stay out of the others.

Weaver smoked and waited until they were out of sight. Then he walked over to the rock and put his palm right where she had sat. Of course, granite had no properties that would allow it to hold any of her body's heat. . . .

And to think she preferred this surface—rough, hard, and almost as cold to the touch as if it had been chipped from a glacier—to the warm, dark pew where her husband and daughter had sat through the last hour. For his part, Weaver preferred a faith founded on a rock like this one.

This was the wager Harriet Weaver made with herself as she watched from the second-story window: If the woman standing at the bottom of the driveway came up to the house by way of the rutted track on the left, Ned would take the woman to Paris. If she chose the right track, they would visit London. If she walked the grassy mound between, she would do no better than New York. Most certainly he would take her to Chicago. But if she wanted more, she had only to set a foot forward on the right, left, or middle path.

Yes, Chicago was assured, as much a part of the pattern as the art itself. Pencil first. Rapid sketches in pencil and perhaps charcoal, lines hardly enough to flatter. But then a few would be washed in with watercolor. More sketches, possibly a pen-and-ink drawing, and in the cross-hatching she might see how close her shadows were to her sunlit spaces. Finally, if she made it that far, oils. And if something in her remained uncaptured, perhaps he would move back through the entire process. The next time, however, each rendering might be sparser, more austere, as he put more pressure on each individual line or stroke, asking it to reveal as much of her essence as possible.

And how would Harriet remember the terms of her wager? It was simple—the track on the left was the trip to Paris. Paris, famous for its Left Bank, the site, oddly enough, of Harriet's happiest night. And what a quiet, unadorned set of hours it was, if any hour spent in Paris can be said to exist without adornment. It was May, and they walked from their hotel—back then they stayed at the tiny Hotel Antinea on rue Cujas—to Violon, their favorite restaurant, for a meal they could barely afford. After dinner, in the soft, everlasting light of a Paris spring evening, they simply wandered through the streets near the Sorbonne. Ned never spoke of art or ambition, and he never stopped touching her, whether it was to hold her hand or drape his arm across her shoulder and caress the top of her breast. And when dark finally fell, back at their room, after love-making, Harriet stood at the window, looking out at the empty street. From the window box the smell of geraniums and fresh dirt rose to her nostrils. He came up behind her and pulled open her robe, under which she wore nothing. She tried to scold him and cover herself, but he would have none of it. From her thighs to her throat, his hands slowly traveled. The curtain's open, she protested, and Ned said, What of it? Let all of Paris see what's mine.

The month was May, she was sure of that, but what was the year? It was before the girls were born—if nothing else, the way she remembered her body told her that. They had no money. Ned had no fame. My God, shouldn't she be able to recall more than the month when her happiness was at its greatest height?

If she won this bet she made with herself, her reward, Harriet decided, would be a meal of Ned's favorite foods, not a particularly easy thing to do since food gave him so little pleasure. But she recalled that once he admired a roast duck that Sheila Hartwick prepared—or was he merely flattering Sheila?—and on their Friday-night excursions to the Ship and Shore for boiled whitefish, Ned frequently ate nothing but cherry pie. So, Harriet would roast a duck and bake a cherry pie.

Since eating this meal would mean she had won her wager and would therefore be eating alone, Harriet would indulge herself. She would eat only the breast of the duck, and even then, if so much as a single bite was in the least stringy or dry, she would throw the rest away. With the pie, she would break through the center of the crust and spoon out as many mouthfuls of the tart cherries and sweet syrup as she liked. When she tired of it, the rest of the pie, tin and all, would go into the garbage. Others might gratify themselves with excess; Harriet's extravagance would be waste.

She was tempted to make another bet—how long from this date would it be until the results of her first wager played out?—when the woman at the bottom of the hill suddenly turned and began to walk back the way she came. Her stride was long and purposeful, yet for all the vigor of the woman's forward motion, the thick braid that hung down her back swung from side to side.

Harriet supposed she could make another wager—would the woman return?—but what was the point? That, as Ned liked to say, was a sucker's bet.

The first time Henry House walked Sonja Skordahl home, he led her through one of his family's orchards. It was a warm evening in late summer, and the trees were heavy with fully grown apples.

She reached up and touched an apple lightly as if she were testing its weight upon the bough. She had just finished a day of work and was wearing the dirndl and apron that all the women at Axel's Norske Inn were required to wear. Henry thought she looked, dressed that way and cupping an apple in her hand, like an illustration from a book of fairy tales.

"These must all come down?" she asked.

"Beg pardon?" Henry had spent most of the war years as an artillery range instructor in Fort Sill, Oklahoma, and an accident with a defective 105-millimeter howitzer shell left him with a perforated eardrum and the loss of hearing in one ear. He bent closer to her and turned his head slightly.

"They must all come off the tree?" she repeated.

"Every last one of them."

"And you will pick them?"

"Well, not all. But I'll pick a hell of a lot of them."

"They are for eating?"

"Eating. Baking. Sauce. Cider. That's a good all-purpose apple."

She touched it again, tapping it as if she were testing the strength of the stem's hold. "They will come down easy?"

"See for yourself. Go ahead. Give it a pull."

At the first feel of resistance, Sonja turned her head as if she feared with a harder tug the tree would release a torrent of apples. Then, when the apple popped free, she laughed in surprise. She brought it to her nose and inhaled deeply. "Christmas," she said with her eyes closed. "The smell of apples is Christmas to me. In Norway, Uncle Karl—my mother's brother—would come to our home for Christmas, and he would bring a small sack of apples for my brothers and me."

"Did he grow them? Your uncle Karl—was he an apple grower?"

She laughed again. "I believe he stole them!"

She brought the apple to her mouth and pretended she was about to take a bite. Her eyes widened in mock apprehension as if she feared Henry would scold her.

"Go ahead," he said. "Help yourself."

Sonja first rubbed the apple on her apron, then took a small, side-of-the-mouth bite. Immediately her face puckered.

"Too tart?"

She nodded.

Henry pulled another apple from the tree. When the branch whipped back into place, he heard the crackle and muffled thump of another apple falling to the ground. "Here," he said. "Try this one. Give us another chance."

This time she made no attempt to clean the apple before biting into it. Once again she winced at the taste.

"That one too?"

"It's better, I think."

He brushed that apple from her hand. "Come on. Let's try another tree."

They were losing light, but Henry still took the time to select a tree slightly taller than those on either side of it. Although he had never thoroughly tested his theory, he believed that a tree's larger share of sunlight resulted in sweeter fruit. He pulled a branch down so close to Sonja's face, she asked merrily, "Shall I bite it on the bough?"

"Pick one of the darkest," he said. "And one of the roundest."

She reached for an apple, hesitated, then moved her hand toward another. Henry shook the branch, hoping that an apple would fall off in her hand and make the decision for her.

"They all look like the best," she said.

"That one there. I guarantee that one."

As soon as she picked it, Henry had his doubts. She had to work too hard to pull it free, and the ripest apples always seemed to jump into your hand.

After a small, tentative bite, she meekly declared, "It's very good."

Henry took it from her. Her teeth had not sunk far beneath the skin. He turned the apple around, opened his mouth as wide as his jaws would allow, and snapped off an oval of apple flesh. It made a sound like cracking wood. The texture was just what it should have been, crisp and distinct, but the taste was so sour it seemed to bite back. He let the apple fall.

"Here. I'm going to find you one, goddammit."

He led her farther down the row to a tree so thick with apples that every branch sagged under the weight. He pulled off one that was as large as a softball and thrust it close to her face. She bent down to bite it while it was still in his hand. Droplets of apple juice sprayed onto Henry's fingers.

"Well?"

"The best," she said, but Henry suspected she was only being polite.

He tossed it aside and picked another. "Is this one better still?"

She opened her mouth, but Henry pulled the apple back. "Make sure the taste of the other is gone."

She exaggerated both her chewing and swallowing motions before closing her eyes, leaning forward, and opening her mouth wide. She trusted him to put an apple in her mouth, even if she was behaving as though she had to take a dose of bitter medicine.

Once again the bite she took was so small he wondered if something might be wrong with her teeth. Henry had an uncle who, because of his bridgework, always bit into an apple from the side.

"Also very good," she said.

"You're not just saying that?"

"Your family grows very good apples."

"Come on. We'll try some more." Henry had, for the moment, set aside his notions of romance. The reputation of his family's apples was more important.

They walked down the darkening corridor of trees, sampling apple after apple as they went and then casting the bitten fruit aside. Sonja continued to compliment each apple's excellence, and although Henry did not mistrust her exactly, he wished he could see in her expression a sign that the fruit gave her the pleasure she said it did. But since they were nearing the end of the orchard, Henry supposed he had no choice but to believe her.

The trees gave out, and Henry and Sonja stood by a dirt road across which the lights of the Singstad farm shone. Since her husband had died a few years earlier, Dagny Singstad rented rooms to young women who came to Door County to work but had difficulty finding a place to live, much less one they could afford. As it was, Sonja shared a room with a woman who clerked at Mast's Pharmacy.

As they stepped onto the road, the smell of wood smoke replaced the aroma of apples. From Mrs. Singstad's chimney smoke rose as straight as a plumb line in the windless evening air.

Henry nodded in the direction of the house. "A little warm for a fire, isn't it?"

"Probably she has the furnace on too. She says she is cold in her bones. She keeps it so hot it is suffocating in that house. We must have our window open always just to have air to breathe."

"Where's your room?"

"You can't see it from here. It's in the back above the kitchen. Do you see that tree? Its branches are right outside our window."

"Maybe I'll climb up that tree some night. Sneak in through your window and surprise you while you're sleeping."

Sonja laughed. "You might have a very bad surprise if you do. Dottie keeps a hammer by her bed."

"Dottie expecting trouble, is she?"

"Dagny's boys. When they come to the house, they look at you like . . . like I don't know what."

"You tell Dottie she doesn't have to worry about Nils. But she better keep her hammer handy when Bjorn's around."

In the distance, a car's headlights appeared. Henry and Sonja both turned to watch, wondering if they would have to move from the middle of the road. When the car was a good quarter of a mile away, however, it turned off at the Lonsdorf place.

"I must go in," she said. "Dagny waits up." Sonja took a step back and bowed slightly. "So I will thank you now for the . . . for the wonderful apple feast."

She had barely finished her little speech when Henry moved to close the distance between them. He tried to kiss her, but Sonja had time to lift her fingers into the space between their lips.

"No, I think tonight—just apples."

Before Henry could form a response, either argument or apology, she was gone, hastening toward her little room under Dagny Singstad's roof. For another moment, Henry remained in the road, analyzing the language of her rebuff. *Tonight—just apples.* Was any other meaning possible—on another night, there would be more than apples?

Henry walked back the way they came. Even in the dark, he could tell when he reached the place in the orchard where he was as far from any path leading in as any leading out. Here he stepped into the space between two trees that grew so close their upper branches tangled and made it impossible to tell which apples belonged on which tree. Henry unbuckled his trousers. He spit twice into his hand to oil its motion up and down his cock. He had had women before, but now he scarcely went further in his mind than the thought of coming up behind Sonja Skordahl, pulling her dress from her shoulders, and baring her bosom. Just when he imagined reaching around her to cup her breasts, ripe and heavy in his hands as fruit about to fall, his semen burst from him with such force that he was staggered on his feet.

The following morning, Sonja left the house at first light. She entered once again the House family orchard, and she gathered up in her apron as many of the apples as she could find that she and Henry had scattered the night before. She worried that someone from Henry's family might be able to follow the trail of once- or twice-bitten fruit and see that it led toward Dagny's. Eventually they would learn that Sonja herself was responsible for such thievery and worse, such waste. They would never approve of such a woman.

She found a mound of soft dirt between two apple trees, and with her fingers she scraped out a depression deep enough to bury the apples. Each apple bore either a small or large scar, depending on whether the teeth that sunk into it had been hers or Henry's. The last apple she pushed into the hole was his, and before she covered it, she ran her finger around the rim of the bite mark where the peel, like human skin, puckered around its wound and tried to heal itself.

When Sonja reported to work, Axel banished her to the kitchen to wash dishes for the remainder of her shift. He had noticed her hands, and he would not allow someone with dirt under her fingernails to serve food to his paying customers.

Mrs. *House could have taken her prospective daughter-in-law* aside almost any time in the weeks before the wedding. She could still have spoken to Sonja at the church, in the hour before the ceremony, when the two of them were alone together in the women's rest room. But Mrs. House adjusted Sonja's veil in silence. She might have talked to Sonja moments after Sonja became Henry's wife, when they all gathered in the basement of the church for the reception. Instead, Mrs. House waited until the wedding party and guests had driven in a caravan to Sturgeon Bay, to the Knights of Columbus Hall, where the wedding dance was to take place. She waited until everyone had eaten and drunk their fill, until they had all stepped and twirled around the hot second-story dance floor with such intensity that coats were tossed aside, ties loosened, buttons unbuttoned, until sweat glistened on the flushed cheeks of both women and men. Mrs. House waited until she herself was drunk. . . .

Sonja sat alone in a row of folding chairs near an open window, where she had gone with the vain hope of finding a little moving air. She watched Mrs. House approach, a tall, raw-boned woman in a navy-blue dress that Sonja was sure the woman would have worn had she attended a funeral that afternoon. Nor would Mrs. House's expression likely have been more dour at a funeral, though what Dagny Singstad said was true: It would be a cold day in hell when you saw Lucille House smile, but it would be an even colder one when you saw her cry.

Holding a drink in one hand and a cigarette in the other, Mrs. House loomed over her daughter-in-law. "Mind if I sit?"

Sonja moved closer to the edge of her own chair. "Please." Mrs. House left an empty chair between them.

"Looks like we fastened that veil down good and tight."

Sonja raised her hand and gently touched the netting to confirm that it was still in place.

"I have to ask you," Mrs. House said. "Are there any old country names you have to give that child of yours?"

Sonja looked frantically for her husband. The cigar and cigarette smoke, the steam coming off the dancers, the early darkness from the approaching storm—it seemed to Sonja as though she had to squint through a fog to see across the room. Was that Henry's back in the group by the makeshift bar? The white-shirted men circling there reminded Sonja of ships with their sails full, but she could not be certain her husband was among them.

Sonja knew she didn't show, and Henry had assured her he'd told no one of her condition. Had Mrs. House guessed? Or was Sonja mistaken—perhaps the little gesture that Mrs. House made in the direction of Sonja's stomach was not intended to accompany the question. Or maybe Mrs. House simply knew that someday Sonja and Henry would have children.

"My father's name," Sonja softly said, "is Hans. My mother is Ulrikka."

"Hansy House. Jesus. The boy'd never live that down. And Ulrikka, you say? You wouldn't saddle a child with that one, would you?"

Sonja shook her head.

Lucille House drew deeply on her cigarette and then exhaled, creating one more cloud for Sonja to try to see through. "It was Henry's father's wish," Mrs. House said, "that one day a child would be named after him."

"He was John?"

"That he was. John House. A boy could go through the world with worse."

Sonja nodded.

"That's that, then. If it's a girl, you're on your own. Though I'd be real surprised if your firstborn turns out to be a girl. Now, as long as I've got your ear," Mrs. House continued, "do you mind if I give you some advice about living the married life with that son of mine?"

The language still harbored mysteries for Sonja. She knew, for instance, that the drink Mrs. House favored, and was likely drinking now, was a brandy old-fashioned. But wasn't that the wrong order— shouldn't it be old-fashioned brandy? And the way Mrs. House phrased her question—it sounded as though she had once been married to her own son!

"Make him get rid of that horse of his."

"Buck?" Sonja asked.

"Hell yes, Buck. Tell Henry he can keep his fishing rods and his rifle, but he's got to sell his horse." Mrs. House shook her head at a memory that bobbed to the surface. "John took the boy's gun from him one year. Damn near broke his heart . . . But it's up to you: Henry's heart or yours. A civilized husband or a wild horseman."

Sonja should have been able to shrug off Mrs. House's advice as nothing more than a drunk's windy false wisdom, but after her mother-in-law's prescience regarding Sonja's pregnancy, Mrs. House's words seemed to carry the force of prophecy.

Mrs. House finished her drink, cracking between her back teeth the ice that had slid into her mouth with the last of the liquor. She stood, and when she was looking down once again at Sonja, Mrs. House said, "But you won't be saying anything to him, will you?"

Sonja shook her head.

"I didn't think so," Mrs. House said, and walked unsteadily away.

Mr. and Mrs. Henry House spent their wedding night at the Crittendon Inn at the far northern tip of the county. The old hotel was situated high on a bluff overlooking the narrow strait between the peninsula and Washington Island, right where the battle between lake currents and prevailing winds made the waters so treacherous—and the site of so many shipwrecks—that the early sailors named the passage Porte des Morts.

But that night the lake was calm. The thunderstorm that had raced through earlier did nothing more than wash away the heat and haze that had been lingering for days. Moonlight entered the third-floor room where Sonja House lay on the four-poster bed next to a window, and her husband of only a few hours sat in a chair next to the bed. The night breeze cooled her body, naked and still sweaty from lovemaking, and she pulled the sheet up to her shoulders.

"Could I ask a favor?"

Henry laughed. "I guess you know I'm not about to say no. Not tonight! But be ready: Those that ask for favors have to be willing to grant them."

"Would you sell Buck? Please—I'm not asking you to. But would you *if* I asked."

"If this doesn't sound like a trap . . . If I say yes, then you'll go ahead and ask for real."

"No, no. Please. I don't mean it like that."

"Then what? Are you trying to find out if I'd obey you?" He picked up his cigarettes from the window ledge, lit one, and blew smoke out toward the strait. "Or is this some kind of test to see which one I'd choose? Jesus!"

"I'm sorry. I shouldn't have said this."

"You've been around Buck. You know he's gentle. He's not going to cost us much in feed. We've got the barn and room for him to run. I don't know what the hell this is about. Are you afraid of him?"

"It was just something your mother said, and I . . . Never mind."

Henry slapped his bare thigh. "Mom! I should have known! She was against my having a horse in the first place. It was Dad's and my idea all the way, and she never wanted to have a damn thing to do with Buck. She resented having to take care of him when I was in the Army. She tried to get me to sell him before I went in, but I told her I'd just as soon take Buck out and shoot him as see someone else own him."

She didn't know what to say but to repeat her apology. "I shouldn't have said anything."

"No, *Mom* shouldn't have said anything. Was she drunk? I bet she was drunk."

Sonja nodded.

"A lot of men around here have boats. Boats never much interested me. I've got a horse. It's nothing to make a fuss about."

She could tell he was trying now to rid his voice of anger, but he had not entirely succeeded. Beneath this new cheerful note she heard another, unyielding as stone. Sonja had grown up in the home of a fisherman—she knew more about men and boats than about men and horses—and early in life she learned the lesson the seaside teaches: Water can avoid being broken on rocks only by finding a way to flow around them.

The sheet was not enough to keep Sonja warm, and she reached for the blanket, but as she did, Henry stopped her hand. She hoped his intention was to cover her body with his, but instead he yanked the sheet from her and leaned back in his chair.

"I'm cold."

"Well, you're just going to have to stay cold until I get my eyes full. That's the favor I want."

"Very well," Sonja said, rolling over and turning her back to her husband. She drew up her knees for warmth.

Henry laughed. "That view suits me too!"

He reached out and put his hand on her backside, and in spite of the intimacies of the previous hour—he had touched her in places and ways she had never touched herself—she flinched at his caress.

Their firstborn child was named for neither her parents nor his. Henry and Sonja favored the first month of summer above all others, and though their daughter was born in the dead of 1947's winter, she was christened June Marie House. If Henry's mother had any opinions about her granddaughter's name, she did not voice them. Two years later, Henry and Sonja had a son, whom they named John in honor of Henry's father. If this pleased Henry's mother, she did not say so. However, by this time she no longer consumed alcohol, and many people noticed what a poor memory she had for what she had said and done during her drinking years.

Harriet Weaver feared that if she didn't draw a breath of cool air soon she would faint. She pushed herself up from the overstuffed chair and crossed the room. She was alone, so she didn't have to ask anyone's permission to open the window.

She lifted, she pressed, she thumped with the heels of her hands, but the window wouldn't budge. Whoever had last painted the room had made no effort to keep paint from sealing the window shut. She returned to her chair, but instead of sitting back, she perched on the front edge and hung her head to the level of her waist.

October had been unusually warm, but last night temperatures had dropped into the twenties, so perhaps when John Feeney, Attorney at Law, came into his office that morning he had turned the heat as high as it would go. But hadn't any other client complained? Hadn't Mr. Feeney or his receptionist noticed the heat? For that matter, where were they? Over an hour ago, the secretary escorted Harriet in here, a room with a small wooden table and two places to sit, this chunk of mauvy brown velour currently soaking up her sweat and a straight-backed chair that could have come from the same kitchen as the table. A reproduction of a three-masted schooner hung on the wall, but that was the room's only decoration. On the table was a six-week-old copy of *Life* that Harriet had already perused. The only window looked out on nothing but the blank brick wall of a building across the alley, so Harriet did not even have a view of Sturgeon Bay's main street to help her pass the time.

Could they have forgotten her? Every time she put her ear to the door she heard nothing from the other side. She wasn't sure what prevented her from opening the door. It might have been the fear that she would try the knob, find it locked, and then know she was truly trapped.

Perhaps she was undergoing a procedure to which John Feeney subjected all clients who came to him seeking a way out of their marriage. *You say you want a divorce? Well, you sit in this room and sweat over what that might mean.* Or was Harriet left alone so she could gather herself and think about how she might present her case? Then, when the time came, she could speak calmly and rationally to Mr. Feeney and not take up any of his time with her weeping.

Yet when Harriet tried to imagine talking to anyone about her wish to divorce Ned, she inevitably found herself trying to answer, in her mind, the questions her mother would put to her.

You say you still love the man, then why—

It's his philandering, Mother. For years I could ignore it, but somewhere I lost that power, and I don't believe I can regain it. Besides, the girls are grown now. Their parents' divorce might upset them, but their lives will remain intact.

These affairs . . . they're doubtless only matters of the flesh. Now, where men are concerned—

Please. Don't lecture me on who or what men are. On this subject, I'm afraid I have more knowledge and experience than you.

You know, don't you, that you'd be walking away from fame, from greatness? From having your name in the art history books.

Only as a footnote, Mother. And that has always impressed you more than me.

Then you think you could be happy with an ordinary *man?*

Don't say that with such scorn, Mother. But I don't deceive myself; I know I couldn't be happy with any other man but Ned.

Then why—

Because I once was necessary to him, and now I'm not. Now I'm habit.

At this point, Harriet could imagine her mother's face puckering into an expression of derision and scorn, the look that some of Sargent's imperious dowagers wore. *Daughter, whatever gave you the idea that you could expect so much from life?*

Not you, Mother. Certainly not you.

Just as she had on two other occasions in the past hour, Harriet took cigarettes and matches from her purse, and just as she had twice before, she put them back when she noticed again there was no ashtray in the room.

She picked up the copy of *Life* again: September 8, 1947. She began to page through the magazine, but now she was not seeking a story or article to help her pass the time; she was searching for anyplace there might be room for a divorced, middle-aged woman. She imagined herself as one of the paper dolls that Emma and Betsy used to play with, and on page after page, Harriet tried to insert an image of herself into scenes.

"Tourists swim at Phantom Ranch after a mule ride down into the Grand Canyon. . . . Coeds break cakes of ice on an engine to promote Toledo, Peoria, and Western Railroad's refrigerator car service. . . . Dorothy Dolan of Racine, Wisconsin"—why, she lived not two hundred miles from Harriet!—"twirls her baton and marches in circles in New York's Legionnaire's Parade up Fifth Avenue. . . ." It was no use; these lives seemed as unlike Harriet's as that of Hedy Lamarr, who lent her beauty to the makers of Royal Crown Cola.

Harriet flipped more pages, concentrating now on the advertisements, those depictions of ostensibly normal lives. Ah, but this was even worse! She couldn't seem to find a woman who wasn't at a man's side—both of them wearing their Koroseal raincoats or their Stetson hats, sleeping contentedly under a General Electric automatic blanket, staying happily within their budget with Cheney fabrics, waking together to the on-the-dot alarm of a Telechron electric clock. . . .

She tossed the magazine back on the table, stood, and began to pace the perimeter of the room.

Could she die in this room? The notion was absurd, but she couldn't help but think that she had been forgotten. Or was she sealed up here as part of a deliberate plan—one more whiny wife whose tired, trite complaints no one really wanted to hear.

These thoughts panicked her, though it was a completely different prospect that finally propelled her out the door. She didn't want Ned to wonder, after she was dead, *What was she doing at a lawyer's office?* She thought she had been fully prepared to say to Ned: You are a self-centered, skirt-chasing son of a bitch, and I want a divorce. But when she realized she didn't want him to deduce, all on his own, why she was visiting John Feeney, she had to admit that her commitment to this enterprise was not as strong as it needed to be.

Harriet found herself once again in that abrupt little hall she had walked down earlier. To her right was the door the secretary had led her through on the way to the waiting room. To her left was a narrow stairway that led down to the street, and though the stairs were steep, Harriet still rushed her descent.

She worried that once she reached the bottom the glass door would be locked, and she would have accomplished nothing more than enlarging her prison, but the door pushed open easily. As soon as she was outside, she felt the sweat cooling on her forehead and at the back of her neck. The door sighed slowly shut, and Harriet knew it sealed a pact she had just made with herself. Never again would she climb the stairs to John Feeney's, or any other lawyer's, offices, at least not on her own initiative. The day might come when Ned would abandon her, but she would not be the one to make the first move to dissolve their marriage. It was strange; she was out in the open now, and she should have been able to breathe in great gulps of chilly air, but some force still seemed to press on her ribs and chest, preventing her from taking in any more oxygen than she might sip from a thimble.

She had parked blocks away so no one would recognize her car and wonder why it was in front of the building with John Feeney's name stenciled in gilt on the door. She walked slowly down the street, and soon her breathing eased to the point where she believed she could smoke a cigarette without collapsing a lung. But before she could reach into her purse, there was her mother's voice again. *Ladies do not chew gum or smoke in public.* She was approaching the Shamrock Bar, its green neon sign burning through the gloom. Now, *there* was a solution. . . . She could enter the Shamrock, order a whiskey and water, and light up a cigarette. Would that satisfy her mother? But of course Harriet's mother not only had an extensive set of rules for behavior; they were ranked according to the degree to which they branded a woman unladylike. Smoking on the street was high on the list, but it was still below entering a tavern without escort. And now that Harriet thought about it, divorcing one's husband might have been at the very top of her mother's list.

Harriet's Studebaker was parked under a streetlamp, and its light enabled her to see, from almost a block away, someone leaning against the car. It didn't take her long to realize who it was, and once she did, she didn't quicken her stride but instead slowed and glanced about frantically for a doorway to duck into.

And then Harriet had to laugh out loud. Only the Shamrock Bar offered sanctuary—now, this was surely a circumstance for which not even her mother had formulated a prohibition: Could a woman enter a tavern without escort in order to avoid the husband she had intended to divorce only an hour earlier?

Ned watched her approach, and she knew she was being appraised. She could still turn men's heads—she didn't have to walk through the Shamrock for confirmation of that—but she was no longer certain her husband's was one of them. Should she walk past him? No, she had made her decision when she ran from the lawyer's offices. She had no choice now.

Harriet took Ned's cigarette from him and inhaled deeply before asking, "What are you doing in town?"

"I ordered some brushes from Snow's, and Sid called to say they were in."

"Snow's is on the other side of town."

Ned shrugged. "I was going to stop for a drink, then I saw your car and thought I'd wait a few minutes to see if you wanted to join me."

"Have you been waiting long?"

"I'm on my third cigarette," he said, taking the butt from her for the final drag.

"Well, here I am. Is the drink offer still good?"

In spite of Harriet's layers of coat, dress, and slip, Ned's fingertips still unerringly found the hollow where her spine dipped, and with the slightest pressure there he guided her back the way she came.

Inside the Shamrock, they sat at the bar, smoked, and drank brandy and soda, Ned's drink of choice when the weather turned cool. Ned needed consolation and encouragement, in that order. He had been working outside all day, trying to capture in watercolor the drab tones of an untended meadow backed by a stand of hardwoods. But the sun refused to cooperate; colors brightened and shadowed at will, and Ned ended up ripping apart sheet after sheet in frustration.

Harriet knew exactly what the script required of her. Don't despair, she told Ned; tomorrow the light will be as constant as a lover. Don't worry; a talent as great as yours can stop the sun in the heavens. Don't give up; the world is waiting for your work. When they left the bar, Harriet was certain that Ned would return to the meadow the next day, determined and confident of his powers.

For years, for decades, the artist serves an apprenticeship, practicing lines, lines, lines—spoken, written, or drawn—so that he may one day deliver them without a trace of artifice to an audience. Harriet had rehearsed her role so well that not even she could discern a difference between performance and belief.

Why had Ned never asked her what she was doing in town that day?

Over the years, Harriet concocted her own explanation, which she brought out from time to time. It was a fantasy, she knew, tiny but durable; it was like the pretty pebble a child picks up, its beauty and utility available only to its owner. Harriet told herself that Ned didn't ask because he knew. John Feeney and Ned were friends, or acquaintances at least, and Mr. Feeney called Ned when Harriet arrived at the office. "Don't talk to her," Ned had said. "Put her in the waiting room and let her cool her heels. She'll come to her senses." In Harriet's construction, Ned acted from love and knowledge of his wife's character. He knew she'd bolt from the building, and he would be waiting for her. Occasionally, Harriet would indulge herself further: If she had not run out when she did, Ned would have come in and saved their marriage.

The problem was, in order to preserve this fantasy, Harriet could never say, in the midst of a quarrel, "Do you know why I was in Sturgeon Bay that day? Do you? I was there to file for divorce!" She couldn't bear to think of Ned answering yes or no. Thus do our own fantasies cripple us.

"I had an uncle once who was blind," Henry's mother said, "and I swear he didn't go by touch as much as that child."

The child she referred to was her grandson, John, and she remarked so frequently on his propensity for feeling his way through the world that his mother was driven to concocting little tests to verify her son's sight. Sonja would wiggle her fingers before his eyes, or hold his favorite toy just out of reach. She would wave a brightly colored cloth, or—once, and she was immediately ashamed—flare a match at the edge of his vision just to watch him startle. Of course he passed every one of these tests, as Sonja knew he would, yet he was so precious to her that she could not keep from worrying at the least suggestion that something might be wrong with her child.

And certainly it was true that from infancy, John House seemed to rely on touch more than any other sense. He liked to lay his cheek against his mother's hand for comfort, an action that reminded Sonja of how, when she nursed him, he wanted to remain pressed against her breast even when he was no longer suckling. He ruffled the dog's fur endlessly, feeling the hair rise and fall under his fingers. When he lay in bed at night, he ran his knuckles back and forth against the cool sheet. Summer or winter, he would press his forehead against a window as though he were gauging the weather by the feel of the glass. Occasionally, his hands would happen upon something—the crenellated base of a floor lamp, the tufts of chenille on his parents' bedspread, the carved wooden leg of the couch, a stone, a handkerchief-size square of tanned deer hide—whose feel would put him in a reverie. The deerskin he found on his father's workbench—Henry thought that he might stitch it into a pouch to hold June's ball and jacks—but when it became apparent that no use that patch of leather could be put to would match the pleasure that John House got from folding it over and over and brushing its nap, Henry decided to give it to the boy. In truth, anyone who observed John House in one of his brown studies of touch might believe the boy was blind; his eyes would glaze and he seemed unable to move until he had taken in all the knowledge and satisfaction his fingers could bring.

So sudden and complete were these spells that as John grew older Sonja worried what would happen when he started school. He was a bright child and a ready learner, but suppose he became so taken with the texture of the paper on which he was instructed to draw a tree that he never touched pencil to paper. For that matter, the grain of the pencil itself might engross him and keep him from his arithmetic.

Sonja's fears were not without basis. When John was three years old and his sister was five, their father lifted them both onto Buck's back. Henry told Sonja to stand next to the children, and he made sure their house was in the background. Henry had a new box camera, and that day he planned to capture on film what he loved most in life.

John had never been on Buck before, and the horse's textures—the short hair growing tight against the skin, the fluttery softness of the ears— were almost too much for the boy. June sat behind her brother and held him tight, but John was supposed to hold on too. Henry showed him how to twine his fingers into Buck's mane, but John could not keep his hands still. He was patting and stroking Buck everywhere, searching for that spot where he could lose himself in feeling.

Henry hardly had time to step back and line up his family in the viewfinder when John disturbed the composition. He leaned forward and to the side, probably in an attempt to lay his cheek against Buck's long, muscular neck, so sleek in the sunlight it looked wet. June scooted forward, trying contradictorily both to tighten her grip on her brother and to allow him to go where he wanted to go. She must have dug her heels into Buck's ribs in a way that made him wonder if he were being spurred, but to the horse's credit, he did not step forward with his riders. He turned his head as if to ask June if she was sure of her command. The horse's great head looming toward him startled John and caused him to jerk back, and that movement was probably enough to keep him on Buck's back for another instant, time enough for Sonja to grab her son and keep him from falling.

Henry scolded his daughter, and she began to cry. John held back his tears, but he clung to his mother and buried his face in the hollow of her neck. Sonja wouldn't put him back on the horse, and Henry gave up on his family portrait.

Sonja struggled with the urge to push the boy's hand away every time he fell into one of his tactile trances. She hated to see him let the world slip away while he rubbed his thumbnail along the hem of his sweater, yet he obviously took in such pleasure through his fingertips that it seemed equally wrong to stop him. The dilemma was difficult because her love for her son was so great—yes, greater than the love she felt for her daughter, but June didn't depend on her mother's love the way John did—and Sonja wanted what was best for her son. But, paradoxically, this problem caused Sonja to turn away from him at times. When he sat at the kitchen table worrying the frayed corner of the oilcloth with an enraptured but witless look in his eyes, she was so uncertain of what to do that she pretended not to notice him at all. Occasionally she would leave the room altogether, thereby absenting herself voluntarily from the person in this world she cared most about.

That pain could result from being a mother came as no surprise to Sonja. Her own parents, after all, had sent her away from home so that Sonja might have what they believed would be a better life in America. Whether anguish had to be a part of all love, Sonja was not sure, and she did not care to speculate on the matter.

There was a knock on Weaver's studio door, and when he opened it, she said, as if months had not intervened between his proposal and her reply, "I'm here to pose. For money."

Weaver did not hesitate. "Two dollars an hour. But I'll seldom need you for the entire day."

"How many days a week?"

"Perhaps as many as six, depending on what I'm working on. Some weeks perhaps not at all."

"Daylight hours?"

Weaver had tried different combinations of blinds and shades on his studio's many windows until he finally found the coverings that allowed in as much or as little light as he desired. "All right. Daylight hours."

She hesitated, and Weaver could see in her eyes that she was making the final computations. "Yes," she said. "I agree."

"And you'll begin today?"

"Yes."

Weaver wanted her, to be sure, but he would forgo any physical contact if it was the only way she would pose for him. If he had to choose between her being available to his sight or his touch, he would choose, as always, his eyes and his art. If he were patient, however, if he did nothing to offend, frighten, or anger her, he might one day have her for both. Therefore, on that first day, Weaver would not even allow her inside his studio. He made her wait outside while he gathered his pencils and a sketch pad.

He led her a half mile away to a hollow between two hills, a tree-ringed grassy area not much larger than a small room. The spot was so secluded that Weaver always felt, as he pushed aside the branches of a stunted birch and stepped forward, that a curtain closed behind him. The

grass was soft enough to sit or lie in, and a fallen tree gave him a place
to arrange his materials. Only at high noon did light flood this space; at
every other hour, the sun shone fitfully through the leaves, shadows blinking first from one direction, then another.

It was in this little vale that Weaver fucked the sharp-faced slattern
he'd picked up in the Lakeside Tavern. He had scarcely asked her if she
would be willing to pose in the nude and she was stripping off her clothes.
On that autumn day he had her lie on her back in a pile of fallen leaves. In
the painting, he wanted to make it seem as if she had risen up through the
earth, but right from the start he had trouble making reality match his vision. He could not find the right arrangement of leaves on her naked body,
and her expressions were wrong—either she looked blank, so it seemed as
if she were a corpse partially buried, or she looked coy, a stripper working
on a new outdoor-themed routine. When Weaver tried to brush the leaves
from her small hard breasts, she misinterpreted his action and reached for
his fly. Soon Weaver was thrusting into her, and as he did the leaves under
her crackled and the smell of tannin and leaf mold rose to his nostrils. She
did not model for him again.

Today, however, he asked Sonja House to do nothing more than lean
back against a tree and tilt her head up as though she were searching for a
bird whose song she heard in the highest branches.

He made two sketches, and when he stepped back, he said, "You can
relax. Move around if you like." Weaver had marked by eye a knot on the
tree so he could duplicate the pose exactly.

She knelt in the grass.

"You know, don't you, that the day will come when I'll ask you to disrobe?"

"Yes."

"I have to make certain you understand what you've agreed to."

"I understand."

When he asked her to resume her pose, Weaver did not have to align
her with the knot on the tree. Without direction, she posed precisely as
before.

Weaver was accustomed to working quickly, and he had not yet learned of Sonja's ability to hold a pose, so he sketched rapidly that first day, concentrating on the lines and proportions—the distance between her eyes, the height of her cheekbones, the width of her jaw, the length of her neck, the asymmetry of her lips—that he would have to get right if he was ever going to reveal her character and her beauty and still convey the mystery of both. As soon as he set his pencil down, the question that always troubled him and his art came back to him: Must one understand an enigma in order to portray it to others?

Weeks later they were in his studio, and the thin steady rain made it seem as though a veil had dropped over the building, and Weaver decided that would be the day he would ask her to undress.

First he posed her, fully clothed, in an old wooden office chair that he sometimes worked from when he did not stand at his easel. The chair squeaked when it swiveled and clattered when its heavy casters rolled over the floor's uneven planks, but of course she sat so still the chair made no noise. Weaver had her turned slightly from him, a partial profile, with one foot on the seat of the chair and the other leg extended. After a very quick watercolor washed with a pale gray that made it seem as though rain had fallen on the paper, Weaver at last said, "If you would please, take off your clothes and then sit again in the chair just as you are now." Oddly enough, the chair had inspired him as much as she had. He wanted the contrast between the chair and its unyielding wood—a chair that a lawyer or a bookkeeper might once have sat in before his rolltop desk—and her body, as languid as she might be in her bath. For the first nude studies, he would switch to a new medium—charcoal, in keeping with the day's somber expression.

Weaver was fifteen years old when his father was killed on a Chicago sidewalk. An iceman became enraged because a hotel doorman would not allow him to park in front of the Monroe House. The iceman drove his wagon around the block for no other reason than to pick up speed; he then jumped the curb and careened down the sidewalk with his brace of horses, driving right into Arthur Weaver and the small group of jurists with whom Mr. Weaver dined weekly. Arthur Weaver hit his head on a fireplug and died soon thereafter; the accident also left a district judge paralyzed from the waist down.

Two of his older brothers woke Ned with news of their father's death, and then told him to come downstairs to join the rest of the grieving family. Weaver, however, remained in his darkened room, too confused at that moment to face another human being, much less his sisters, brothers, mother, or any of the mourners who had come to the house.

The need to draw and paint had already inflamed Weaver, and while he was determined on a career in art, his father, a practical public man and an enormously successful one at that, ceaselessly cross-examined his son on how art would enable him to make his way in the world. The questioning was good-natured, but rigorous all the same, and as frustrated as Weaver became over these interrogations, he knew their purpose: His father wanted to make certain his son did not answer his vocation half-heartedly. If Weaver could not stand up to his father's questions, how could he overcome the obstacles that stood in the way of anyone who sought a career in the arts?

So, while his siblings' sorrow no doubt centered on the deprivation of happiness that was sure to be the result of a life without their father— no more sailing on Lake Michigan, no more endless summer picnics, no more walks on Lake Shore Drive, in short no more of those occasions made memorable and pleasurable by Arthur Weaver's humor, wit, and generosity—Ned Weaver lamented that his father would never again say, upon viewing one of his son's watercolors, "Pretty enough, I imagine, but why that line of green at the water's edge? Will that put food on the table or clothes on your back?" Weaver loved his father, but he also needed him the way an oyster needs a grain of sand.

Weaver rolled onto his side, but before rising from his bed he stretched to his nightstand, and in a fit of anger, grief, and despair, clamped his fingernails into the table's varnished soft pine. He squeezed down so hard that the wood forever bore the faint imprint of his nails.

Sonja House rose from the swivel chair and walked to the iron cot that

Weaver kept in the studio. With her back to Weaver, she proceeded to undress, spreading out her garments from the top of the mattress to the bottom, as if, without having them thus singly arranged, she might not remember the correct order when it was time to clothe herself again.

When she turned, Weaver did not gasp, though he was unprepared for the plenitude and power that he saw in her when she appeared naked before him for the first time. This was a woman in whom he had seldom seen anything far from sorrow, a woman whose careless beauty brought her no joy, a woman whom he felt he had to capture quickly, so inexorably was her vitality draining away. But all those impressions were the result of seeing too much the spirit that held sway over her being. When her body came into play . . .

Her breasts were round, heavy, her shoulders and hips wide. The shadows of muscles faintly wavered in her arms and legs, and he could see other signs of how a working life had marked her—a V of sunburn at her throat, tanned and freckled limbs—yet when she was naked she looked so eros-charged that any other use of her body—mothering, laboring—any purpose other than the pleasures of love was waste, waste, waste. Reflexively he made a fist, and his nails bit into his palm just as they had gouged his nightstand so many years before.

Once she was seated again, and Weaver's hand was scuffing charcoal across the paper, he said, "When most people look at one of my drawings or paintings, what they fail to see is the story. They see a scene. Lines and shapes. Something existing in space. A man or a woman. Objects. But everything I draw or paint has its own story. A past. A future. Never only the moment on the canvas."

Weaver sometimes talked as he drew, using his tongue to occupy his brain and thereby allowing his hand to work free of his mind's judgments.

"And what"—her speech came slowly, as though the model was concentrating harder than the artist—"is the story you're telling now?"

Weaver tore off a sheet and began another drawing, experimenting with a change of scale. "This will be the story of a woman who stayed away for a long time, but now that she's here . . ."

"Yes?"

"Suppose you tell me. You never explained: Why did you finally decide to pose for me?"

"It was as I said. For money. My husband couldn't work. He had an accident."

"Is he working now?"

"Some. But not like before."

"But there are other things you could have done for money."

"I didn't wish to wait on people again. And you pay better."

Weaver ripped away another sheet. Perhaps he would try a series of drawings, all on the same sheet, but in each one she would be turned toward him a bit more. "It's not that you like posing?"

"I don't mind."

"But do you enjoy it?"

"You've had such models?"

"Certainly."

"And what is it they enjoy?"

"Oh, any number of things. Some simply like to be looked at. They might feel that no one has ever taken time to really look at them, to give them the attention that every human being needs and deserves. Some think I'll make them beautiful, and that I'll make their beauty available to the world. Some only want their likeness preserved, a record that says nothing more than 'I was here. This is what I looked like.' And some pose in order to seduce."

"Who is it they wish to seduce?"

"Me. The viewer—anyone who looks at their image. It's a kind of power." Though her hair hung straight down, Weaver drew strands twining in and out of the slats of the chair back. "And some believe they will become works of art themselves. This has nothing to do with vanity. This is a wish for immortality."

"And that is not vanity?"

"Could I ask you to turn toward the right a few inches? There. That's good." This movement brought the nipple of one breast into view.

"These stories you draw and paint," she said. "They are yours alone? Is this why you ask me nothing about myself?"

All afternoon the gentle rain had made faint brushing sounds at the window, but now the drops, gathering volume, tapped louder. Weaver's concentration did not falter. While he drew, her nipple grew erect, and the stiffening did not subside. For the time being, Weaver made no attempt to incorporate this detail into the drawing.

"I could ask you as well," he said. "Why do you volunteer nothing about yourself?"

For a long time she said nothing. Then Weaver heard what might have been the softest laughter, followed by her voice. "Perhaps I want my story to be only the one you paint." Then again, the sound may not have been laughter at all but merely rain against the glass.

The father's lessons were not lost on the son. As soon as his art began to find favor with the buying public, Weaver never let pass an opportunity to make a sale. He placed most of his work with the Lear Gallery in Chicago, and though Edmund Lear could get top prices for Ned Weaver originals, Weaver eventually opened his own small gallery in Door County. Here Weaver sold the miniature watercolors that Edmund did not care for, as well as the work of a few local artists whose landscapes appealed to tourists.

Not a single work of art by Ned Weaver was on display in the Weaver home, and his paintings and drawings stayed in the studio only until they were complete. Once they were signed, they were for sale, and if they weren't fit for the market, Weaver destroyed them.

Weaver kept for himself only the images of Sonja House, and these he stored in a trunk in the studio. No one else knew of the existence or location of these works, though Weaver always meant to tell Ed Lear about them. He meant to.

From the kitchen window she saw him coming out of the barn, and she smiled when he stopped to sneeze twice, because she always did the same thing when she stepped out into the sunlight.

She couldn't watch him long, however, because her hands were in the soapy water with that sharp paring knife that had once sliced her thumb when she was not paying attention to the task at hand.

Why was he now walking backward, lurching away from the open barn door? Was he gazing back at the site of some mischief? She didn't like either of the children playing in the barn, but she finally gave up trying to keep them out. Instead, she made these rules: They could bring their playthings into the barn, but they could not play with anything they found there. And they could not enter Buck's stall.

Spring and early summer had been unusually hot, and the county was overdue for rain. Farmers and orchardists both feared for their crops, and the resort owners worried that tourists would cancel or cut short their vacations—why travel north and pay to stay in cottages that were hotter than city houses?

Sonja disliked the heat, and when she could escape it no other way, she tried to imagine herself in surroundings unlike those pressing in on her. On days as stifling as these, she thought back to the winters of her childhood when icy gales blew down from the Norwegian Sea and snow as fine-grained as salt could pelt you even from a blue sky. John sat down heavily in the path between the house and the barn, and Sonja recalled how when her father walked back and forth from the house to the boat shed his boots kicked up powdery clouds of snow like the dry puff of dust that rose just now from her son's rump.

Was it this memory of her father? Was it Sonja's wish to leave this moment when the morning was already so warm she felt as though she were wrapped in a membrane of her own sweat? Or was it nothing more than her concern for that paring knife hiding in the dishwater that made her miss the exact moment when her son flopped onto his back and began to convulse, thrashing against the ground so violently it seemed as if his intent was to raise a cloud of dust dense enough to conceal him during this embarrassing episode?

The dog arrived at John's twitching body before Sonja did, but Sandy, usually as placid and even-tempered as a pet could be, was plainly agitated at the sight of the boy and began to bark excitedly. Sonja felt as if she had to quiet Sandy as well as care for her son, but then she stopped herself just as she was about to shush the dog—what if John thought she was telling him he should be quiet, and at that moment she wanted nothing more fiercely than for her son to speak to her. No, he didn't even have to speak—he could cry out, wail, he could make any sound other than that faint gurgling at the back of his throat that made it seem as though he were drowning, drowning in the dust between the house and the barn.

His spasms stopped abruptly, and Sonja was about to pick him up, but John's arms were thrust out from his body with a rigidity that seemed to warn away her touch.

She put her hands on his cheeks, and that was when she noticed the bits of chaff in his hair, mingled so well with the reddish-blond strands it looked as if straw were taking root in his scalp. When she brushed these out, John's eyes blinked open and he spoke his last words, or at least Sonja believed the sounds were shaped into words, but his voice was so faint she couldn't be sure. She thought he said, "It's far."

Sonja House never shared with anyone what John said, nor did she confess that in her son's last living moment she had been afraid to lift him in her arms, thereby depriving him of what all human beings must wish for: to die in their mother's embrace.

Although John had a large bump on the back of his head, Dr. Van Voort would not—could not—say with absolute certainty that this injury was responsible for the boy's death. He had a hematoma, that was sure, and yes, a bump or blow could cause have caused the brain to bleed and swell, but perhaps John House simply had a weak blood vessel that would have burst that day no matter what the circumstances.

The doctor would go no further in his explanation to the boy's parents. His voice trailed off into silence, and he put up his hands. He did not wish to seem unfeeling, but he had been practicing medicine for many years—during Henry House's childhood Dr. Van Voort had been the only year-round physician in the county north of Sturgeon Bay, and he had practically lived with the Houses when young Henry fell ill with pneumonia—and in his view it was best for parents to accept as quickly as possible the finality of their child's demise. If Henry and Sonja believed that they could have done something to prevent their son's death, they would flagellate themselves and each other until they were stripped down to nothing but bone, guilt, and grief. And what could they have done? Well, of course there were any number of things. They could have put the horse out in the pasture when the children were around. They might have kept the boy out of the barn. They could have sold the horse once they decided to have a family. The doctor didn't know exactly what caused the boy's death—only an autopsy could settle the matter, and he sure as hell wouldn't put the parents through that—but he was fairly certain the horse was involved. Dr. Van Voort hadn't found any mark on the child that a shod hoof might have made, but even a glancing kick or bump from a thousand-pound creature could be fatal to a four-year-old boy. But what would be gained by assigning blame to that gentle beast? The child might have teased him, startled him, come up on the wrong side of him. Why not let the horse be as guiltless as the parents? Dr. Van Voort couldn't say to Henry and Sonja that their boy's brain was destined to rupture on June 29, 1953, no matter what the circumstances, but that could have been the truth. And finally the doctor wished that that was the conclusion on which they would settle. They might go on then to believe that it was a cruel, godless world in which a child's death was inevitable, but in the long run there would be less torment in that faith. Losing a child was pain enough to undo any parent; adding guilt and recrimination frequently doomed the marriage as well.

Sonja knew the form in the doorway was Henry's, but since she saw him only in silhouette, she could not figure out how he was posed. Where were his arms? Had he bundled himself in a blanket, the chill of grief finally overcoming the season's heat? Was he embracing himself? Were his hands clasped behind his back, so he might approach as a supplicant?

She turned her head away, though less to avoid her husband and more to escape her own thoughts. Dr. Van Voort had given her pills intended to make her sleep. "If I could," he said, "I'd have you sleep for a year. Then, when you woke, the pain wouldn't be gone—God knows that's not possible—but the hurt wouldn't be quite so sharp. Just remember that—every hour, every minute you can get past will make it a little better. I know that doesn't seem possible either, not now, but it's so." Yet she didn't sleep, not exactly. She lay on her bed, and while her head, arms, and legs felt so heavy she hadn't sufficient strength to lift them, her thoughts churned like the wildest sea, and she would have given anything to stop her own thinking.

The winter before, Henry, Sonja, June, and John had driven down to Green Bay on a Sunday afternoon to visit Henry's mother in her apartment. They returned in a snowstorm, which Henry steered them through without incident until the truck began to climb the driveway toward home. Then a tire slipped into the ditch, and they were stuck. The wheels spun and whined but wouldn't catch. Henry only laughed, and they walked through the drifts to the house, John riding high on Henry's shoulders. And under the influence of Dr. Van Voort's pills, that was what happened with Sonja's thoughts. They slipped the track and spun uselessly.

"Are you awake?" asked Henry.

She turned her face once again in his direction, hoping he would see her open eyes and spare her the effort of using her voice to answer him.

He took a step into the room and let his hands fall to his sides. "Can I ask you a question?"

"Yes."

He wrapped himself once again in his own arms. "If you want to sleep . . ."

"No, no. What is it?"

He walked over to the bed and sat down beside her. She didn't see the motion his hand made, but she sensed that he had reached out to her, then drew back.

"I know you probably don't want to think about such things," he said, "but we have to. So here goes." His intake of breath was doubled, as if a sob was concealed inside it. "Do you want me to dig the grave myself? I know that might sound strange to you, but the Houses have done it before. Not regularly, I mean. But my dad did it. Twice. He and his brother did it for their father. And then when my uncle died, Dad dug his grave too. So if you want . . ."

What if John had not died? Would Sonja never have known that she was married to a man willing to pick up a shovel for such a purpose?

"You don't have to decide just yet," Henry said. "Give it some thought, and I'll check back. Maybe after you've had a rest . . ."

But she couldn't decide, not when her mind kept getting stuck, this time spinning on two words. Dig . . . grave. Grave . . . dig. *Grave* was the Norwegian word for dig.

Sonja could trace her confusion over the word to the day she left her home and climbed into a boat to begin her journey to America.

"Grave! Grave!" The man in the prow shouted at the men who immediately obeyed, pulling back even harder on the oars in an attempt to carry the boat and its passengers beyond the waves that wanted to push them all back to the shore.

Dig? thought Sonja. Surrounded by nothing but water and he commands them to dig? Then she noticed how the oar's blade plunged again and again into the froth, and she knew: Digging was exactly right. Her older brother had taught her some English, and she could see the connection—the effort to displace water was not so different from the gravedigger's as he worked to move dirt.

And what did young Sonja Skordahl believe would go into that watery grave? She was insufficiently versed in irony to think it possible her life could end exactly when so many people told her it was about to start anew. But then neither had she ever thought it possible that the day would come when her mother and father would place their twelve-year-old daughter in a small, unsteady boat that would row her to the ship on which she would sail to a country Sonja had never seen to live with an aunt and uncle she had never met. "To a better life, Sonja," they told her again and again. "We are sending you to a better life." But how could that life be better when it hurt like death to leave the present one?

Ah, so that must have been it! The oarsman gouged a grave in the ocean to bury the past. In went the village and the little house! Under the waves with the friends and all the familiar faces of childhood! Down, down went Father and Mother and brothers, as surely as if they were going into coffins, never to be seen again!

She never saw her parents again. Two years after she left Norway her father was dead. He slipped from the roof when he was making repairs on the chimney, and though he was not killed instantly, he never woke from the coma he lay in for eleven days. One week before Sonja's sixteenth birthday she learned that her mother was dead of a cancer that bloomed in her brain with such rapidity there was scarcely any time between diagnosis and demise. Both her brothers, Anders and Viktor, she met again, but so many years after their first parting that when they entered the room without introduction she wondered who these strange men were.

And now, into her life again—dig, grave . . . grave dig. Could he mean it—Henry was willing to dig the hole into which their baby boy would go? Only a man could think such a thing! If she stood in that empty space in the earth, she would never climb out. It would be too easy to pull the dirt in on top of herself, to pull and scrape until the stony, sandy soil began to tumble over her of its own accord, the way ocean waves rush to fill in their own hollows and troughs.

She knew what her decision was, what it had to be. It came to her as she thought again of Henry's silhouette in the doorway. On unsteady legs she rose to go and find her husband, to tell him he should not have to use his muscles to dig their son's grave.

Sonja was not interested in assigning blame, at least not beyond the sizable portion she heaped upon her own plate for not keeping John out of the barn altogether, but she could not quell her curiosity. Something had happened when John was in the barn, and she meant to know what.

She had reason to believe that the horse was involved, not only because of the straw in John's hair—possibly indicating that he had been in Buck's stall—but also because the boy died with his hands clenched into fists and twined tight between the fingers of one hand were filaments that Sonja thought could have been horsehair. That was all it took. A bit of chaff. A strand of hair. She imagined her little boy sneaking up behind Buck in order to run his fingers through the tangle of the horse's tail. The horse, startled or annoyed or both, kicked out, and his hoof either hit John and caused that bump on the back of head or caused him to fall back and strike his head.

Sonja did not present this theory to her husband, not right away, but on the night of the funeral, she asked Henry to accompany her to the barn. Their home was still brimming with family and friends who had come over with cakes and casseroles and their own bewildered hearts to try to help Henry, Sonja, and June through their grief.

Henry did not at first understand his wife's request; furthermore, he seemed uncomfortable being alone with her. "The barn? With all these people here? You want to go out to the barn?"

"Perhaps we can know what happened out there."

Henry moaned and let his weight fall back against the wall. "Honey. No, no. Don't. Let it go. You heard what the doctor said. Sometimes you can't know."

Perhaps if Henry had put a hand on Sonja—a touch on the wrist might have been enough—he could have kept her in the house.

"I'm going out there," she said. "You stay if you like."

Henry walked with her to a point midway between the house and the barn, but there he stopped. Did he know that this was where John collapsed? No, Sonja was sure she had told him no more than that John fell in the yard.

"I can't," Henry said. "Not tonight."

"But you've already been in there. Feeding Buck. The chores."

"That was different. I wasn't . . . Look, we have people here. We can do this another time."

"Go back, then. They are your family anyway." Sonja knew she angered him with this remark, but when he turned and wordlessly walked back toward the house, she felt no inclination to go after him.

Although Henry and his friend Reuben Rosicky had brought electricity out to the barn two years earlier, Sonja did not turn on any lights. John had no doubt come there to touch, and only by denying herself the use of her eyes could Sonja take in through her hands, her fingertips, as much as her son did every day of his brief life.

She walked slowly forward, her hands held out in front of her. A barn cat, or one of its prey, made a scurrying sound in the straw. The pigeons that Sonja would have thought fell asleep hours before burbled high in the rafters. The heat had swirled all the barn's smells into the single overpowering odor of rot, and breathing it in brought unbidden to Sonja's mind the image of her son in his child-size coffin, her son at the mercy of decay's inexorable powers. She rushed forward to frighten away such thoughts, and when she stopped she was standing next to Buck's stall. She felt his warmth and heard his deep-lunged breathing. He snorted softly.

Perhaps if you stood in the barn next to Sonja House that night, perhaps if you stood so close to her that her lips were almost touching your ear, perhaps if you were that close and you also understood the Norwegian tongue, then you might have heard her whisper, "Horse, did you kill my baby boy?"

Sonja did not want to go back in the house, not right away. The lights there were too bright, and after three days of tears her eyes felt like open wounds. The barn was too dark—its blackness seemed to have substance—but standing out in the yard was a comfort. The warm night asked nothing of her, neither sorrow nor soothing, and the crickets' scraping made no attempt to question or console.

She began to count silently to herself, though she had no idea what number she would have to reach before reentering the house. Twenty-five, twenty-six . . . Just as this afternoon, seated in the hard pew, she had counted—one hundred, two hundred. . . . How high she had to go before the hymns and prayers and the young minister's words words words would stop she couldn't know. Three hundred twenty-five, twenty-six. He spoke about the impossibility of knowing God's unknowable reasons and of the futility of even approaching God by way of reason: "God's ways are mysterious and many." How many, Sonja echoed, and counted higher. By then, she had stopped believing in God and instead believed in what she desired—silence, since it was silence that surrounded her son now and forever five hundred forty-one . . .

From the house came the sound of laughter, bass notes sung by Henry's uncle Alvin, a man who could not remain somber any longer than a child. Sonja liked to hear him laugh, but she did not want to come too close for fear his joviality might be contagious.

She counted the squares and rectangles, the house's windows and doors, three, four, five blank portals of light . . . and while she watched, one of the spaces filled. In an upstairs window a figure appeared, a child-size body in the exact place where John used to stand and watch for his father's truck winding up the hill toward home.

That was June silhouetted in the upstairs window, and while Sonja stared up at her daughter another figure joined June. Henry had searched the house and found his daughter alone looking out at the night. He put his arm around her, and their separate bodies became one shadow.

They didn't know Sonja was out there—they were simply standing together, each taking comfort in the nearness of the other—but to Sonja it seemed as if they had linked their bodies for strength, and thus joined they could block the way to anyone threatening their home.

Who might such an intruder be? Only Sonja stood outside.

Henry's father taught him how to thin the fruit by hand, leaving at least twelve inches between each apple. This would mean fewer but larger apples—equal at harvest. Pluck the fruit *like this,* Henry's father said, with thumb and two fingers, *like this, like this.* . . .

When his life fell in on itself after John's death, Henry found, among his many difficulties, that he could not keep grief and love and work separate. The three fingers with which he pulled incipient apples from the boughs—*like this*—were the same fingers with which he teased Sonja's nipples, and when he thought of the act of thinning fruit it came to him that when God took John He was thinning the House crop and when Henry thought of putting his hands on his wife—*like this, like this*—he held back because that would lead to Henry planting his seed deep enough in her to yield and that could result in heartbreak. Nonetheless, while Henry could force himself to pluck fruit from his trees, he could not make love to his wife, and to hide from her his lack of desire he tried to avoid touching her altogether.

However, six weeks to the day after John was placed in the earth and dirt packed around and over his small coffin, as Henry and Sonja lay in bed together, Sonja pulled her nightgown up to her neck and pressed her body against his.

While Henry pretended to sleep, Sonja ran her hand down his outstretched arm as if she were trying him on like a garment. In so doing, she increased the pressure of her breasts against his back.

He tried to mimic a sleeper's regular breathing, but she must have known he was awake because she said softly, "There is nothing between us."

Henry did not reply. How could he? Her words could have two sets of meanings, each the opposite of the other. She may have wanted to entice him into sex by pointing out that since nothing intervened between her flesh and his, why shouldn't they complete the process—logical between man and wife—and become one? Or she may have been making a declaration, advising Henry that since they shared neither desire nor love there was no reason for him to turn her way. If she spoke the language like a native, perhaps then she would have inflected her sentence in a way to make her meaning clear.

Before long, she moved her body until it no longer touched Henry's. A moment later, she raised and lowered herself quickly on the mattress; she was, he knew, pulling her nightgown back down.

Two days later, Henry and Sonja were alone in the house. For the first time since her brother's death, June had accepted an invitation to play with a friend.

Henry smoked and drank coffee while Sonja rinsed the plates, behavior that struck Henry as odd. She usually cleared everything before starting on the dishes, but there were the leftover boiled potatoes still on the table. Shouldn't Sonja cover them, put them in the icebox, and tomorrow grate them and make potato pancakes for lunch?

She raised her voice to be heard over the running water, and then it was too late for Henry to escape—he had no choice but to finish his coffee and listen.

"My father had a friend—Thorvald Norstog—who wanted to make contracts over every little thing. If you borrowed a cup of sugar, Thorvald wanted to write a contract saying how and when it would be repaid. If he said he would help you repair your boat, Thorvald would write down the agreement saying exactly what work he would do."

Henry lit another cigarette and waited for her to arrive at her point.

She shut off the water and turned to him, wiping her hands on her apron. "Would you like to make a contract between us?" she asked. "We would sign this and then we would be agreed: We will sleep in the same bed, eat under the same roof"—she looked up as if to verify that the roof had not blown off since she began her speech—"but we will not put our hands on each other. Then you won't have to pretend to be asleep when we lie together."

Strange that she should mention sleep just at the moment when Henry felt he would rather put his head down on the table and try to sleep than have this conversation.

"People who love each other," he said, "don't draw up contracts like that."

"People who love each other don't need them."

"Sonja, look—I just need a little time. It's too soon after—"

"Too soon? Are you sure it's not too late?"

"You're angry," he said. "What's the point of anger? Do you think you can scold a man into . . . That's not how a man works."

"You want to talk to me about how a man works? A man does not even need love."

Patches of color—raspberry interrupted with white—crept up her throat and settled in her cheeks. The irregular shape of those blotches reminded Henry of countries on a map; at moments like these she seemed so much a creature of a foreign land that he despaired of finding the means by which he could make himself understood to her.

"The time will come," he said. "But right now I can't."

"You won't."

"No, I *can't*."

"You think I am asking something more of you. I want your touch. Nothing more."

Henry stabbed out his cigarette, and the tin ashtray wobbled and spun on the tabletop. "I told you. Not just yet."

Sonja crossed the room and stood next to Henry's chair. While he watched, she unbuttoned two of the buttons on her housedress and pulled the dress and the strap of her brassiere off one shoulder, leaving the flesh bare and unmarked but for the narrow pink notch that the strap had made. She did this with such deliberation she could have been exposing her shoulder for a doctor who had asked to see the site of her pain.

She bent closer to him. "There," she said. "I've done almost everything for you. All you have to do is lift your hand. Touch me and no more."

Henry had to slide off his chair on the side away from Sonja; otherwise, he would have bumped into her when he stood and walked from the house.

Buck had not been ridden for days, but he was not eager for exercise. Instead, when Henry saddled him the horse acted as though he were being unduly put upon. He kept looking back at Henry in inquiry: *It's late in the day—are you sure you want to do this?* When the bridle came over his head he sniffed hard for air. He worked his jaw as though he had never had a bit between his teeth, and when Henry tightened the cinch, Buck whoofed in protest. Nevertheless, once Henry took up the reins and swung into the saddle, Buck stepped smartly out of the barn.

For the next few hours, Henry rode through his family's three orchards, starting with the one adjoining his place—he thought, each time he turned Buck down a new lane, that he might see Sonja walking out through the tall grass to meet him—and then moving on until at dusk he was among the apple trees farthest from his home. He patrolled the aisles listlessly. The only real job to be done at this time of year was thinning fruit, and Henry had performed that task until his fingers and heart cramped from the effort.

So there he was, astride the horse that might have killed his son, at the hour when the day was useless save for demonstrating the dark blue and emerald beauty with which a summer evening can softly descend. Henry clicked his tongue and wheeled Buck into a trot toward the lake, where the day's light would linger longest.

Neither horse nor rider had a destination in mind, yet they eventually found themselves on the narrow beach in front of Henry's sister's home.

Henry was concentrating on helping Buck pick his way through the rocks when someone shouted Henry's name.

The voice belonged to Russell Kaye, Henry's brother-in-law, and he called out from the back porch overlooking the lake. "Henry? Is that you?"

Henry waved in acknowledgment.

"Henry? Where?" He heard his sister's question, but before he could answer, a screen door slammed and then Phyllis was jogging across the lawn toward him.

"What are you doing out here?" Phyllis asked.

"Just out for a ride. Watching the sunset."

She ducked under Buck's head to look at the western sky. "You didn't see much of one, did you?" A bank of thunderheads had slid in from the southwest and then stalled, obscuring the horizon precisely at the hour when it would have been most brilliant.

Henry shrugged. "It was enough."

"Come on up to the house. Have a beer. Russell's folks are here."

"I should keep moving."

"Oh, come on. Were you trying to sneak past us? It's hard to miss a horse going by, you know." Phyllis stroked Buck's forehead, and he pushed his head in her direction in order to receive as much affection as she was willing to give.

"Sonja doesn't know I'm here."

"You can call her."

Henry said nothing, and Phyllis quickly added, "I'll call and tell her you're here."

Before he could offer further argument, Phyllis grabbed the reins and began to walk toward the house. Buck went along so willingly it seemed as though Henry's horse and his sister had previously formed an alliance and a plan that was only now taking effect.

This tanned, slender woman leading him looked as though she might have been golfing that afternoon at the private country club to which she and Russell belonged. Indeed, the club could have used Henry's sister's

smiling, stylish image on the cover of its brochure advertising the pleasures of membership. The country club, convertible, sailboat, and extrava-
gant home on the lake all came Phyllis's way through her marriage to
Russell, and Russell's wealth had showered down on him from that cloud
of cigar smoke on the porch. Russell's father, Bernard Kaye, owned a
chain of Midwest grocery stores (O-Kaye Foods).

Phyllis led Henry and Buck behind the garage, and once Henry had
dismounted, she quietly asked, "How are you?"

He knew what her question meant: Has grief loosened its grip at all?
"I'm all right."

"Why don't you join the others?" Phyllis said. "I'll call Sonja."

Henry nodded and looped the reins around a drainpipe, even though
he knew Buck would never wander off.

When Henry stepped onto the open porch, Bernard Kaye didn't rise—his
massive girth made that too difficult—but he tilted forward in his Adiron-
dack chair, removed his cigar from his mouth, and patted the vacant chair
next to him. "Henry. Sit yourself down, son."

Henry sat and said hello to Mrs. Kaye, seated primly at her husband's
side.

In front of Bernard Kaye rested a galvanized tub packed with ice and
bristling with bottles of Pabst Blue Ribbon. He pulled a beer from the tub,
wiped off the chips of ice clinging to the brown glass, and handed it to
Henry. Then Bernard asked the question he asked every time he and
Henry met. "How are those apples doing?"

Mr. Kaye did not carry apples from the House family's orchards in
the produce bins of any of the Kaye groceries, but he stocked House
cider, and in the fall, Russell allowed Henry and Sonja to sell bushels of
apples in the parking lot of Door County's O-Kaye Foods.

"I expect we'll have a decent crop," Henry said.

"This heat don't make trouble for you?"

"My father knew about the weather extremes we could have up here.
He made sure we planted only the hardiest varieties."

"He was a wise man." Bernard raised his beer bottle to the memory of Henry's father.

Phyllis returned, and when she walked past Henry she touched him lightly on the arm and said softly, "She knows you're here."

Henry guessed he was in Phyllis's chair, but he made no move to rise. He was tired, and tired especially of being a husband and a father, those roles that had brought him so much confusion and heartache. He wished he could be a boy again, and perhaps in the bargain, the son of a man like Bernard Kaye whose fortune and influence made it possible for him to ease the lives of those close to him.

Phyllis leaned back against the porch rail. "How's the apple thinning going?" she asked Henry.

"Done."

"Why didn't you say something? You know Russ and I would have helped."

Henry waved away her offer. "You've got the store to mind."

"Well, come fall," Russell said, "you know we'll be there with our baskets strapped on."

Now it was Henry's turn to raise his bottle in salute. "I thank you. But I'm thinking this fall I might hire that crew of Indians who pick over in Fairchild's cherry orchards."

Talk soon turned to the familiar and tired topic of the county's need for tourists, yet its worry that too many outsiders would alter the beauty and character of the peninsula. Even carpetbaggers like Bernard Kaye could feel possessive and protective toward Door County. Henry had heard it all before, and he let his mind wander from the conversation.

A desultory rain began to fall, drops so widely spaced and random that no one felt the need to pull a chair back to shelter. It was in just such a rain that Henry had first seen Sonja. . . .

He and a group of his friends, newly reunited after the war, left the Three Arrows Bar late one evening. Drunk, they decided they wanted something to eat before calling it a night. They walked down the hill to Axel's Norske Inn, only to find it closed. Under a streetlamp in front of the restaurant stood a tall young woman wearing the dirndl that Axel made all his female employees wear. By the way she kept glancing down the road, Henry guessed she was waiting for a ride. Henry's friends moved on in their search for food, but Henry lingered, trying to think of a way to engage this woman in conversation.

Just then a few drops of rain began to fall, and she lifted her face to the night sky. Henry was standing close enough to see her flinch when a drop hit her upturned cheek. She looked away, blinking as if she were puzzled by what was happening.

Henry said, "What's the matter—don't they have rain where you come from?"

She turned to Henry as if he were as bewildering as the rain, and Henry, who seldom had trouble coming up with words to fling in the direction of an attractive woman, suddenly could think of nothing else to say. In fact, he found himself backing away, and he wasn't sure why. Perhaps her foreignness made communication seem impossibly complicated to someone in his drunken state. Perhaps her rain-spattered beauty intimidated him.

That memory of Sonja standing in the rain revived his desire, but of course she was not there, at his side, and no matter how swiftly Henry might gallop back to her, he knew his passion would subside as soon as he led Buck into his stall. Henry wondered if he would ever again have an erection strong enough to survive the walk from the barn to the house.

He reached for another beer, pulling the bottle from the ice with his thumb and two fingers. *Like this. Like this. Like this.*

Sometime in the weeks and months after her brother's death, June House realized she had a new job: She had to watch her father and mother to make sure they didn't drift in the direction of the far-off look in their eyes and become lost forever. And almost as soon as she knew this was a job she alone could perform, she realized she had already failed at half of it— her dad was away from home as much as he was there, and every night June fell asleep to the worry that the next morning he would be gone for good.

But June could not keep watch every moment, and when she decided to attend the St. Adalbert's Carnival with the Engerson family, she became more and more nervous the longer she was away. Yes, she had fun, but then she felt guilty because she had forgotten for a few hours that sorrow had taken up residence in her home, and from then on she couldn't wait to return. It was close to midnight when the Engersons pulled up in front of her house, and June was so eager to get out of the station wagon the she forgot to hold on to the string of her helium balloon.

The balloon, as if it had a mind that understood the meaning of escape, flew from the car and into the night sky. June's step faltered, but only for an instant. Almost immediately, she became reconciled to her loss and continued running toward the house.

When she woke the next morning, she discovered that her balloon was not gone, not entirely. Its string had tangled in the high branches of the maple, and there the balloon was caught, bobbling in the wind and bumping against the scarlet leaves. June knew the balloon would not hold its air, nor could it be retrieved from that height, yet in a way she still possessed it. After all, the balloon was still on the property, even though it was available only to sight. She felt the same way when she saw her father's jacket by the back door or smelled the smoke from his cigarette or heard the *thunk* of his boots on the stairs—any sign that he still lived in their home. Her relief, however, lasted only until the next time he walked out the door.

But even if June could not keep her father there, she could still be a maple branch for her mother, snagging her when she started to go away. June knew the signs. In the midst of an activity—chopping vegetables, sewing a button, drying a glass—her mother's hands would suddenly stop, the knife poised over the celery stalk, the towel stuck in the glass. Her eyes would lose their focus, and she seemed to be listening to a sound only she could hear. June developed special tricks to keep her mother there, in the moment. June would turn up the volume on the radio. "This song, Mama, do you like this song?" And then for a few minutes they would listen to Nat King Cole sing "Pretend" or Eddie Fisher "O Mein Papa." June drew and colored picture after picture for her mother, scenes of forests and lakes, sunsets and lightning storms. But June found the very best way to bring her mother back to the present was by way of the past.

"Mama!" June called. "What's the Norwegian word for 'school'?"

After a moment, Sonja answered, "*Skole*. But the school you attend is *grunnskole*. Elementary school."

"What about 'doll'? How do you say 'doll' in Norwegian?"

"*Dukke.*"

"And did you have one—a doll? Did you have a doll when you were a little girl in the old country?"

"I had a little boy doll that was almost flat because I took him to bed with me, and I slept on him."

"Did you give your doll a name?"

Sonja laughed, and June knew she had done what she set out to do. "Oskar," Sonja said. "I named him Oskar, after a boy who lived up the road."

Then June might wince—how could she have been so stupid as to ask a question that wound around to the subject of a little boy!—and she would rush to move her mother in another direction: "Did you have to leave your doll behind when you got on the boat to come to America?"

Had June blundered again—leading her mother to the topic of abandonment—and didn't her mother feel, didn't they all feel, that they had abandoned John, left him alone in the land of the dead? Oh, on some days every trail seemed to end at her brother's grave!

But June needn't have worried. Her mother smiled that smile that said she was wholly there, there in the kitchen with June at that late-afternoon hour when the sun finally harried the shadows from the room's far corner.

At the MFA exhibit of June House-Chen's oils and acrylics, the large painting of a balloon caught in the branches of a tree drew the most comment. The balloon, its slack, creased surface rendered so it resembled human skin, commanded not only the viewer's eye but seemed the element in the picture that had the greatest force, as if it were the trees that were mostly air and required balloons to anchor them, tether them, pull their trunks straight, and unfurl their foliage.

Certainly the painting—a canvas the size and dimension of a door—belonged to the surrealist tradition, yet because of the way the tree and balloon were centered on the panel, the painting looked as if it might be a family's crest or coat of arms, its motto *Nihil est quid videtur,* "Nothing is what it seems."

Henry walked through the back door just after dark. He had missed another meal, and he had not called to explain why, where he was, or when he might come home, but this was behavior Sonja had grown accustomed to. More and more frequently he came home late or else he rose from the table immediately after eating and went out to the barn. He saddled Buck and rode for hours—or so he said—through the orchards. Whether she was in bed when he came home or, as now, standing over the sink shelling peas, she often smelled beer on his breath.

This time he didn't say anything to her when he came in. He simply walked up behind her, put his hands on her hips, and buried his face in her neck as if he meant to inhale her whole.

She lifted her shoulder to push his face away. Since that night when Henry refused her, she had begun to think he might be right: In the aftermath of a child's death, it was best to deny oneself any pleasure.

But now Henry would not be deterred. He simply abandoned the side of her neck for her back. He lifted her hair and began to kiss the top vertebra, reasoning, perhaps, if he could win over that one spot then the rest of her spine would relax and she would relent.

Sonja slid away from him and shook her head to make sure her hair covered her neck once again. Why now? The supper dishes were not dry. There was still light in the western sky. June was playing in the living room. *Why now?* She would have asked this aloud, but she could not entirely trust her voice to keep a moan out of the question.

Henry persisted. He followed her along the kitchen counter, and when Sonja turned to face him—ostensibly to tell him this was neither the time nor the place—he simply took that as an invitation to help himself to another part of her. His hands came up to her breasts, and he pressed his kisses so hard against her collarbone she felt his teeth.

She asked him to stop, but he did not, perhaps because she whispered her plea into his deaf ear, and perhaps because her body gave lie to her request. She leaned back against the cupboard, leaving herself open to his urgent caresses.

He didn't try to unbutton the four imitation pearl buttons at the top of her housedress. Instead, he plucked at them as if they were tight little blossoms that would somehow open in his fingers.

Sonja knew they should not go on, yet for another moment she let him continue, all the while keeping her eyes open to make sure June didn't appear in the doorway.

When Henry tried to lift the hem of her dress, however, she had to push him away. "Hsst! What are you doing—with your daughter in the next room!"

Henry still said nothing but simply came toward her again. She knew she could not allow him to corner her in the kitchen, and when she slipped past him this time, she kept right on going, out the back door and to the porch.

The night air felt as steamy as the kitchen had hours earlier when she stood over a sink of close-to-scalding dishwater. There was no wind, yet she grabbed hold of the porch post as if the house could pitch like the ship that brought her to this country.

Henry tried to tug her loose, and when he couldn't he too grabbed the post, encircling Sonja with his arms and pressing himself hard against her.

After John died, Sonja wanted no one to speak to her. She did not want anyone to try to make things better for her with words when it was plain no language contained such words. Yet now she wanted speech from Henry—say anything, she thought, and I'm yours, even here, now, clinging to this post.

The literal terms of her wish were granted. "Come with me," he said, and she let him take her by the hand, keeping herself ready to yank free if he tried to pull her toward the barn.

He did not. Only grief could have kept them away when every impulse of the blood wanted them to move toward one of those piles of straw.

Between the barn and a small shed that had once been a chicken coop was a tree stump almost three feet high and with a top the size of a small table. The farm's previous owners had used the stump as a chopping block—the blood of chickens who there lost their heads still stained the wood—but Henry used the surface to split logs and cut up kindling.

It was to the stump that Henry brought Sonja. He sat down and pulled her onto his lap, arranging her dress in such a way as to cover them and conceal what Henry hoped to do.

Not only did Sonja raise no objection, she rearranged her undergarments so Henry could enter her. The only concession she made to propriety was to move them around on the stump so she could watch the house over Henry's shoulder.

When they finished, it was Sonja who led them back to the house, one hand holding her skirt up between her legs like a diaper.

"*Now, I'm not going to touch you,*" Weaver said, as he unbuttoned his shirt, "but I'm going to undress and lie down beside you."

He took off his shirt and held it up against the sky. The chambray was so worn that it barely filtered the light, yet it was also dotted and smeared with paint, and these splotches blocked the sun completely. Weaver's art had always been representational, but lately it seemed as though he had been seeing more and more possibilities for abstract works. And what would Weaver do for a shirt-inspired painting—try to approximate on canvas the sun-whitened blue of his shirt dotted with a palette of colors? Or would the shirt itself be the work, gallery-hung and brightly backlit to simulate sunlight?

Weaver unbuckled his trousers. "I'm doing this because I not only need to know what you look like lying in the sun, I need to know what it feels like."

Weaver and his model were alone on the beach, but Sonja still moved her naked body over a foot or two as though she were making room for him on the sand. Or was she trying to tell him not to lie too close? She lay on her stomach, as Weaver had instructed her to do, but she turned her head away from him as though she did not want to see him naked.

"If I just stand back and draw and paint you from a distance," Weaver continued, "I'm working only with my eyes. I have to find ways to involve the other senses. Otherwise the work's dead. A goddamn pretty picture. Nothing more. I tried something like this once before. Someone sat for me, and the entire time I worked on her portrait, we were both naked." He was aware that he was rambling, but he feared that if he stopped or slowed down, she might object to what he was doing.

Only someone in a boat, cruising the bay and veering dangerously close to shore, or—even more improbable—someone in an airplane, flying too low, would be able to see Weaver and his model. They lay on a private beach, a stretch of sand so fine it seemed sifted, on property owned by Edith Shurman, art collector and heiress to the Shur-Fit Auto Parts fortune. She and Weaver were friends, and she had given him permission to wander as he pleased on her grounds, fenced off so the public had no access to the beach or the acres of woods surrounding her home.

When Weaver lowered himself facedown, the hot sand molded itself to his body and yet gave slightly under his weight. He imagined he was lying in the depression Sonja's body made, and his cock stirred at the thought.

"As a child," Sonja said, "I used to confuse sand and the sea."

He was unaccustomed to her starting a conversation, and her willingness to speak, even though her voice traveled out toward the water, almost made him rush the moment and reach out to touch her. He remembered, however, the vow of patience he had taken months before; he could screw himself into the sand and wait a little longer.

"You confused the words?" he asked. "Or was the confusion in your eye? I remember the first time I visited the ocean. I couldn't get used to what seemed to be the sight of the sand rushing out to sea."

"No, no. I thought—I knew the sea was salt. I tasted it. And when my father came home from his day out on his fishing boat, in his—what do you call them? In his face? Folds? Wrinkles? In the wrinkles on his face and in his hair would be lines and grains of white—salt from the sea and the wind. So then when I walked on the beach I thought the sand was salt, tossed up by the ocean. This was when I was very young, but I still get them a little mixed up in my mind. Like when I hear the expression 'salt of the earth'—I think 'sea of the earth'? That makes no sense."

"The sand of your beaches must have been very white."

"I think maybe our salt was not so white."

Weaver laughed and then realized she may not have been joking. "Where did you grow up?"

"Takla. A small fishing village on the northwest coast of Norway. When fishing was poor, life there was very hard."

"And life here?" Weaver asked. "With the lake all around—does it remind you of your childhood home?"

She said nothing for a long time, and Weaver wondered if she had fallen asleep. A gull hovered then landed on a flat rock nearby. It picked up its feet a few times, as if it had to adjust to the stone's hot surface. When it swiveled its head in Sonja's direction, she began to speak again.

"In our village there was a man whose son begged to fish with his father's fleet. The father finally gave in, though everyone knew this boy was too young to do a man's work. On his first day on the ocean, a great storm rose and the boy—who was not on his father's boat because the father did not want to favor his child—was washed overboard.

"The father never fished again, but he kept going out to sea. He rowed out alone in a small boat, and then pulled in the oars and sat there, drifting and bouncing on the waves. From the shore we watched him. Everyone said he was looking for his son, and each day he searched farther and farther out. Soon he was beyond the rocks, and people whispered that someday he would not return in the evening with the other boats. When that day came, my mother, who wanted every story to end happily, said to my brothers and me so we would not be frightened by too much death in our little village, 'Einar has found his boy. . . .' "

Sonja fell silent, and the gull, as if it knew there was nothing more to the story, blinked its black oily eye and then jumped into flight. The lake made small sipping sounds among the rocks, and under the heat of the sun Weaver felt the skin along his backside tighten like a drumhead. He was burning, he knew, but he did not change his position or speak. He wondered if there was anything he could do but wait with this woman.

Since she began posing for him, Weaver felt as though he had produced some of his finest work, yet his frustration had also increased, as if he were incapable of reaching a new, higher standard that this model set for him.

Sonja raised up on her elbows and turned to look at Weaver. Sand stuck to her breast, and while he watched, the grains began to drop away, but slowly, as if she and nature had concocted a little striptease. "Have you lay here long enough?" she asked. "Do you know now what it feels like to be me?"

The following day, Weaver returned to the beach alone, and he brought with him the necessary materials for working on either an oil or a water-color. His idea was this: He would take a pinch of sand from the spot where Sonja had lain, and he would mix the grains into the swirled paint on his palette. If he were moved to work on a watercolor, he would use lake water as a wash and as a rinse for his brushes.

The night before, as Weaver lay in a cool bath drinking gin and try-ing to soothe his sunburn, he decided that Sonja had somehow crossed a boundary. Without either of them willing it to be so, the model had passed from inspiration to control, and Weaver would not be controlled—not in society, not in his marriage, and certainly not in his art.

Therefore, the work that Weaver began that day—an oil, as it happened—was of a stretch of sand without a human being on it.

And yet as empty as that beach was, the completed painting is full of—is there any other word for it?—presence. Those wide, flat, sun-bleached and waterworn stones seem to be waiting for the next bird to land or for the next foot to step down to the lake's edge. The sand is as rippled and scalloped as water on a windy day. But look again—wouldn't some of those dents and impressions in the sand conform themselves exactly to the concavity of a woman's breasts or thighs? The brush-strokes themselves seem to shimmer, a perfect joining of subject—the sun scorches almost all the blue from the cloudless sky—with emotion; cer-tainly the artist as he painted blazed with more than the sun's heat.

The only tranquillity in the painting comes from the lake itself, so calm that any boat that might once have stirred the surface has drifted far from sight.

The work is titled "Absence and Desire."

Harriet Weaver was not allowed to enter her husband's studio unless he brought her there, and that he was likely to do only when he had new work he needed her help with. Harriet had learned over the years that when he showed her a painting it meant it wasn't finished, not quite, and it would not leave the studio until Weaver was certain he could do nothing to make it better. A completed work he might bring to the house before shipping it out, but by then he was generally indifferent to her opinion.

Harriet, however, had reached the point where she no longer trusted her ability to see a painting for the first time and instantly offer an assessment, at least one that might truly aid her husband and not enrage or disappoint him. That was why for years now she had been sneaking into the studio, not only so she could prepare her critical response but also so she might see into the life he walled off from her. She always waited until she could be absolutely certain he would not return for hours or perhaps even days—a business trip (or so Ned termed it) to Chicago usually, but also to London, Paris, New York, Santa Fe, Minneapolis. Ned enjoyed attending any new exhibition of his work, if for no other reason than to needle the critics and charm the patrons, and he used the same rough-edged, plainspoken, prickly persona for both purposes.

On this sunny afternoon in late September, Harriet decided to visit the studio as soon as her husband climbed into the station wagon to drive into Fox Harbor. She knew she had at least two hours. At the end of a workday, Ned liked to drink, and he preferred to do his drinking in the company of other men, talking about baseball or fishing, mocking the tourists, complaining about the weather. He had a few favorite taverns, though Harriet doubted it was known in any of them that Ned Weaver was an artist of international reputation. At the Lakeside Tavern they probably thought that the short man standing at the end of the bar drinking gin was a housepainter or a carpenter, and that suited Ned just fine.

Ned's studio was forty yards from the main house, up a slope lined with lilac and spirea bushes, their white and lavender petals in spring strewing the artist's stony path as he walked to his work. The studio itself, a century-old, rough-hewn, chinked log cabin, was snugged up against a steep hill overhung by an apple orchard.

The cabin, built by one of the county's first white settlers, was the only building on the property when Ned and Harriet bought it, and for two summers that was where they lived while the main house was being built. Then they sold their town house in Chicago and moved to Wisconsin to live year-round. Harriet had a sentimental impulse that made her want to say she and her family were never happier than when they lived in the cabin's small rooms, but she knew it wasn't true. A hundred years of dust clung to the splinters of the open beams and unfinished timbers. Insects found their way in through every open crevice. The plumbing and cookstove were primitive, and the stone fireplace did not draw properly. The girls lamented the lack of privacy in the cabin, and they liked even less that they had to leave for hours if Ned decided to work indoors. They were all happier when the big house was ready for them, though in that brief period when they lived in the cabin's cramped quarters, both Ned's life and work were open to Harriet in a way they had not been before or since.

Ned converted the cabin to a studio. He knocked down an interior wall. He increased the size and number of the windows. He put a padlock on the door. After Harriet found the key, hidden in a mustache cup that belonged to Ned's father, she still waited almost a year before going into the studio. Even then, she might have continued to obey his command to stay out if she had not been certain that Ned took to England with him the woman who wrote the catalog for his show at the Sand Gallery in St. Louis.

Now Harriet stepped inside, feeling as always a mixture of both fear and anticipation. She never knew what she might find. Last year she walked in and gasped, sure she had stepped into a booby trap. A rifle, its barrel pointing at the door, lay on a table. But there were no trip wires attached to the trigger; the rifle was simply another of Ned's props. Six months later it appeared in a painting. She could as easily discover that Ned had begun an exciting new phase—the watercolor series of weather over the lake, for example, each painting representing the storm of a different season. Or she might happen upon the evidence that Ned had found a new model, as when Harriet saw the painting of a familiar-looking woman seated naked on Ned's footlocker. Harriet finally placed her as Dr. Van Voort's nurse. Ned had cut his ankle scrambling around the rocks below the Egg Island lighthouse, and his leg became infected, necessitating frequent visits to Dr. Van Voort's office. Obviously those trips had also provided Ned the opportunity to persuade the dark-haired nurse to pose, not that women usually needed much persuading. Either they knew of his stature as an artist or they succumbed to his charm, which he knew how to wield almost as well as a drawing pencil. Harriet had long ago reconciled herself to the fact that when Ned's models were females and attractive, the chances were excellent that he fucked them. How did she know this? She knew her husband, and how his art—the act of making it rather than the made object—stimulated him almost beyond release. She remembered well the demonstration he had once given. He picked up a red sable brush, spread its hairs, then wet them between his lips so they came together in a stiletto point. He held up his forearm, and while she and others watched, he somehow made the hairs on his arm stand up, though there was no chill in the room. "See," Ned said to those assembled around the Weavers' dining room table—Harriet, the novelist Jake Bram and his wife, Caroline, along with the writer from *Art and Artists* there to do the article on Ned—"that's what painting does to me. It's as if my whole body is trying to turn into a brush, and if I could figure out a way to paint with *these* hairs, I'd do it." The entire episode (none of which made it into the printed article unless one counted the sentence "Weaver brings his entire being to every work") seemed to Harriet akin to a parlor trick, but it expressed, no matter how crudely, a truth about Ned and his attitude toward his art.

She also knew, from those long-ago years of posing for him herself, of how in Ned the wires connecting art and sex were hopelessly crossed. In her memory, it seemed as if most sessions ended with Ned saying, "That's it. You can relax. We're done for the day," followed by the sound of his belt unbuckling. Some days she had been posing for only minutes before Ned made his way out from behind the easel.

But it wasn't only Harriet's insight into Ned's artistic soul that provided her with proof of his infidelity. She needn't be so lofty. Ned seldom cleaned the studio, and on more than one occasion she found his discarded condoms under the iron cot next to the window. She had long since given up trying to gather evidence to convict her husband of cheating on her. She had never made use of what she already found—why would she wish to gather more? No, on that day, it was art she was looking for, not adultery.

She stepped carefully through the usual detritus of the studio—the coffee cans filled with brushes, the piles of rags, the empty paint tubes, the palettes so clotted with paint they were no longer usable, the paper balled up and tossed aside, the ashtrays brimming with cigarette butts, the empty coffee cups and Coca-Cola bottles. If Ned were to die, Harriet would immediately run to this place, where his presence was so strong it felt as if it could ward off death. Then, when it seemed at last as though his spirit had left even the studio, when she could walk through these rooms without feeling she might at any moment hear his voice—his basso profundo voice demanding to know what the hell she was doing in here—she would leave the building and perhaps Door County forever.

Now, however, the easel held new work, and Harriet made her way toward it as surely as if it were lit by a spotlight and hanging in a gallery.

It was an oil, and it was larger than most of Ned's works, maybe three feet high and four feet wide. On the canvas was a reclining nude, the young woman lying on the cot under the studio's east window.

Ned liked to pose his subjects next to a window—to take advantage of natural light, he said—and Harriet didn't doubt that was so, although he had another motivation as well. He liked to expose his models, as this woman's backside was exposed to anyone in a position to look through the window, as unlikely as that might be considering how close the cabin was to the wooded hillside. Nevertheless . . .

Years ago, the Weavers lived briefly in Manhattan while Ned taught at the New York School of Art, his only brush with academia, such as it was. They lived on the eighteenth floor of a Midtown apartment building, and it was there that Ned painted "Solstice," which featured Harriet lying naked on the bed while the afternoon sun bathed her in its dying light. Harriet asked Ned to close the curtains—if she could see people in the surrounding office and apartment buildings then certainly they could see her. Ned refused. The light, he said, the city sunlight glancing off glass and stone before finding her, could not be duplicated.

Ned posed her with her head hanging over the foot of the bed staring up at the sky—and at the banks of windows where she was sure innumerable eyes were trained on her. At least they didn't know who she was, she told herself; at least her body looked good.

"You're blushing," Ned said. "Perfect!" He loved the way her embarrassment pinked her pale flesh and contrasted with the sun's efforts to leach all the color from her and the rest of the room. What he called her blush, she thought, might have been blood rushing to her head.

The next day Ned put his brushes aside early, but before he undressed to join Harriet on the bed, he drew the curtains.

"So," she said, "people can see me, but they can't see you."

"That's right," Ned said. "They can see you, but they can't see me."

She knew too that this statement was not only a literal fact but also had something to do with his desire for his work to be seen while he remained invisible. What she didn't know was whether she, as she lay revealed on that bed, counted as one of his works. She could not brood on the question for long; during those years, Ned's sexual needs had an urgency that took her breath away and left her feeling as though she should search herself for bruises in the aftermath of love.

Back then, Harriet had both posed and offered suggestions on the painting. It had been years now since Ned had wanted to draw or paint her, but thank God he still valued her opinions. She didn't know what she'd do if the day came when he no longer needed her on either side of the easel.

The nude woman in the new painting lay on her side, stretched out with one hand tucked under her cheek, the other hand extended off the bed. She lay as unselfconsciously exposed as a sleeper.

Ned had done something in this painting that Harriet had never seen before. The portrait was filled with his signature photographic details— the veins standing out in her long, bony feet, the scuffs of dirt on her knees as if she had recently been kneeling on the earth, the rust-colored pubic patch so sharply rendered the coils of individual hairs were visible, the tracks where childbearing had stretched her skin beyond its ability to spring back, and her breasts, her breasts, detailed down to the tiny milk slit in each nipple, painted so that—my God, how did Ned do it!—it seemed as though the viewer could know the weight and feel of each one in hand. But for all the exactitude of this woman's interior lines, Ned had blurred her outline in places so it seemed as though she were losing herself to the world outside her body. The fingers of her outstretched arm were losing their individuation. The curve of her hip seemed to vanish in the colors of the wall behind her. Her shoulder was losing its definition of muscularity. The pillow bunched under her head was draining the ruddy color from her cheek.

Harriet had seen Ned do something like this with watercolors, but this was different. And the painting did not seem unfinished. No, Ned saw that this woman was in danger of dissolving, whether from her own sense of self or from Ned's sight, Harriet couldn't be sure.

She looked away from the blurred borders and returned her attention to the woman's wide-eyed gaze. Ned had done her eyes with such care that Harriet could see the striations of the iris, the glint of light in the pupil. The woman stared straight ahead, as if she could see into the future, and nothing there promised any end to her sorrow.

Harriet stepped forward and tentatively touched a spot on the canvas that seemed to glisten. She hoped the surface would be tacky, the paint still wet. That would mean the portrait was definitely not finished; Ned might decide yet to alter her expression. And if Harriet's finger came back dotted with ocher that would mean Ned had worked on the painting that afternoon. Harriet was sure no model had entered today—perhaps Ned was working not from life but from memory. Perhaps, as he put brush to canvas, he was thinking of no one but Harriet. God knew, Ned could have seen that look often enough in her eyes.

The paint was dry.

Nearly two years before, Henry, Nils Singstad, and Reuben Rosicky were fishing the early ice down on the Oxbow, a kink in the backwaters of the Grouse River, when they realized they had the wrong bait. Henry volunteered to drive back into town to pick up some wax worms, and since they had all ridden down in Reuben's truck, it was Reuben's truck Henry drove back up the hill.

There was fresh snow that day too; it had fallen all night, and when it finally ended, more than six inches of heavy, wet snow covered the ground. Henry had to gear down and gun it hard to make it up the steep, twisting trail. Halfway up, the narrow path veered sharply to the right, but the truck slid to the left, heading for the trunk of a massive oak. No matter how hard Henry turned the wheel, he couldn't do anything to alter the course of what seemed the certain collision of truck and tree. Strangely, Henry did not think at all of his own safety or survival at this moment, but only about what would be his shame over wrecking Reuben's truck.

But the next thing Henry knew, he fishtailed past the tree and slipped back on course up the hill. He had not asked for the aid of providence, yet it seemed as though nothing less than the hand of God could have kept him from crashing into that oak tree.

Similarly, Henry could think of nothing—no impediment, force, or spirit—that might have halted his feetfirst slide toward the cabin's chinked walls, but halt he did and once again a collision that seemed fated was averted.

Nevertheless, even though his fall was stopped, Henry did not get back on his feet, not right away. He scooted forward on his backside until he was up against the cabin. If anyone had seen him stumbling, scraping, and sliding down the hill, they would certainly appear soon, so Henry stood slowly, kept his back pressed to the log wall, and listened for a window to raise or a door to slam. While he waited, Henry did inventory. He did not have to feel for the pistol; its weight in his pocket was so unfamiliar its presence unbalanced him. He patted his other pocket to make sure the box of kitchen matches was there. If no one came out in the next minute or two, Henry would proceed with his plan.

He was on the east side of the cabin, and he thought Max had said it was through an east window he had seen her. But that hill Henry came down was so steep and overgrown—could Max have looked in through a window on the north or south? Henry would simply have to peer in each one until he saw her for himself.

The children were lined up at the back of the school gymnasium, waiting for the piano chord that signaled they were to begin marching up the aisles. Sonja was twisted around in her folding chair, trying to find June, and that was the very moment Henry chose to tell her that the previous Saturday he'd almost wrecked Reuben Rosicky's truck driving up from the Oxbow.

Sonja spun quickly back to face her husband.

"That's right," Henry said. "I thought for sure I was going to pile into a tree." He shook his head and chuckled at the memory. "I looked up and there it was, like it had been planted smack-dab in my path. Of course, it was there first, so there wasn't much I could do but try to go around it."

Sonja leaned forward to try to determine if he had been drinking, but that made no sense—it was not now she wanted to know about, but then.

"And you know what I was thinking when I was headed for that tree?"

That within a year's time I would have lost both my son and my husband, Sonja thought to say, but instead she shook her head. Perhaps he wasn't really talking to her. She could hardly be the right audience for Henry's little story, because he plainly considered it humorous, yet while she listened she felt her stomach tighten and go cold while her scalp hotly prickled.

Mrs. Manserus, the music teacher, began to play "Joy to the World," and the children started to sing and march forward. Their voices wobbled and teetered at first, but by the time they reached "The Lord is come," they found their balance. Similarly, their initial steps up the aisle were bunched and halting, but that rhythm soon returned to them as well. The angels, of which June was one, came last, and because of their wings, they had to keep a greater distance between each other than Joseph and Mary, the shepherds, the wise men, or the children without costume.

"I thought," Henry said, "Reuben's going to kill me when he sees what I did to his truck. But just as sudden it came to me—what the hell does it matter? I'll likely be dead myself."

Sonja placed her hand gently over her husband's mouth, but she did not stop his speech for the sake of their daughter, who was coming closer, or for the rest of the children or for their parents seated nearby or for the holiday itself or for any reason except that she could not hear any more of accidents or death.

When June marched past, she did not look in her parents' direction, but that was all right; Sonja knew June was concentrating on remembering the words to the carol and on keeping the proper spacing between herself and the angel in front of her. June looked so lovely that no real angel could equal her beauty, but then Sonja had to banish that thought. If there were angels in heaven such as these, they could only be the souls of dead children, like her son, and therefore, to keep from thinking of June and death in such proximity, Sonja had to tell herself that these were merely earth's children, the sons and daughters of the mothers and fathers who helped build those wings of wire, cardboard, and aluminum foil.

Snow had been falling when they entered the school for the program, but it was coming down much harder now, a heavy, wet snow that resisted the rising wind's efforts to blow the flakes off their fast, vertical descent. Henry and Sonja sat in the truck waiting for June. The heater ran full strength, but so far it wheezed out only cold air. Henry turned on the windshield wipers, but they could not keep up with the snow that seemed to splat against the glass in clumps. They had only a thirteen-mile drive home, but Henry knew the road would be slick and he'd be lucky if he could see a hundred yards.

He began to bounce his legs impatiently.

"Are you cold?" Sonja asked.

"Not especially, but I'd like to start before it gets worse."

"The teacher has gifts for them. Do you want me to go in and hurry her along?"

Henry could have said, yes, we have to get going. He could have pointed out that they didn't have any weight in the back of the truck for traction, and he hadn't gotten around to putting on the snow tires. He was worried they might not get out of the parking lot, or, worse, start for home and slide off the road. But although he was still angry with Sonja for shushing him when he tried to tell her about driving up from the Oxbow, he kept all his concerns about the weather and the roads to himself.

"Let her get her present," he said.

In another moment, June came running toward the truck, her knees lifting high to help her clear the ridges of snow made by the tires of the cars that had already left the lot. Once June was inside the truck, both her father and mother edged closer to her so their bodies might help warm their daughter.

Outside town, conditions were worse. The wind was having its way now, hurling snow at the truck as if its motion were an affront to the storm. Henry gripped the steering wheel and tried to keep the truck aimed toward the double track that vanished and appeared at the wind's caprice.

Henry wished he would have gone ahead and told Sonja about what happened with Reuben's truck. He hadn't meant to alarm her with the story. Just the opposite—it had a theme that he thought might hearten her. When he was heading for that oak tree, he had no doubt: He was going to hit the tree head-on, and all his efforts to avoid it would come to naught. And then he was past, safe, not so much as a scrape of fender and bark.

And that was what he wanted to convey to Sonja, that perhaps a measure of power and control was edging back into their lives. The lesson of John's death was wrong. They didn't have to lie down and submit. What looked to be inevitable might not be, and if Sonja could have been with him in Reuben's truck, if she could have felt what he felt when he arrived intact at the top of the hill—the exhilaration!—she'd understand.

The episode had been so seductive that Henry couldn't help but flirt with its counterpart out here on the snow-packed hills, curves, and straightaways of Highway 42. He drove a little too fast for the reach of his headlights, and when the truck's tires began to slide he waited just an instant longer than he should have, letting the danger rise into his throat before he steered them back on track.

From the corner of his eye he could see Sonja lean forward and cast a questioning look his way. He didn't say anything, but he wanted to tell her to sit back and relax. *If something happens, at least it will happen to all three of us.*

No one spoke from the time they left the school parking lot until they pulled up in front of their home, and then it was Henry who broke the long silence. "Well, I got us here," he said. "Safe and sound."

He half-expected to hear an expression of gratitude or admiration for his driving skill, but none was forthcoming.

Later, when June lay in bed with her unopened peppermint stick on the nightstand, her mother crept quietly into the room. She sat on the bed and gently stroked her daughter's hair. "I could hear you," Sonja said. "Out of all those children, I could still hear my baby's voice. You sang so beautifully."

June could think of nothing to say in response to her mother's compliment. At more than one rehearsal, Mrs. Manserus had corrected June for singing off-key. June did not understand what it meant to be either on- or off-key, so after she was chastised a third time, June rectified the problem the only way she knew how. She sang softer and softer until tonight at the actual performance, she was no longer singing at all but only mouthing the words to every song.

*N*ed *Weaver lifted his cup to propose a toast.* "*What is it—two* o'clock? We're barely half a day into the new year and we've already had a taste of failure."

The only patrons in the Top Deck Tavern were Weaver and his friend Jake Bram. They sat in barrel-backed chairs in front of a fire so low it did not blaze but glow. Both men were smoking and drinking brandy and coffee.

Two hours earlier, they had parked their cars behind the Moravian church and set out on what had become for them a New Year's Day ritual—snowshoeing a four-mile trail that took them through a small forest, along a high ridge that looked out over the frozen harbor, and back through a golf course. Today, however, the weather got the better of them. They had been dressed for the cold—the temperature never rose above ten below that day—but once they left the shelter of the trees and stood on the high bluff above the lake, the north wind had unobstructed access to the two men, and within minutes they felt as if they had been lacerated with whips of ice. They altered their course and made for the Top Deck, the nearest establishment they could be sure would be open on the holiday.

Jake Bram raised his own glass. "To 1954. May failure not be its theme."

"Yes," Weaver said, "I don't need another year like the last one."

"The work doesn't go well?"

"It does not."

"Have you ever thought the problem might be your standards? Now me, I'll accept any kind of crap that rolls out of my typewriter." Under his own name, Jake Bram wrote paperback Westerns; under the name J. B. Fall he wrote hard-boiled detective novels.

"And it all sells," Weaver said.

Jake shrugged and put a match to his pipe. "It does. But I keep my standards low in that regard as well."

Weaver scraped his chair closer to the fire. "I don't give a good goddamn if I never sell another work. If I'm not making something new—and making the discoveries that go with it—life isn't worth shit. Making art—that's all there is. The rest is just killing time and keeping myself amused."

"Maybe having become a successful merchant is obscuring your artistic vision."

Weaver waved away the suggestion. "I could do that shit with one hand behind my back and one eye closed."

"Paint it or sell it?"

"Either one." He tossed his cigarette butt into the fire. "No, I need something to shake me up. Something to scare the hell out of me. To mystify me. Something to help me get someplace I haven't been before."

"Try painting with your left hand."

"I take that remark to mean I should try a new technique. This has nothing to do with technique. I'm talking about vision."

"Well, hell. Why didn't you say so?" Jake rolled the brandy around his glass. "Drink up. Vision guaranteed. Followed by blindness."

"Come on, goddammit. I'm putting myself at your mercy here. What works for you?"

Jake stirred and packed the tobacco in the bowl of his pipe with a kitchen match. He scraped the match into flame on the underside of the table and relit his pipe. "I sign a contract."

Weaver stood and, taking the poker from the rack, pushed and rearranged the logs to allow more air into the fire. When one of the logs threatened to roll from the grate, Weaver shoved it back with the toe of his boot. He had a brief impulse to hold his foot in the fire to impress Jake with the seriousness of the matter at hand. Instead, he sat back down, leaning forward as if he were speaking to the rising flames and not to the man at his side.

"I need a new model," Weaver said. "Someone who has a face and a body I can find stories in."

"Are you sure you're not confusing the muse with fresh pussy?"

Weaver turned to his friend. "Are you sure they're supposed to be separate?"

Before Jake could answer, from behind the bar Frankie Rawling, the owner's wife, called out to the two men, "Hey! Either of you want a baked potato? I got an oven full of them, and I'm going to have to throw them out otherwise."

"Baked potatoes?" Weaver and Jake Bram asked in unison.

Frankie approached them carrying a bottle of brandy. "I don't know what the hell happened," she said. "I miscounted or something. I ran out of prime rib early last night, but I got all these goddamn baked potatoes left over."

Without a request from either man, she poured brandy into their glasses.

"Frankie," Jake said, "do us a favor. Stand over there by the fire."

She seemed to know instinctively that she was being asked to pose, for she positioned herself in front of the mantel, faced the two men, held the bottle in one hand, and with the other balanced an imaginary tray. She cocked her head to one side and smiled.

"What about it?" Jake asked Weaver. "Feeling inspired?"

Frankie was Owen Rawling's second wife, and she waited on tables and tended bar both before and after her marriage to the owner. She was younger than her husband, and the rumors about her as an adulteress were both numerous and specific: She took many lovers but only one at a time, and after she wore a man out, she'd move on to another and never go back. These men had to be of her choosing; walking into the Top Deck and making a pass at Frankie Rawling would get you nowhere. She favored men who lived in the county, but occasionally she would select a summer tourist if she knew he would be around for at least a week.

"I don't know if it's inspiration," Weaver said, "but I'm definitely feeling something."

Frankie had black hair, wide hips, large breasts, and a face that looked a little pushed in. She was a woman you might not look twice at were it not for the fact that she carried herself with the unapologetic confidence of someone sure of her attributes. Then, when you looked again, she returned your gaze directly, and the dark of her eyes held out promise of more darkness and directness.

"Make up your mind," Frankie said. "And decide about the potatoes too. If I don't get any takers I'll start chucking them into the snow."

"Patience," Jake said. "Some things can't be rushed."

"Mind telling me what part I'm up for here?" she asked. "I'm not exactly dressed for the audition." She wore a man's white shirt, stained from her work in the kitchen, and a pair of stiff dark blue dungarees turned up at the cuff.

"This role you'd undoubtedly *undress* for," Jake told her. "You're being appraised by Mr. Ned Weaver himself, and he is in search of a model, a muse."

"All right," Weaver said softly to his friend. "Enough."

"Yeah?" Frankie said to Weaver. "I thought you only painted landscapes."

"Those," Jake said, "are his lesser efforts."

"I almost bought one—the church in the snow?—but the price! Jesus, you aren't shy, are you?"

"Perhaps an arrangement can be made," suggested Jake. "In return for inspiration, Mr. Weaver here might give you one of those watercolors you admire. Or perhaps he might paint one especially for you."

"Jesus," Weaver said, "are you my business manager now?"

At this moment, Owen Rawling came out of the kitchen to see his wife standing in front of the fireplace while two men stared at her. "Do them two want any of the goddamn potatoes?"

With the brandy bottle still in hand, Frankie made hurrying gestures to the two men. "Well?"

"Are they hot?"

"Hot? You're fussy, aren't you? No, they're not hot. They're left-overs, for Christ's sake."

"Tell you what," Weaver said. "Bring us a platter of those potatoes, along with some butter and salt, and we'll see how much damage we can do. And draw us a pitcher of beer."

As Frankie scurried off to fill their order, she said to her husband, "Step to it. A pitcher—and it's on the house. Small price if we can unload those potatoes. Nothing I hate more than seeing food go to waste."

"I told you," Owen said. "We could take those over to Kirking's tonight."

Frankie's laugh sounded as though it could take at least two inches off a man's height. "Now, what the hell do you think they'd say if we showed up with *potatoes?*"

Jake waited until both Frankie and Owen were in the kitchen. "Well?"

"That hair . . . Who's that supposed to be in imitation of? Jane Russell? Ava Gardner?"

"Don't evade the issue. You think you could do anything with her? Because she'd sure as hell do it."

Weaver shook another cigarette from the pack, put a match to it, and inhaled deeply.

"Too zaftig?" Jake asked. "You looking for something that lives closer to the bone?"

"No mystery," Weaver said.

"By God, she was right. You are fussy."

Weaver hadn't told the entire truth. On this subzero day, Frankie Rawling still had a touch of summer tan. She was likely one of those women who lay out for hours under the sun, baking until her skin was as dark as saddle leather, and Weaver was mildly curious to know whether she sunbathed in the nude or if her body was striped with flesh as pale as the soles of her feet.

"It's not that I don't appreciate your efforts," Weaver said. "But I already have a candidate in mind."

Jake tilted back in his chair, balancing like one of the western marshals he wrote about. "And here I've been working my ass off on your behalf."

"I was thinking of Caroline," Weaver said. Caroline was Jake Bram's young wife.

Jake continued to teeter back and forth. "I don't know if I should be amused or offended."

"Why not flattered?"

"Maybe because I know your track record with your models. Has there been one yet you've failed to fuck?"

"That's not the kind of count a man is supposed to keep, is it?"

Jake's pipe had gone out again, and he took it from between his teeth and stared into the bowl. "You wouldn't mind if I sat in on the sessions, would you?"

"Hell, yes, I'd mind. How would you like it if I looked over your shoulder while you wrote?"

"You could sit on my fucking lap, for all I care."

Frankie returned from the kitchen, and the two men stopped talking and turned in her direction. She pulled the tap and expertly filled a pitcher with a minimum of foam. She brought the beer, along with two glasses, to the small table. "I know I'm fascinating to watch, but you two don't have to stop talking every time I walk into the room."

"We're struck dumb by your beauty," Weaver said. He watched her closely for a trace of blush, but he saw none. Perhaps she caught the trace of irony he couldn't keep out of his voice.

"I'll believe half that." She poured beer into each glass. "Owen will bring the potatoes in a few minutes."

Both men continued to watch Frankie as she walked away. The January wind that had cut short their trek gusted hard, trembling the window in its casement. A sudden draft of air found its way down the chimney, and for an instant, the fire raised its voice above a murmur.

Weaver crushed out his half-smoked cigarette, and when he began to speak, he directed his remarks to the ashtray. "So let's see if I have this right: You'll offer up Frankie Rawling because you're sure she's slut enough to take off her clothes for any man. It would never occur to you I'd want a model for any other reason. Just as it wouldn't occur to you that your wife might pose for me but choose not to disrobe. Or that I might not ask her to. Or that she might not choose to sleep with me. Or that she has any choice at all in any of these matters. My God, you have a low opinion of the woman you married. And it's no wonder you're a hack. You have absolutely no goddamn understanding of art or artistry whatsoever."

Without disturbing the position of his chair, Weaver stood slowly. "Don't get up," he said to Jake Bram. "You sit there. Sit there and eat potatoes until they come out your ass."

Weaver did not count this quarrel with his friend as the second failure of the day. That occurred later, after dark, when the wind finally subsided, and Weaver strapped on his snowshoes again. With the aid of a flashlight, and by cutting through the windswept corridors of an apple orchard, he made his slow, high-stepping way back to the Top Deck. He hoped that Frankie Rawling might be there alone, that her husband had taken the leftover potatoes and fulfilled their social obligation without his wife.

The Top Deck's windows, however, were dark, both in the first-floor business establishment and in the second-floor apartment where the Rawlings lived. Weaver knocked on the door anyway, by that time thinking as much about the fireplace as Frankie Rawling's combustible nature. There was no answer. Halfway home, the batteries in his flashlight flickered, grew faint, and finally gave out, but he had no trouble following his own trail of darker indentations in the dark snow.

Weaver's friendship with Jake Bram was restored within the month when Jake came to visit and brought with him, as a goodwill offering, his wife, Caroline, who expressed her eagerness to pose for Weaver.

As it turned out, she was not the model he had been hoping for. She had about her certain physical features—an especially elongated philtrum and a waist unusually thick for a woman so boyishly slender—so that when Weaver tried to render her, first in pencil and then in pastel, the resulting image seemed to be a mistake, an artist's failure of proportion.

When Weaver tried to correct these anomalies, a different, even more un-satisfactory distortion occurred—he was prettying up reality, rounding its corners, smoothing its rough edges, and that was something he refused to do in his art.

A physical relationship between artist and model did not eventuate until Weaver persuaded Caroline to run off to Chicago with him. They phoned their spouses and told them that Weaver had found himself unable to paint, so they decided to drive to Chicago in hopes of finding inspira-tion in one of the city's museums. They would have returned that night, but a snowstorm suddenly skidded in across Lake Michigan trapping them in the city.

The two of them toured the Art Institute, ate jaeger schnitzel and drank dark beer at Berghoff's, and then checked into the Drake. That evening they went for a walk, and Weaver showed Caroline Bram where his father was run over and killed. Later, they made love in a room so high above Michigan Avenue the sounds of traffic could barely reach them.

Making love to Caroline Bram was a singular experience, for in her Weaver found a body eerily similar to his own in size and shape. Hence, his every move—every squeeze, flex, thrust, and roll, every push and every pull—found an almost synchronous response, as if her body was answering his mind rather than his physical being. For the night, Weaver could not get enough of Caroline Bram, yet when they checked out of the hotel the following day, he had no regrets about driving her back to her home and her husband. Weaver was finished with her as both model and lover.

The only painting of consequence to come out of this set of circum-stances was "Another New Year." In it, half of a snowshoe is visible, as its wearer would see it looking down. The painting somehow captures mo-tion, as if we are glimpsing a booted, bound, webbed foot just before it strides off the canvas.

The details, as they so often are in a Ned Weaver work, are uncannily precise: the snow curling and scattering over the edge and tip of the snowshoe; the cracks in the leather binding; the bent and sere grasses poking through the snow. It's apparent that this walker in the snow is following in the tracks that another—or the walker himself—earlier made: In front of the snowshoe is a cavity in the snow that could only have been formed by another snowshoe. These footprints, along with the painting's "tired" title, inclined one critic to interpret the work as "an indication that the artist has come to a dead end and has no other path available but to return to the subjects and styles which have served him in the past."

Harriet was already in bed when the telephone rang.

When she answered, Jake Bram asked, as if he were continuing an earlier conversation, "What do you think? Any reason we should drink alone tonight?"

"You'll have to come here," Harriet said. "It's too late for me to go out." The sleeping pill had already taken effect, and she wasn't entirely sure she was responding correctly to his question.

"You have the requisite supplies?"

"I believe we're adequately equipped."

"If I'm not there in half an hour, call out the dogs."

Harriet did not get dressed, not exactly. She did, however, take off her flannel nightgown and instead put on the silk peignoir set she'd bought at Bergdorf's the last time Ned invited her to go to New York with him. She brushed her hair and applied a little lipstick and rouge. Her plan was quickly conceived and only dimly outlined—perhaps she wouldn't go through with it—but she wanted to make the necessary preparations just in case. Then she poured herself a drink—she knew Jake would be well ahead of her. She was smoking her second cigarette and watching from an upstairs window when headlights loomed at the base of the long drive-way. She hurried down so she could be standing in the open doorway when he arrived.

As soon as Jake stepped onto the porch, he reached into his coat pocket, pulled out a bottle of Martini & Rossi, and held it aloft. Under the porch light, the green glass glinted icily in the night air. He took his pipe from between his teeth. "I know, I know," he said. "But I have a new drink of choice, and I couldn't take a chance on being left high and dry."

"Oh ye of little faith."

He followed her into the house. "You got that? High and dry?"

"I got it. Come along. Let's see to your needs."

They were sitting in the darkened living room, each working on a second martini, before the name of either missing spouse was spoken, and it was Jake who hung the name *Ned Weaver* in the air between them.

"I swear to God," Jake said, "there are days when I think I'm the luckiest man in the world to count Ned Weaver as my friend. Other days it's all I can do to keep track of the ways I'd like to kill the son of a bitch."

Harriet reached over and touched the rim of Jake's glass with her own. "Congratulations. You're now a full member of the Ned Weaver Fan Club with all attendant rights and privileges."

"Yeah? What finally got me in? Turning my wife over to him?"

"If it were only that simple." She finished her drink. "No, no. You have to go further than that. You must actually contemplate bringing on his demise."

Jake jumped up from the couch and took Harriet's glass from her hand. "Let's get to it, then! I'll refill these, and we can begin plotting!"

Alone on the couch, Harriet closed her eyes and clasped her hands over her stomach, the tip of each index finger touching her navel. She always assumed this position when she began to get drunk. She thought she could steady herself by locating her body's center. She silently said the word *equilibrium* three times, confident she could say it aloud without difficulty.

When Jake returned with Harriet's drink, he sat closer to her than before. "Tell me what you think of this," he said. "Ned told me he sometimes uses his own saliva when he's doing a watercolor. Now, if someone could get ahold of one of his brushes, they could dip the hairs in poison, and when he puts it in his mouth—"

Before he finished, Harriet was shaking her head. "I believe he spits on the palette. Besides, isn't that a little iffy? You don't want to sacrifice certainty for the sake of ingenuity."

"Hmmm. Then you'll probably put the kibosh on the elaborate set of tubing through which carbon monoxide is piped back into the car while he's driving?"

"How can you be sure I won't be in the car that day?"

Jake's pipe made a slurping sound as he drew on it. "Potentially the same problem with draining the brake fluid . . ."

Harriet put her hand on Jake's wrist. The span and knob of bone felt large and hard, but then she was comparing him to Ned, whose underpinnings always reminded her of a bird's. "Simplify, simplify," Harriet said. "See if you can't figure out a way to get the job done without so much . . . engineering."

Jake leaned back but made no move to pull his hand out from under hers. "You're right. We're not plotting a novel here, are we?"

She moved her fingers around, feeling for Jake's pulse. Her father had been a doctor who practiced out of an office in their home, and one summer he hired Harriet to be his assistant, to answer the phone, greet patients, and conduct a few of a routine examination's simplest tasks. He hoped his daughter might follow him into a career in medicine, yet this hope soon faded. Harriet could never find the pulse in any man, woman, or child. She could not locate Jake's either, but it didn't matter. If his heartbeat seemed to quicken, she wouldn't know if it was from her touch or from planning the murder of her husband.

Jake put a finger in the air as if he were checking the wind's direction. "I think I've got it. It'll take a little time, but if we can be patient, this will work. Guaranteed. Okay, we wait until hunting season—deer hunting— and when he goes out for his daily walk, we line him up in the crosshairs of a high-powered rifle and—*boom*. Looks like an accident. A stray bullet from a hunter's gun. Happens all the time."

Harriet tightened her hold on Jake's wrist. "This is so sweet of you. But tell me, Jake—who will pull the trigger?"

"Another minor detail. Nothing we can't work out."

"Do you own a gun?"

"We could buy one."

"Would you even know how to load and fire one?"

"All right, all right. Suppose you come up with your own goddamn plan, instead of just raining on everyone's parade."

Harriet had to release Jake's wrist in order to put down her drink and draw herself up straight. "Very well. I personally think for sheer simplicity and effectiveness this cannot be topped. One would wait until Ned's asleep, very soundly asleep at that, in his bed on a night when he's had too much to drink. One walks stealthfully—*stealthily*—into the room and brings crashing down on his head a brick. It wouldn't have to be a brick, of course. A large stone would do. A crowbar. Something of suffice—sufficient—weight that even a person without much strength could deliver a mortal blow. Or blows, I should say. One wants to leave nothing to chance. Not when one has come that far."

Throughout this little exercise in make-believe, Jake had kept a straight face, but now the lines in his face seemed more deeply drawn. What had she done! This man whom Harriet thought she might seduce now regarded her with equal parts pity and horror.

Jake took two quick swallows from his drink, and that seemed to lubricate the machinery of his speech, although he spoke much more solemnly than before. "Harriet, I can call down there. I have friends in Chicago. I can call someone, and they can tell us if it's really snowing down there."

"Oh, Jake, Jake. Where's your faith? They told us it was snowing, so that's what we must believe. Didn't Caroline describe the conditions for you?"

"She just said it was coming down hard."

"See now, Ned went into great detail. They started out, he said, but north of the city, just past Evanston, it really got bad. The snow was coming down sideways and drifting across the highway." Harriet put up her hands to grip an imaginary steering wheel, and as she did, her robe fell open, but then that no longer mattered. "Ned was fighting to keep the car on the road, but he could feel it sliding out of control. He crossed the center line, but fortunately, no car was coming." Here Harriet twisted the wheel so hard she lost her balance and toppled from the sofa.

"See?" she said, trying to act as though she intended to end up on her knees next to the coffee table. "See how dangerous conditions are?"

Jake reached out to help her up, but Harriet twisted away from any assistance. She pushed herself up from the floor. Her nightgown had ridden up high on her thighs, but she was too exhausted to rearrange or cover herself. Not that Jake was looking.

"The thing is," Jake said sheepishly, "I love her. The little bitch doesn't deserve it, but there you have it."

"Well, you see? You *are* a believer. A high priest in the Church of Caroline."

Jake's expression brightened once again. "Ah, if only my dear mother were alive. She always hoped one of her sons might enter the priesthood. Hell, she didn't give up on me until my divorce."

Harriet reached over and traced with her fingernail the crease that ran from the corner of Jake's eye toward his ear, exactly the path a tear would follow if he were to lie flat on his back and weep for his wife who was at that very moment probably enfolded in another man's arms. "Just remember your creed," Harriet said. "Your Caroline creed. Repeat it every day. 'The little bitch doesn't deserve it, but I love her.' "

After Jake left, Harriet sat up for another hour, waiting, she told herself, to feel a little steadier before she climbed the stairs. Another thought, however, tried to hide itself behind that practical consideration: If Jake decided to come back, she didn't want the house's darkened windows to discourage him.

When she finally headed for bed, she left the living room as it was. The thought had occurred to her: For her strategem to succeed she didn't have to actually seduce Jake Bram; she only had to allow Ned to believe that she had. Let Ned come home and find empty martini glasses and an ashtray brimming with her cigarette butts and the half-burnt kitchen matches that Jake used to light and relight his pipe. Let Ned find these when he returned, and see if his faith would waver.

Harriet's original intent had been to stay in bed until Ned returned, but she woke early and, though her head felt as though it were filled with a viscous, toxic fluid, she rose and hurried downstairs.

First, she emptied the ashtray, making sure to bury its contents deep in the garbage. Next, she put the liquor bottles away, hiding Jake's Martini & Rossi in the back of the cupboard. She washed and dried the glasses and the cocktail shaker and put them away. Finally, though the morning was cold, she opened all the windows in the kitchen and living room in order to air out the place. Because Ned had insisted that the house's design let in as much light and air as possible, the winter wind instantly blew through the house as freely as it would across an open field.

As Harriet worked, the straps from her nightgown kept slipping from her shoulders, just as they had while she slept. Finally, frustrated and partially recalling the previous night's dreams that had over and over assumed a theme of entanglement, she shrugged out of the garment and let it fall to the floor. The silk had so little weight, she almost expected the breeze to carry it away. She stood in the middle of the living room and shivered, but she waited until she could be reasonably confident that the aroma of pipe smoke no longer lingered in the room. Then she closed the windows and made once again for her bed.

When she stopped on the landing, she looked down on that beautiful paisley puddle of silk. Left on the floor like that, her nightgown might have been more damning than martini glasses or a few burnt matches, but she could not make herself go back down to pick it up. She no longer entertained any thoughts of trying to make Ned jealous. What if she succeeded and as a consequence his ability to concentrate on his art became impaired? Besides, what would be gained by doubling the suffering in a marriage? But the nightgown's colors looked so brilliant against the hardwood planks it just had to remain where it was. It was as close as Harriet could come to the making of art, and she could not help but wonder if it was also as close as she could come to understanding what Mr. Ned Weaver felt before his easel.

"What's that," Henry asked, "on your back?"

Instantly Sonja knew the mistakes she had made. Assuming he was asleep, she had undressed in the bedroom instead of the bathroom. The moon was almost full, and she stood close to the window. Too close, and enough light shone in to reveal the continent-shaped areas of paler flesh on her back and shoulders.

"Come over here," he said.

She walked to the bed, clutching her nightgown to her chest.

"Turn around," Henry said.

She turned, and he snapped on the lamp. "Jesus," he said. "Your back. You've peeled."

The night before she had pulled off the last of the dried skin. It was a wonder he hadn't noticed earlier.

"I was . . . I got a bad sunburn. Going out too long with bare shoulders."

"I guess you got burned. What were you wearing?"

She didn't answer. She simply stood still, knowing he was examining her.

"Because I have to tell you, I don't see any marks where your straps were."

She still said nothing.

"Back up here."

With one long backward step she placed herself within his reach.

"Your whole backside is burned. Christ."

"Yes."

He blew his cooling breath across the small of her back. "Does it hurt?"

"Now not so much."

Delicately, he slipped a finger inside the elastic of her underpants. He tugged them down until her buttocks were partially exposed, and though she knew he was not blowing on her anymore, she felt goose bumps form as surely as if a chill had found its way into the room.

"You're burned all over." He let go of the elastic and traced his finger down the back of her leg. "Jesus. Turn around. Let me see the front of you."

Once more she turned, still covering her torso with the bunched cloth of her nightgown.

"You can let go of that," he said. "One way or the other, I'm going to see."

She dropped the garment and let her arms fall to her sides. She was tanned and burned on this side as well, but in no area had her skin blistered and peeled. Weaver had not made her pose as long lying on her back as on her stomach.

Henry stared at her a long time before he began to nod, understanding at last. "You've been lying naked out in the sun, haven't you?"

"Yes."

He slapped the mattress with such force Sonja flinched and stared at the sheet, expecting to see the imprint of his hand as if the bedsheet were wet sand.

"Where?" Henry asked. "Was this where people could see you?"

"By the lake."

"By the lake *where*? For Christ's sake, what did you do—strip right there in front of everybody and just plop down on the goddamn sand?"

"I was . . . It was deserted."

"I know this shoreline a hell of a lot better than you do. There aren't many goddamn spots left where you can be sure no one's watching you."

"I was careful." She remembered when she lay on her back, and the sun beat down on her with such ferocity it seemed as though it had just been waiting to get at those parts of her that had always been covered to its heat and light. Her breasts had tingled, and her nipples puckered and hardened. Just as they were doing now when Henry stared hotly at her. That was it! The sun had been like an eye, looking down on her so intently that she became aroused under its gaze, and then, when there was nothing to do with her arousal, her flesh simply burned with the sun's heat and her own.

"Do you want to tell me where you were," Henry said, "and let me decide how alone you were likely to be?"

"It was a private beach. The owners were not at home."

"So you were trespassing."

She shook her head, pretending not to know the meaning of the word.

"You know what I'd do if I saw someone coming on my property without permission?"

"You would load up your shotgun."

"Don't joke about this."

"I won't." In fact, she had meant nothing humorous by her remark.

"What the hell got into your head to try something like that?"

"I wanted . . . I wanted to feel the sun."

"If somebody would have seen you . . . Do you know what people would be saying about you? About me? Maybe you don't know it, but we've got reputations in the county."

That seemed much funnier than what she said about his shotgun, but she knew she mustn't laugh.

"You keep yourself decent outside this house," Henry said. "Now turn around again. I want another look at your back."

Sonja did as she was told, and immediately Henry slapped her buttocks so hard the blow swayed her back.

"There," he said. "And that wouldn't have hurt nearly so bad if you weren't red as a lobster back there."

Did the air behind her vibrate as Henry prepared to strike her again, or did she simply know her husband well enough to be certain that, having spanked her once, he would do it again? She didn't wait to find out. She walked from the room with such speed that for the only time in her life she felt as though she and the horse in the barn had something in common, as Buck, when he was slapped in the rump, always took that blow as a command to move forward.

Harriet was about to climb into bed when her husband called her into the bathroom.

Ned was sitting in the bathtub, smoking and drinking what she presumed to be gin. At the sight of her, he leaned forward and stiffly pointed toward his back. "Can you pull off this loose skin?" he asked. "It's driving me nuts, and I can't reach it."

She walked around behind him and looked down at his back. He had gotten a sunburn so severe that the skin had blistered, popped loose, and then cracked like parchment.

"My God, Ned." She knew the water was cool—at the end of these hot summer days he always soaked in a bath as cold as he could stand before going to bed—but she still reached down to confirm that his burned flesh had not heated the water.

"It doesn't hurt," he said. "It's just a goddamn nuisance. I feel like I'm molting, for Christ's sake."

His upper back and shoulders had taken most of the sun, but as far down as Harriet could see, Ned's back was red. "Bend over a bit," she said. Yes, it looked as though his buttocks had been burned. "Have you found a nude beach somewhere?"

"Over at Edith's. I've been working over there, and one day, I just thought, well, hell: I know what the light on the sand *looks* like. What do you suppose it feels like?"

"Let me guess. Hot."

"There you have it. If you had only been there you could have saved me some time and a nasty sunburn. Hot. By God, you're right. It *was* hot. I might go a bit further: It was very fucking hot."

She crouched down behind the tub. "Do you want me to do this or not?"

Weaver drank off the last of the gin and then dumped the ice cubes in the water. "Go ahead. Skin me. Here's your chance. It's probably what you've always wanted to do. Skin me alive."

The analogous behavior should have been peeling fruit, something that actually had a protective skin and a fleshy interior—a pear, a peach. An apple. But pulling Ned's loose skin away instead reminded Harriet of a household chore she had not done for years: removing wallpaper. And she remembered the special satisfaction that came when the wallpaper peeled away in an especially large swatch. The key, then as now, was to pull slowly, not to become impatient or greedy. Like that, like that—with the thumb and two fingers working under the skin's hard, dried outer edge and then simultaneously lifting and pulling.

Harriet had long known—Ned said it himself—that only to his art did he bring his best self. All the other hours of his life he simply tried to slay as pleasantly as he could until it came time to pick up his brush again. Nevertheless, Harriet kept waiting for Ned to display that capacity for generosity, honesty, and wholeness that he revealed when he put images on paper or canvas and thereby translated his private visions to public truths. If these qualities were in him, Harriet frequently wondered, why didn't they come out in his relationships as well? In the end, she loved him not for what he was but for what he could be. Did Ned similarly love the weeds growing in the ditch—the burdock, for example, depicted in his dry-brush painting "Road to Loyal Farm"—not for what they were but for what he could make of them in art?

As she carefully, gently pulled away Ned's outer layer, she looked closely at the blotchy, pink-tinged skin beneath—was that where his goodness lay? Could she peel and keep peeling until only the decent Ned was exposed to the world?

The question she finally asked him, however, had nothing to do with Ned's potential for goodness or her patient willingness to wait for it. "Were you alone on Edith's beach?"

He didn't answer, but Harriet felt his spine stiffen under her fingertips.

"Tell me," she said, "is there someone out there with a sunburn that matches yours—only, her arms and legs and knees are burned instead of her backside?"

"Jesus, Harriet. What the hell kind of question is that?"

"The kind that I'm usually able to bite back and keep from asking. But even I have my limits, Ned."

"I told you. I was working. And you are not allowed to question my methods of working."

"I believe I'm allowed to ask, Ned. But you're under no obligation to answer. Or you feel no obligation."

"Look, I asked you in here to help me get this loose skin off my back. If you can't even do that without trying to start something, then get the hell out."

Harriet pinched a horny little tab of skin and pulled it hard, hoping a yard of Ned's flesh would rip away. What came loose, however, wasn't much larger than a fingernail, and she doubted she had caused Ned any pain.

She stood and looked down on his narrow, hunched shoulders. The ragged border of peeled skin looked like a faded tattoo, as if Ned had long ago had his back illustrated with a map of the country where he alone lived.

The bathwater was murky and of course distorted everything below its surface, but when Harriet glanced down on her way out of the room, it looked as though Ned had an erection. If she could have been sure not only that it was there but also what caused it—whether her touch teasing away tiny patches of his skin or his memory of a woman with whom he'd lain under the sun—she might have stayed.

It was a Friday night, and the Top Deck Tavern was full of the men and women who spent the week waiting on, serving, guiding, or cleaning up after tourists. Even at the height of summer, the Top Deck remained a bar for locals, one of the only spots in the county where they could take the edge off their frustrations and spend a night cursing and mocking the summer people who drove up from Milwaukee or Chicago, rich bastards and their kids who may have had money in their pockets but didn't know their asses from their elbows.

The four or five glasses of beer Henry had drunk were just enough to make it seem as if the dim light and the haze of cigarette smoke, rather than the noise, kept him from hearing clearly the remark Jimmy Lauer tossed Henry's way. Henry waved a hand in front of his face and peered down the bar to where Jimmy stood, then he cupped a hand to his good ear and shouted back, "I know you're talking to me, but I can't hear a damn thing you're saying."

"I said, What do you think this is—some kind of Wild West saloon?"

This time Jimmy's words got through, but Henry still didn't understand. He turned to Frankie Rawling, who was leaning across the bar from him.

"Ignore him," Frankie said. "He's just trying to get under your skin."

"How's he going to do that when I can't hear what the hell he's saying?"

Frankie reached across the bar and put her palm on Henry's cheek. She turned his head until his vision was once again fixed on her and away from the group of four men standing halfway down the bar. "Ignore him," she repeated, and kept her hand on Henry's face a moment longer.

For months Henry and Frankie Rawling had been moving steadily toward a destination at which Henry was still not sure he wanted to arrive.

It began with Frankie's teasing, which was harmless enough, since for years she had been reddening Henry's and every other man's ears with her bold talk. Soon, however, they moved to new stages of playful, joking intimacy. As she passed, Frankie would snap Henry's ass with a bar towel. She would pick up his cigarette, take a deep drag, and put it back in the ashtray, and when he brought it to his own lips, he couldn't help but put his mouth on her lipstick stain. And finally, when Henry rode up to the Top Deck on Buck not long ago, Frankie, seeing that he had not bothered with saddle or bridle, said, "A bareback rider, eh? Maybe I've finally found a man who can stay on for the full ride." "I guess," Henry said, "you've bucked off a few, huh?" She looked him up and down. "Just hang on tight, cowboy, when it comes your turn."

Since that night, Henry had not bothered to saddle Buck for their evening ride if he thought he'd be stopping at the Top Deck. Tonight, however, he had taken a few extra minutes and slipped a bit between Buck's teeth, noticing, in the process, how hooked and pointed they had become and chastising himself for not having them floated. Perhaps that was the real reason why, on most nights, Henry simply climbed on Buck without bothering with tack, not because he was in such a hurry to get to Frankie's place but because he didn't want to be reminded of how neglectful he had become in the care of his animal.

It had been almost a year since John's death, and during those months, Henry had drifted from one extreme to the other in trying to get past the grief.

He had tried to handle it as he thought his father would, by standing up to it and trying to face it down. This Henry was the responsible citizen, the sober-sided husband and father and the dutiful churchgoer. This was the hardworking Henry who put in long hours in the orchard and then came home to attack the chores that needed to be done there. But then, when all his strenuous efforts still could not accomplish the task that most needed to be done—banishing heartache from his own house—Henry turned from his father's model and instead ran away to lose himself in a boy-man's diversions. Fishing. Riding horseback. Playing cards. Drinking beer. Flirting with Frankie Rawling.

Henry was fairly certain all he had to do to take the next step with
Frankie was to say, "Let's go upstairs," and she would lead him off by the
hand, even if it meant telling Owen that he'd have to mind the bar alone
for a while. So what was holding Henry back? Perhaps it was the fact that
sometimes his attempts to find pleasure tasted so flat and stale that a life
salted with sorrow seemed preferable.

But ignoring Jimmy Lauer was not making him go away. "Did you always want to be a cowboy?" Jimmy said. "Is that it? Is that why you ride
up on your horse and tie up outside the saloon like a goddamn movie cowboy?"

People generally made allowances for Jimmy's behavior because of
the tragedy that befell his family years ago. Jimmy's father and two uncles
had been professional herring fishermen, and in 1930, on the day after
Thanksgiving, they were caught out on the lake when a terrible storm
blew in. Their boat ran aground on Plum Reef, and all rescue attempts
failed. The three Lauers, along with Eldon Gottschalk, drowned. The incident happened when Jimmy was a boy, and it seemed to strand him in
early adolescence. He never married, he jumped from job to job, he spent
every evening in one of the county's taverns, and after he had a few beers,
he usually settled on his victim for the night, someone to receive his in-
sults. Most people laughed off these taunts—Jimmy just being Jimmy.

Which was exactly what Henry usually would have done, but on this
night, he decided to answer Jimmy. "Not jealous, are you? Seeing as how
you can't stay on anything faster than that leaky rowboat of yours."

Obviously pleased that he'd found someone to take the bait, Jimmy
walked toward Henry. "Why would anyone even want to sit on that old
swayback? A man can likely walk faster'n that nag can gallop."

When Henry moved away from the bar to meet Jimmy, Frankie muttered, "Shit."

"Buck might surprise you," Henry said. Face-to-face with Jimmy,
Henry was struck once again by the prominence of Jimmy's lower jaw and
the way it turned Jimmy's smile upside down, reminding Henry of a bass.

"Hell, he's surprised me by still being able to stand up. I recall you
traipsing around on that horse back in high school."

This reference to their past made Henry wonder if Jimmy's banter was not entirely good-natured. In the fall of their senior year, Henry, Jimmy, Nils Singstad, and Phil Trent had gone duck hunting down at Horicon on land owned by Phil's uncle. Henry drove, but with the stipulation that the others would have to pitch in for gas. On their first night out, as they sat around a campfire drinking, Jimmy began to grouse about sharing expenses. "It ain't fair, goddammit. Henry's old man owns half the apple orchards in the county while my mom had to go ask Pastor Sunvold if the church would help us out last winter. I wouldn't mind kicking in, but a gallon of gas ain't nothing to the Houses." The House family was never as prosperous as Jimmy supposed, but in the years since Henry's father dropped dead of a stroke outside Bill Tufte's bait shop, the House family's fortune, such as it was, had declined. Many of those orchards that Jimmy referred to had long since been sold off.

Vernon Brack pushed himself between the two men. "How about a race," Vernon suggested. "What say?" He turned back to Jimmy. "See if you can outwalk Henry and his horse?"

"I'm game," Henry said. "Time and place. We'll be there."

"That makes a lot of fucking sense," said Jimmy. "That's bullshit."

"Maybe so, but it's your bullshit."

"Fuck you both," Jimmy said and stepped back to his waiting beer.

From behind him, Henry heard a voice say, "How about your boat, Jimmy?"

The suggestion came from Frankie. Henry thought she had turned away from this little argument, but she was pushing her way forward. She stopped next to Henry, put an arm on his shoulder, and pushed her hip out until it pressed against his thigh. "You think you could row your boat across the bay faster than Henry could gallop his way around to Cooley's Landing?"

The feel of Frankie at his side made Henry wonder if she were offering herself up as the prize.

And that was how Henry came to be sitting astride Buck on a warm, humid night when the bar's haze seemed to follow all the patrons outside. Above the waters of the bay, fog hung motionlessly as if it too were waiting for a signal.

The evening reminded Henry of those summer nights when he and his father used to climb a hill to look out across this same bay and watch thunderheads march in from the west. Henry liked it best when the storm would stall over the water, and lightning, confined to the clouds, would give off a soft flickering like a candle inside a paper lantern. Then, even the rumble of thunder seemed benign, a sound no more threatening than the drumbeat of his father's heart when he held Henry close.

Now, from down at the dock, one of Jimmy Lauer's supporters called up to Henry and his men standing around Buck. "Hey, who's going to say when to go?"

"I will." Once again, Frankie stepped forward and stood at Henry's side.

Looking up at Henry, she said, "They're ready down there. How about you?"

"I suppose. But I got to say, this is feeling dumber by the minute."

Nils Singstad was gently stroking Buck's forehead. "Did it ever get decided what you're racing for?"

"Damned if I know," Henry said. "To shut Jimmy's mouth, maybe."

"Well, hell, that ain't going to happen."

With his knees, Henry tightened his hold on Buck. He could feel that great barrel of ribs expand and contract as the horse tried to find a rhythm of breathing that matched this bewildering situation.

Bob Banville, although he was certainly one of those rooting for Henry to win, said, "God damn, it doesn't look from here like Jimmy's got that far to row. You can see the lights over at Cooley's. It's a straight shot across the bay." The expanse of water he pointed across was dead calm.

"Does anyone know," Henry asked, "can I stay on the beach all the way?"

Nils said, "Someone's building a place next to Voldt's. You want to watch out there in case they got their shit all over the beach."

Henry looked down at Frankie. A cigarette jutted from the corner of her mouth, and she was squinting through the smoke and fingering through a scattering of coins in her palm. Tip money, Henry thought. She had already lost interest in the race and was trying to count how much she'd made by scooping nickels and dimes out of the beer slop on the bar.

"This is crazy," he said to anyone who was willing to hear him and say, It sure as hell is; now climb down and let's go back inside where we belong. But Henry no more belonged in the Top Deck than out here on the back of Buck. He should have been home, putting the screen on the back door and propping open the upstairs windows so electric fans could be set right on the ledges, drawing in a little night air and perhaps making sleep a little easier.

Frankie sucked in her breath to slip the coins back into the pocket of her dungarees. "Crazy? Yeah, ain't it," she said. "Okay. It looks like Jimmy's ready down there, so I'm giving the signal he can push off."

Nils patted Buck's forehead one more time then stepped aside.

"Yeah, all right," said Henry.

Frankie made a few backhand waves as though she were trying to shoo Jimmy Lauer from the dock. To Henry she said, "This is it, cowboy," and swatted Buck.

The horse could probably be excused for not immediately striding out at a speed appropriate to a race, because Frankie's gentle slap on his rump was exactly the kind of blow that Henry used when he opened the gate and released Buck into his own small corral. Confused and longing for home himself, the horse may not have understood what was being asked of him.

Within seconds however, because Buck was trained to put human impulses before his own, he had broken into a trot and soon was galloping as fast as the beach's broken stretches of sand and rock allowed.

Falling off Buck was nothing like the experience of almost driving into a tree with Reuben Rosicky's truck. On that occasion, Henry thought the collision was inevitable, and even after he missed the tree, he was unaware of having done anything to avoid the crash. Now, however, even as he was slipping from his horse's back, he continued to feel confident that he'd be able to right himself. When he finally realized that wouldn't be possible, he was still able to think through a sequence of thoughts that were remarkably coherent and calm considering the circumstances. *I have not fallen or been thrown from a horse since I was ten years old,* Henry thought, *and it's goddamn embarrassing to be doing it at my age.* He chastised himself further: Racing like this, on a horse's bare back—it's something a boastful, strutting man would do . . . or a drunk who had turned away from the obligations of his home and family and business in order to take up a dare that any sane and responsible man would have walked away from.

Finally, when it was obvious that he would not be able to stop his slide from Buck, Henry still believed he could dictate the terms of the fall itself—where and how he would land—thereby forgetting the lesson that failing to give in to what lies beyond human power to alter frequently worsens a situation.

Henry let go of the reins—he didn't want the panic and confusion of the moment to cause him to forget and hold on and perhaps pull Buck over on top of himself—and thrust out an arm to break his fall, aiming for an area of the beach free of rocks and debris. But Henry was not falling from a stationary object. In all his calculations, he had failed to figure in how Buck's galloping speed increased the rate of the fall.

The heel of his hand and his wrist jammed under a driftwood log, and his forward momentum snapped both the ulna and the radius. A branch, sticking out of the log like a horn, tore open the skin of his forehead as if it were paper. When Henry tumbled to the side, he separated his shoulder and bruised his hip on a rock.

As soon as Henry sat up, blood would run down into his eyes and veil his vision in red, but for the moment, lying flat on his back on the sand, he could see clearly. The stars above glittered like dagger points. The shaggy tops of a few tall firs tossed in the wind as if they were nodding heads. Nearby Buck nickered, and Henry arched his head back to try to find his horse, hoping he wouldn't see that Buck too had tumbled onto the sand.

No, there he was, standing at the water's edge where the waves lapped no higher than his fetlocks. He was looking away from Henry, out toward the horizon where, although the sun had long since set, a smudge of lavender lingered. In spite of Buck's unconcern, Henry felt a flood of feeling for the animal. Oh, Jesus, Buck, you poor son of a bitch—now she'll blame you for this too.

His eyelids began to flutter, and Sonja said a silent prayer, directed not to God but to her husband propped in the hospital bed: *Don't make a joke. Please don't make your first words to me a joke.*

Henry's head lolled to the side, which meant that when his eyes finally opened he would not see his wife but a heat lamp drying the plaster encasing his arm from wrist to shoulder. In another moment, he turned back toward her and blinked slowly. He worked his jaw back and forth. To ensure that her prayer was answered, at least temporarily, Sonja pressed her finger to his lips.

He twisted away and spit dryly as if he thought some of the gauze that swathed his head had gotten into his mouth. His eyes flit wildly to as many corners of the room as he could see without moving his head.

"You're in the hospital," Sonja said.

He swallowed with difficulty. "The hospital. Sure, sure."

"Your friends brought you here."

"And called you?"

"Nils came for me."

Henry looked around again, wincing at even this slight movement. "Is it late?"

"Yes, it's very late."

"June's not here?"

Sonja shook her head. She had a sudden fear that this was now her life with Henry, that something in his brain had been jarred loose and now he could do nothing but ask simple little questions. "She's at home."

His eyes widened with concern. "Alone?"

"Dagny is staying with her," Sonja said wearily.

Henry touched his face lightly all over like a blind man trying to see with his fingertips. When he reached the bandages swaddling the top of his head he stopped. He closed his eyes as though he needed to work at remembering his injuries. When recognition came, he looked again at Sonja. "I guess I'm no longer your handsome man."

She was about to tell him there were matters more important than his looks, but perhaps to him that was not so. "Nurse said you were lucky to have Dr. Jim sew you up. She said he does the best stitches because he once wanted to be a . . . a . . ."

Nils, sliding into the room as if he were on skates, finished her sentence. "Plastic surgeon. Yah, that's so. Dr. Jim pulls the stitches so tight you probably won't even see the seam where he sewed your face back on. I saw him when he was about to go to work on you. I think he used four-pound test line."

Henry glanced down at his injured arm and then looked questioningly back to Nils as though he were the best authority on Henry's condition. Sonja caught this silent exchange and stepped back to make room for Nils at the bedside.

"What—they didn't tell you where all your arm was busted?"

"They told me," Henry said. "I'm just not sure I heard right."

Nils tapped his own forearm. "Both bones here, I know. And something in your shoulder. But maybe that's not broken?" He looked to Sonja for confirmation.

"It's . . . separated. Is that the right word? Separated?"

Henry reached across and touched his cast so gingerly it seemed as though he feared he might have feeling in the plaster.

"Come harvest time," Nils said, "you'll have to pick all the low apples. You damn sure won't be reaching."

"I've got two arms."

"And you got friends aplenty who'll lend a hand."

All during the ride to the hospital, right up to the moment when Henry's eyes opened, Sonja had been so brim-full of fear for her husband's life that she hadn't room for any other concern. Then, once she knew that Henry would live, new worries rushed into the open space—he would not be able to work, and there wouldn't be enough money for them to live. At almost the same instant, Sonja made three resolutions, two of them coming from experiences in her own past. She would not ask a minister for help, and she would not, in order to have one less mouth to feed, send her child away to live with another family. Sonja would beg in the streets, she would go back to waiting on tables, before she would leave her door open to the kinds of humiliation and hurt her own mother and father had invited into their home.

"I know I asked this before," Henry said, "but is Buck okay?"

Niles nodded. "Bob took him up to your place and put him back in his stall."

At the mention of the horse's name, Sonja grabbed three fingers on her left hand and squeezed them hard with her right. She thought she had gotten past the trembling, but now here it was, starting up again, this time in her hands. During the previous hours she had been clenching herself so tightly she knew tomorrow her muscles would ache, but she also knew that if she allowed the shaking to start it would not stop until her tendons tore loose from her bones.

Dr. Jim entered the room, his voice so loud Sonja flinched. "Can you tell me," he asked Henry, "is there any place it doesn't hurt?"

Dr. Jim was new to the county, but he had already developed a reputation that made Sonja wish that Dr. Van Voort were treating Henry, no matter how excellent were the stitches Dr. Jim sewed. It was said this young doctor was too sure of himself, that he scolded some patients and insulted others, that he took too little time with the elderly and too much time with pretty young women. Sonja's sister-in-law, Phyllis, had visited Dr. Jim with an earache and walked angrily out of his office when the doctor tried to insist on an examination too thorough for her symptoms.

"My big toe," Henry said. "On my left foot."

"Wait until the anesthetic wears off completely. That toe will be driving you nuts." The doctor had a crew cut that bristled like needles, his eyebrows seemed permanently arched, and the cigarette pinched between his lips angled toward the ceiling. Everything about him, it seemed to Sonja, directed your attention up, up, over his head.

"Then maybe you'll give him a bullet to bite down on, huh, Doc?"

"We don't use bullets," the doctor said to Nils. "We give our patients razor straps to gnaw."

"What—no shot of whiskey?" Henry asked.

The doctor expelled smoke from his nostrils. "We had to curtail the whiskey because Mildred Ryan kept checking into the hospital just to get herself liquored up."

The three men laughed heartily. Sonja wondered if such a person as Mildred Ryan even existed, but then Sonja's own existence at that moment might be in doubt as far as these men were concerned.

To Henry, the doctor said, "So, you were in a race. Did you win or lose?"

"I'm lying here, so I guess that means I lost."

"Jimmy pulled up," Nils said. "He never finished either. He feels terrible about what happened."

Henry pointed to the doctor's cigarette. "Can you spare one of those smokes, Doc?"

Dr. Jim shook out a Chesterfield from the pack in his shirt pocket, put the cigarette between his lips, lit it from his own, then deftly placed the new cigarette between Henry's waiting lips. Nils waved away the offer of the doctor's pack.

Henry inhaled deeply, then with a gentle sigh let the smoke drift slowly from his lungs. "And maybe I'll have to check myself into the hospital just to get someone to light my cigarette." Sonja was right; they didn't see her.

"No lighter?" the doctor asked.

"I always lose 'em."

"Here," Dr. Jim said, "let me show you a little trick."

He brought out a book of matches and, with one hand, opened the cover, tucked it back in, bent a match in half, and scratched it into flame. He held the burning match aloft for a second, then blew it out. "See? The poor man's lighter."

"Or you could use farmer's matches," suggested Nils.

"Little exercises like this," Dr. Jim said, "keep the fingers nimble." He held up both hands and wiggled his fingers. "And people don't realize a doctor works by hand as much as an auto mechanic."

But the mechanic, thought Sonja, does not have such long-fingered, delicate-looking hands. Dr. Jim's hands did not appear to have the strength necessary to set broken bones or sew up split flesh. She remembered her mother's old friend Astrid Hansa, more skilled with needle and thread than anyone in the village. Astrid had fingers so short and blunt they looked like oversize thimbles.

"I'm afraid," Henry said, "an apple grower does most of his work by hand too."

Earlier she had put her finger to his lips to keep her husband from joking about his situation, but she would have preferred jokes to self-pitying remarks like that one. "Excuse me," she said, "I'm going to wait in the hall."

It was close to morning, yet the corridor still held on to the heat of the preceding day. That warmth, along with the odor common to every hospital Sonja had ever been in, made her reel. She rested her forehead against the wall, and fortunately those bricks, smooth rectangles the color of pale, pale flesh, felt soothingly cool.

"Which is it?" The doctor's voice startled her again. "Are you holding up the wall or is it holding you up?"

She turned to face him and found the doctor standing so close she felt trapped, yet if she stepped to the side, he might take that movement as an affront.

"You can head back home," he said. "He'll sleep again soon. No reason for you to stay awake."

"I'm all right."

"Are you? You're looking a little green around the gills."

"The smell. What is that smell?"

The doctor glanced left and right as if the odor had a visual presence. "I think what you smell is ether. Sort of a cheesy aroma? Ether and probably antiseptic."

Looking up at Dr. Jim, Sonja noticed that even the doctor's long eyelashes curved upward. Was it possible he curled them like a woman? "How long," she asked, "until he can go home?"

"Another day or two, I suppose." The doctor leaned his hand on the wall close to Sonja's head. She smelled coffee and tobacco on his breath. "But I must tell you," he said in a lowered, confidential voice, "your husband is going to be out of commission for a while."

"Commission?"

"I'm sure he thinks he's a tough young fellow. But he really banged himself up."

When Nils came to the house to tell her that Henry had been hurt, Sonja dressed hastily. She pulled on the skirt she had worn during the day, and, unable to find her blouse, she grabbed the garment closest at hand, Henry's shirt.

"Do you understand what I'm saying?" the doctor asked, and then, as if he thought she might comprehend action better than speech, he reached out and tugged on Sonja's—Henry's—shirt collar. She pressed herself harder against the wall.

From the time she first came to this country, from that first day standing in the great hall on Ellis Island, under that ceiling that seemed, even after days on the open sea, as high as the sky, Sonja had often been asked if she understood. "Do you need an interpreter? Do you need a translation?" She heard those questions over and over, and she always said no, though months sometimes passed before she knew exactly what people were asking. The odd thing about understanding was how often time alone seemed to bring it about. The meaning of a word she didn't know on Monday was clear on Friday. Sometimes years were necessary for understanding and sometimes only minutes, as now, when she began to realize that when Dr. Jim had boasted of his strong and nimble fingers he may well have been speaking to her. And, just as new understandings often cleared away old misunderstandings, she knew now she had not been in-visible in Henry's room. Dr. Jim had been watching her all along, but in that sidelong way characteristic of so many men. Oh, men were supposed to be so bold, yet they would not look directly at you. Instead, they waited until you bent over, and then if you glanced up quickly you could see where their eyes had been! Truly, it would be better to be invisible.

"I understand," she said softly.

At that moment, Nils came out of Henry's room, and the doctor in-stantly stepped back. "He's asleep," Nils said, smiling as if he were re-sponsible for Henry's state.

"What do you want to do now?" he asked Sonja.

She looked directly at the doctor, but she spoke in Norwegian, the tongue native to her and to Nils. *"Ta meg hjem."*

It was her hope that if she made her request to Nils in the language of their childhood he would take her directly home and not pull the car off the road somewhere and begin tugging at her collar.

Sonja was surprised at how willing Henry was to allow his sister, his friends, and hired men to take over the work of the orchards. Yes, yes, certainly his injuries prevented him from returning to his work routine, but she would have thought the forced inactivity would frustrate him, that he would become so impatient to get back to work that he would tear off his bandages, pull out his stitches, throw away his sling, and crack open his plaster cast.

Instead, for much of the day, Henry gave himself over to invalidism. He slept late and did not dress until midday. He neglected not only the apple business but also the welfare of his animals. He threw no sticks for Sandy to retrieve, and Buck got no more exercise than what he provided himself in his small corral. The doctor advised Henry to raise and rotate his injured shoulder to prevent muscle atrophy, but Henry kept his arm pinched close to his side. He spent so many hours staring out the window that Sonja wondered if grief, unable to get a firm grip on Henry after

John's death, had now finally caught up to her husband and was pulling him down. Only late in the day did Henry come to life.

Then he would get into his truck, and, though it was difficult for him to maneuver the gearshift with his left hand, somehow he would manage and drive off. When Sonja listened for him to return at night, she could sometimes hear him approach because the transmission whined as Henry tried to avoid shifting down. When he came to bed, he smelled of beer and cigarettes.

On one of the evenings when she knew he was about to leave, she followed him out of the house. She didn't say anything to him—she wanted him to *want* to stay home, not to be scolded into it—but when he climbed into the truck's cab, she walked to the passenger's side and stood there, waiting to be explained to, to be invited in, to be merely spoken to. But Henry simply drove away, with Sonja walking alongside the truck until she could not match its speed. Even then, she kept going. June was at a friend's house, so if nothing was going to hold Henry at home, why should Sonja stay?

She walked without a destination in mind until she came to Denmark Road, and only then did she realize she was moving in the direction of the only door that something other than pity or good manners had invited her to enter.

When she arrived at the mailbox bearing the Weaver name, she stopped at the bottom of the long, rutted driveway and stared up at the grand house. She could start up the drive, but what would she say when he answered the door? *You asked me to come, so I came?* And if he didn't remember his offer? She could hardly argue her way inside. Worse yet, what if he looked at her and, like Henry driving away with her beside the truck, simply didn't see her? Twice in one day? That would be too much, too much. She turned and walked back the way she came.

A week later, Sonja repeated her experiment, but this time she did not follow Henry out of the house. She anticipated his departure, and she went out ahead of him. When he came out and climbed into the truck, she hurried to her position right at the point where the drive curved and sloped away from the house, and she did not stand in the weeds beside the gravel but just on the edge of the drive itself and on Henry's side of the truck. He would have to see her and, one way or another, alter his path.

He did not honk his horn or lean out the window and yell at her to step back. Neither did he stop and ask her quietly why she was standing there. All the while staring straight ahead, Henry turned the steering wheel slightly and drove so close to Sonja she could have reached out and touched Henry on the arm. But she did not, and as the truck slowly passed, Sonja caught a glimpse of herself in the side-view mirror. She was sure Henry was not looking at the same reflection.

The following day, when June was in school, Sonja set out again for Denmark Road, and when she came to the Weaver house, she did not hesitate at the bottom of the hill. She walked right up the driveway, past the big house with its many windows, and on to the cabin.

She didn't need to know the right words. She only had to watch the artist's eyes. If his pupils widened at the sight of her, that would be enough.

*E*ven when Henry finally shook off the lethargy he had been draped in following his accident, he still had trouble getting back to work. He set out to prune his trees, and with his first attempt to work a saw back and forth the pain in his shoulder became so severe he had to stop. He tried shifting the tool to his left hand, but if he kept working that way the job would take forever, so the saw was soon back in his right hand and he was trying to push and pull his way through the pain.

It wasn't pain alone that hindered him. Whenever he extended his arm beyond a certain point, something in his shoulder seized, as though bone suddenly jammed against bone, and he had to turn his entire torso to free the joint. Then, for a minute or two, his whole arm hummed with an ache that felt like an electrical current.

Frustrated, he brought the saw down, and stepped back from the tree. He looked up and down the orchard's snowy lanes and wondered when— or if—Max Sherry would appear.

Max Sherry was a sour, tough little man who had worked in the House family's orchards for decades, though not in continuous service. At irregular intervals—just often enough so relying on him became impossible— Max would vanish without warning or explanation. Some said he was running from the family of a man he had come close to killing with a wrench when they worked together at a shipyard in Sturgeon Bay. Another rumor assigned to Max a wife and children somewhere whom he occasionally visited. Still another story, the most improbable of all, made Max a wealthy eccentric who worked only because he wanted to rub elbows with the common folk. Henry's father had dismissed all these theories. "He's a drunk, pure and simple," Mr. House used to say. "And like all drunks, he goes off on a bender now and then. Either that or he's holing up somewhere drying out." But Henry's father also spoke highly of Max

Sherry as a worker. "He knows the apple business, and if he shows up, he'll give you full value for your dollar." When Max wanted to work, the Houses were always willing to hire him.

Today, however, Henry was not at all confident he would see Max. That morning, the thermometer outside the kitchen window read only twelve degrees, and what little relief daylight brought was more than off-set by the wind that rose with the sun. The cold, as if it had teeth, eyes, and a black heart, went unerringly for any exposed skin—Henry's face or wrist when he lifted his arm to saw—and bit hard. Henry couldn't blame Max if he chose to stay indoors and count his fortune, write to his wife, or see how much space he could free up in a fifth of whiskey. Henry wondered too if he had started the job too early. You didn't want to do the dormant pruning until you could be sure the temperature wouldn't drop below zero again. But since he was already out there, and alone, he might as well get on with it.

Just as he reached this moment of resignation, Henry saw someone coming his way. Max was on snowshoes, the only means to navigate the knee-high drifts that filled the pathless woods to the east of the orchard. Henry waved to him, and Max kept trudging forward, though he offered no sign in response.

Max finally stopped ten feet from Henry. Max's dress varied little according to season. He wore the same pac boots and wool cap all year round and the same canvas chore coat September to May. In the coldest weather, the flaps came down on his cap, and he layered as many shirts and sweaters under his coat as he could.

"I thought you'd be coming from the other direction," Henry said. His jaw had stiffened from the cold, and it felt as though words were stones he had to work his mouth around.

"I been staying over at Bertram's lately," Max said.

"How's that boy of theirs?" If Henry remembered correctly, Harv and Mary Bertram had a son born within months of John House.

"They got him rigged up with some kind of special boot to fix his foot. Clumps around the house like a horse with one shod hoof."

Henry nodded toward the few trees he had managed to prune so far. "You can see I haven't made much progress. I don't know how you want to proceed. I've got a lopper, shears, and another saw over there in the truck."

Max took a long look at the tree Henry had been working on, and the expression on his face took Henry back to childhood and his first attempt to help out with the family business. Then, now, and in all the intervening years, Max's coldly appraising eye seemed to find the efforts of the boss's son wanting.

"I didn't come out here to trim trees," Max said.

If the cold had not made speech a special exertion, Henry might have blurted out what came instantly to mind—*then what the hell did you come out here for?*—but given Max's prickly nature a remark like that would probably have done nothing but cause him to turn around and walk back in his own tracks. Henry waited, and Max soon continued.

"You ain't going to like what I got to say. Unless you already know."

Henry guessed that Max no longer wanted to work in the House orchards. Fine. Perhaps Henry couldn't hire a man who knew the labor of apples as well as Max Sherry, but more dependable hands could certainly be found. And a damn sight less peevish. If Henry had to, he'd lean once again on friends and family.

Max said, "I seen your wife naked."

Henry had been standing on that spot long enough to pack down the snow, and he had the sudden strange feeling that he had better remain exactly where he was, that if he stepped onto untrodden snow he might sink through and keep right on sinking, as if firm earth was nowhere but where he stood.

And yet shouldn't he barrel into Max Sherry? Take a swing at him and knock him on his ass? Wasn't that what a man was supposed to do after he heard the kind of remark that Max just made?

And yet Henry still couldn't make himself move. The very idea of a fight out there in the cold seemed ridiculous. Their hands were gloved, and their bodies were padded with layers of clothing. And then there was the problem of Henry's shoulder. If he experienced that much pain sawing a branch, what would throwing a punch feel like?

But if Henry were honest with himself he would admit that neither the temperature nor his shoulder was the real reason he didn't try to hit Max Sherry. The truth was Henry felt immediately defeated, although this feeling was not the type associated with losing a contest or a match. This defeat came before the game even began. It was very similar to what he felt when he learned his son had died.

"I know you didn't even want to hear that," Max said, "so maybe you don't want the rest."

"I'm listening. Go ahead."

"Your wife's been posing for that artist."

Henry feared he knew the answer, but he asked the question anyway. "Who?"

"He's got that big place off Denmark Road. Right below those orchards that used to belong to the Pepperdells."

Max's identification wasn't necessary. Two autumns ago, when Sonja's precarious mental condition made a gun in the house too great a temptation and danger, Henry had sold his Winchester, and that artist was the buyer. And now, so Henry's thinking went, the man had in his possession something else of Henry's.

"All right," Henry said. "I know where the Pepperdell orchard is. Go ahead."

"I guess you didn't know about her, eh? This artist's got a cabin toward the back of his property, and that's where your wife's posing."

It occurred to Henry that Max had not yet spoken her name. "Sonja."

"I know your wife. We ain't been introduced, but I know who she is." Max looked into the distance the way some men glance at their watches. "Maybe you don't want to hear any more until you talk to her."

"I'm still listening."

"If that painter's got shades in that cabin, he don't bother pulling them. Not even on the days your wife's there in her birthday suit."

By monitoring the steam of his breath, Henry could gauge the modulation of his response. As long as the little clouds came out at the same rate, as long as each was the same size as the one preceding it, he was fine.

"Ernie Glaser was the one first discovered her. He was back in those trees for one reason or other—"

"When was this?"

Max looked exasperated at the interruption. "Late summer? Early fall? I ain't sure. There was still plenty of leaves on the trees, I know that. Anyway, Ernie found out there's a spot on that hill where you can see right down into the cabin. And there's enough cover so they ain't likely to spot you from inside."

"And it didn't take Ernie long to spread the word."

Max shrugged. "He didn't tell too many. Ernie didn't want a big crowd back there."

"No, that might close down the show."

"What the hell do you suppose I'm doing now? I tell you about what your wife's been up to, and you're going to bring down the curtain. Ernie won't like it. A few others won't be too happy either. They find out I'm the one told you, they'll kick my ass here to Sunday."

"And what makes you think I'm not going to do the same? A man hears something like this about his wife, it's not like he wants to say thank you to the one who brings the news."

Max simply stared darkly at Henry, and for a long moment, neither man spoke. The boughs of the apple tree creaked with cold, and a knee-high gust of snow blew through the orchard as if it had been swept by a broom. Finally, without taking his eyes from Henry, Max Sherry brought his hand out from his coat pocket. He did not hold the pistol by its grip or trigger guard. Instead, he held it in his palm as if he were proffering an object for inspection.

Henry guessed the revolver to be a .38, and hard-used at that. The plating was worn and chipped in so many places the gun showed as much black as nickel. The bottom half of the grip was wrapped with electrician's tape.

"Looks like you came prepared for anything," Henry said.

"Everything but pruning trees."

"So if I took this message wrong," said Henry, "what were you going to do—kill me?"

Apparently satisfied that Henry was not about to mount a charge, Max slipped the pistol back in his pocket. "Maybe shoot you in the foot."

Henry stared up into the gnarled branches of the tree next to him. And to think that only moments ago the most daunting element in his life was the pruning of apple trees.

Max must have interpreted Henry's long gaze as that of a man whose greatest concern was still his orchard. Max lifted his knees high and walked a few steps closer to the tree. "You let your leader get too tall here."

His father's words came back to Henry: Watch Max when it comes to pruning—he's got a good eye. Mr. House said he himself expected to be a good pruner someday—if he lived to be a hundred.

"I could still use a hand," Henry said.

"Too damn cold. For me and the trees. This wind keeps up and we lose our cloud cover, it'll get down below zero tonight."

Max Sherry's word had been enough for Henry to believe that Sonja was taking her clothes off for another man, yet now Henry needed evidence to confirm the truth of Max's statement about the weather. Henry looked off to the western sky. Sure enough. The clouds were fraying, and patches of pale, icy blue were freezing their way through.

"I'm not sure what to do," Henry said.

"Well, if you can put this pruning business off for another week, I can help you out," Max said. "For now, maybe you ought to get on home and straighten out that wife of yours. Because I have to tell you: If she keeps putting on a show, I ain't going to look the other way."

Henry was twelve the first time his father took him grouse hunting. They had been walking through heavy woods when a bird fewer than ten feet from Henry burst from the leaves and whirred into flight. Not only did Henry fail to raise his shotgun to his shoulder in time to fire, he had jumped back, startled.

"Hey," his father said, laughing, "*we're* hunting *them*—remember?"

His heart still racing, Henry confessed, "It happened so fast—I didn't know what to do!"

The incident stayed with Henry because, typical of remembered moments, it bore little resemblance to most of his life's events. He almost always knew what to do, and it was not reason or planning that showed him the way but instinct, exactly the faculty that failed him that day in the woods. For the most part, Henry moved through his days trusting that when action was required something inside him would automatically bring forth the right one. He no more had to devise in advance what he would say or do in a situation than he had to plan to set a hook or stiff-arm a tackler.

Yet now, as he turned off the road at his own home and saw Sonja—she was shoveling the section of the driveway that always drifted over when the wind blew—he felt just as he had on that day when a ruffed grouse exploded from the dry leaves and frightened Henry into inaction. And if he could not trust that the right response would be ready now when he confronted his wife, perhaps Henry should never have put his faith in that power.

She put up the shovel, and Henry rolled down his window as he drove the truck abreast of her. He stopped, but he did not keep his foot on the brake. He shifted to first and kept the truck in place by giving it just a little gas and holding the clutch just so.

Smiling, Sonja stepped toward him. She wore an old felt hat of his and tied it down with a wool scarf knotted under her chin. The wind and cold had reddened her cheeks. If she didn't put lotion on tonight her face would be chapped and dry for days.

"Are you finished already?" she asked.

"Finished? Jesus. I'll be at that job for weeks. No. I quit. It's too goddamn cold."

She winced at his language.

"For the trees," he added. "If you make any cuts now and the temperature drops, you can damage the tree. And it's going to be cold tonight."

She tilted her head away from the stiffening wind. "The cold gets inside the tree?"

"Something like that. I've explained it to you before." He pointed to the mound of snow she had piled up in her shoveling. "I told you I was going to do this."

"I wanted to help. You said you'd be busy all day—"

"I'm not a goddamn cripple, you know. I can lift a shovel. Or I could if you weren't in such a hurry to beat me to every job around this place."

"I'm helping—"

"Helping? You think you're helping? You're making me feel helpless is what you're doing. A man needs—"

Sonja flicked the shovel up so the flat back of the blade clanged against the truck's door. "A man needs! Don't say to me what a man needs! I'm trying to take care of this family, to see that we are all fed and dressed and warm and that we have electricity and gasoline. . . . I should care about your man's pride? You would have us freezing and wearing rags so you can walk around with your pride!"

Both the suddenness and the intensity of her anger surprised him. It must have been there all along, waiting to be detonated. *Her* anger? What about *his*? All right—if all it took was his presence to set her off, then he wouldn't even give her that. He leaned out the window to look behind him, then pushed the clutch in all the way and let the truck roll slowly back down the drive.

"Yes, go. Go!" Sonja shouted. "Go drink your beers and feel sorry for yourself!"

He hesitated only once and that was to roll up his window. Sonja had charged after him, flinging shovelful after shovelful of snow at the truck. Once the flakes were in the air, however, they turned and flew back at her, as if the wind knew that on this day right was on Henry's side. Where, after all, was the harm in drinking a few beers, especially set alongside the sin of a wife taking off her clothes for another man?

Henry returned at an hour when he could be reasonably certain Sonja would be asleep. He plugged in the truck's head-bolt heater and turned toward the house. From horizon to horizon stars sprinkled the sky. Since the wind had given up its howl hours earlier, nothing competed with the sound of the snow squeaking underfoot. He checked the thermometer nailed to the porch post, but Henry had no doubt Max's prediction had proved out. Yes, there it was: four below.

Sonja was taking advantage of the cold. She had set the folding clothes rack outside the back door and hung a few items out to dry. The towels and washcloths and pillowcases would freeze stiff and then could be brought inside. They had first used this drying method with diapers. June's? John's? To know for certain Henry would have had to recall their birth dates and then work back toward the winter months. But he didn't know for certain how long each child had been in diapers. The hell with it.

He felt like kicking over the rack. She was so goddamn eager to do every job around here, she could do this one twice. But then he noticed: Those were his socks and T-shirts bent over the middle dowel, so it would be his own clothing he would be knocking onto the porch's dirt and packed snow. A similar thought had occurred to him earlier when he was staring into one of the many brandy old-fashioneds he drank at the Lakeside Tavern. Then, he had been contemplating ways he could punish Sonja for posing for that artist. When his anger dropped him into the colder, darker zones, he considered beating her, pummeling her until purple rosettes of bruises bloomed all over her pale body. Or maybe there'd be no beating, just a single punch. He'd break her nose. How would that artist like her then, her beauty smudged by Henry's fist? But wait a minute—exactly whom would Henry be punishing? My God, no one loved Sonja's body more than he did, and after all these years he still found her as exciting to his sight as to his touch. That body, he thought, wasn't it as much his as the socks he wore? If he broke or blemished her body it would be like damaging one of his own possessions. Yet if she was his, how could she have slipped so far from his control?

U*sually when she entered the studio he was busy with something*—mixing paint, moving a chair or a table or a prop so it caught the light just so, or, if they would be working *en plein air*—and what if she dusted her speech with Norwegian the way he dusted his with French?—he might be packing the old toolbox that contained all the supplies he would need for their hours outside. But when Sonja came in today, she saw him nowhere. And yet he had called out for her to come in.

"I'm right here," he said softly. Startled, Sonja turned in the direction of his voice.

He had rolled that old office chair into the darkest corner of the room, and there he sat, one foot up on the seat just as he had once posed her. The smoke from his cigarette rose into a shaft of sunlight, and Sonja found it unsettling that she could see that drifting cloud so clearly when Weaver's face was not visible at all.

"Am I early?" she asked.

"Have you ever been anything but right on time?" He exhaled a great plume of smoke. "No, the workers of the world should all be as punctual and obedient as you."

She wasn't sure—something in his posture or his speech made her think he had been drinking. Although Weaver was never drunk in her presence, this going off to a dark corner to brood and smoke—Henry did that when he had too much to drink.

"Should I make tea?" she asked. On a table by the door was an electric kettle with which Weaver or Sonja made tea when they took a break from the day's work. Really, she only wanted a reason to move closer to the door, so strong was her foreboding.

And he, as if he knew of her fear, pushed the chair out of the corner and rolled himself across the room. The casters rattling over the floor-boards reminded Sonja of chattering teeth.

How could she have had such difficulty seeing him? He was dressed in a white shirt and trousers and his pale little feet were bare.

"We need," he said, "to discuss our arrangement."

Here it came. He would no longer need her to pose for him. No more of those white envelopes into which he carelessly folded the bills that mattered so much to her and so little to him. When he held out her pay, it was all she could do not to grab the envelope from him and run for home and there hide the money in the place where she was sure Henry would never find it—tucked inside the pages of her Norwegian Bible, a book she never opened but to make a deposit or a withdrawal.

"How long have we been working together?" Weaver asked.

Sonja knew, but she kept quiet. If he heard spoken the duration of time, he might have exactly the evidence he needed to confirm their partnership had gone on too long.

He waved away his own question. "Doesn't matter. Long enough. We've gone on like this long enough."

Yes, long enough for her to know what he truly wanted of her. Could she decide, in advance of his offer, what she would accede to in order to keep being paid? This, but not this . . . that, but not that . . .

He rose from the chair, went to the door, opened it, and dropped his cigarette into the soft dirt. When he closed the screen he locked it. He coughed, and when he put his hand to his chest, he discovered that his shirt was halfway undone. He buttoned two of the buttons before he began to speak.

"When our session is over today, I propose"—he coughed again—"I propose that you remain here."

"Here?"

Weaver stood behind his chair and, leaning down on its arms, swiveled back and forth like a boy who could not stand still. "Well, not *here* literally. On the grounds. In the house. Or here—why not, if that's what you prefer."

She glanced at the hook-and-eye latch on the screen door. "I would not go home?"

"Don't put it that way. Certainly you'd go home if you needed to. I'm not talking about imprisoning you. I'm *asking* you to stay."

"To live . . . forever?"

He came out from behind his chair and walked toward Sonja. She had been barefoot on these floors, and she knew how uneven the boards were, how you had to be careful of the nails that had raised their heads over the years, but she didn't warn him. This building, after all, was his.

"Forever? Yes, I suppose that's what I mean. Look, I know I'm not doing a very good job of this. I decided I'd ask you today, but I didn't decide how I'd phrase it. And now I'm not sure if I should present it as an argument or a business proposition or as . . . or if I should simply say how important is it to me that you say yes."

"Tell me," Sonja said, keeping herself between Weaver and the door, "about business."

He backed up and then lowered himself into the chair again. When she posed she could stand tirelessly in one place for more than an hour, yet now she was envious that he could sit while she had to remain on her feet.

"That's not the inducement that I would have hoped you'd most want to hear, but very well." He lit another cigarette, and when he exhaled Sonja was sure she detected the smell of whiskey mingled with tobacco smoke. "I'd continue to pay you for the actual modeling sessions, whether the rate should change—we can discuss that. Living here, you would have no expenses. I'd see to your needs. Your wishes, for that matter. You've never asked me about my finances, but you must know I'm a wealthy man. *Modestly* wealthy, but still. You would be well provided for. Better than at any other time in your life, I'm guessing."

"I have a daughter," Sonja said. "And a husband."

"And I have a wife. Did you think I proposed this in ignorance of the relevant facts? If you feel you can't live without having your daughter with you, bring her along. I've had children under my roof before; I might find it a salutary experience to repeat."

"But my husband—he would not be welcome?"

Weaver looked up at her as if he were trying to gauge her seriousness. "He would not."

"So he and your wife—they would be out in the cold, as they say?"

"They're old enough to know how to keep themselves warm."

"Just—the hell with those two, eh?"

"The hell with them—exactly. If there was a way to do this without anyone being hurt, I'd be all for it. But that's not possible, so let's limit our losses as best we can. The most important consideration here—and I think all parties would agree, no matter how grudgingly—is my art. You, my dear, are essential to that. And that moves you and me to the top rung. If you say it's not fair that the happiness of a few relatively innocent people be sacrificed, I would agree with you. But there you have it."

Sonja turned her back to Weaver and walked to a window. The chair's squeak told her he was swiveling around to watch her.

It was early enough in spring—the trees had not yet fully leafed out—that she could see clear through to the orchard at the top of the hill behind the cabin. Did those apple trees once belong to Henry's family? She wasn't sure; she only knew how scornful Henry was of the people who owned them now, how they neither pruned nor picked properly. Worst of all, Henry suspected they didn't care about or need the apples at all; they wanted the orchard for nothing more than decoration and deer feed.

"I can see you're giving this serious thought," Weaver said. "Is there anything else I can say that might help you decide?"

The pale, barely open buds on the trees looked, when Sonja allowed her vision to blur slightly, as though they were not attached to branches but hovering in the air like a hatch of newly warmed, newly winged insects.

Sonja said, "My husband keeps trying to teach me the difference between a *couple* and a *few*. How many is a few?"

"Your husband sounds like a pedant. If you want to be literal about it, I suppose you'd say a couple is two. A few—three. Maybe more, but not many. Why?"

"So when you say the happiness of a few must be sacrificed for this arrangement. . . . If you said a couple you would have meant two, so that would be the happiness of my Henry and your wife. But you said 'a few,' so more than two. Am I numbered? Is my happiness of no concern?"

She heard the chair roll across the floor again and knew he had stopped behind her. "What if I answer your question with another question: Are you happy now? Perhaps we should set the matter of happiness aside entirely. My wife, for example, is not happy married to me. Nevertheless, she—Harriet, by the way, is her name—wants to remain married to me. By now she probably can't imagine another life. When my daughter Emma was a teenager she hated school, and a day didn't pass but that she left the house in tears. You know what I said to her? 'Baby, I'm sorry you're unhappy, but you've got to go. Some things are more important than your happiness, and education is one of them.' "

"And are you another?"

Weaver's laugh soon disintegrated into a dry, breathy cough. "My dear, I'm not the least bit important. But art is. It's supremely important. And as it happens, in this mix I'm the one who makes art. And you are helping me in the process."

She turned away from the window. Because she stood over him in his chair, he looked even smaller. Older too, and weaker. She had no trouble imagining a future in which he would be hunched down in a wheelchair while a younger woman—Sonja? that daughter who was so unhappy in school?—rolled him from room to room.

"But you want more," she said. "Already you have me posing for you. So you're asking for more."

"Do we need to discuss this? Of course I want something more from you, and I think you know what that something is."

"You want me to be . . . a wife?"

This time Weaver's laugh was a single dry bark. "As I said before, I *have* a wife. I'm in no hurry to acquire another. But if that's what you would require, if that's what it would take to get you to say yes . . . What the hell. You divorce Henry, I'll divorce Harriet, and you'll be my wife. Why not."

Now it was Sonja's turn to laugh. "You make it sound as though you're still talking business."

This time he came out of his chair quickly, and though he moved toward her as if he meant to put his hands on her, he stopped just beyond arm's reach. "What if I told you I adored you? Would that make the difference here? I have the feeling it wouldn't mean a goddamn thing to you. You seem to have no vanity, so I can't appeal to you by pointing out you'd gain a measure of fame by being my . . . my mate. Better still, my inspiration. You'd be more celebrated for that than for being my wife. Let's face it—the artist's wife is never remembered, unless she was his subject as well. You already know that one day your image will adorn the walls of museums, but you're wise enough to realize that the same hands that hang the paintings might someday take them down. A hell of a lot of art that people once thought was great is now gathering dust in the dark. For that matter, canvas can eventually turn to dust. But while I'm alive I want to make the finest art I can, and I want you near me while I do it."

She had grown accustomed to standing unclothed before him, but now it was his gaze that was naked and she couldn't bear it. She whirled around and faced once again the wooded slope behind the studio. At that moment a crow sliced in and out of the trees at a speed so astonishing it didn't seem possible it could avoid crashing into the trunk of an aspen.

"Would you like to travel?" he asked in a rapid, diminished voice. "Would you like to get away from here, where people would talk? I don't give a damn myself, but if that's what you want . . . We could visit Paris. A friend of mine has an apartment in the Latin Quarter overlooking the Luxembourg Gardens. He's seldom there, and he's told me I'm welcome to the place anytime. Or perhaps you'd prefer a fine hotel—maid service and room service so you don't have to lift a finger. The Savoy in London? Do you want to go back to your homeland? Do you have family you'd like to see again?"

She interrupted him to ask, "If I say no, will you still hire me to pose for you?"

Weaver said nothing. He retreated to a worktable, where he busied himself with work that didn't need to be done. Finally, after picking up and putting down five or six paint tubes—he seemed interested only in how neatly crimped the bottoms of the tubes were—Weaver replied, "I won't ask you again, but my offer—my request, my plea, whatever the hell you want to call it—will remain open. If you should ever change your mind." He pushed himself back as if something on one of his own paint-clotted palettes had repulsed him. "But that's not going to happen, is it?"

To Sonja's surprise, Weaver still wanted her to pose that day, although he started a new work rather than continue with the previous sitting, in which she was seated on the edge of the bed, naked but for the blanket draped across her lap, looking impassively at the adjacent small table and its water glass.

Now Weaver pulled the bed away from the corner and aligned it with the north window and the meadow beyond. He stripped the blankets and sheets from the bed and bade Sonja undress and lie flat on her back on the bare mattress.

The end of life has long fascinated the artist—Roman death masks, depictions of the crucified Christ, soldiers mutilated on the field of battle. David's "Death of Marat." Ruskin's deathbed drawing of his beloved Rose. Delacroix. Eakins. And at first glance, Ned Weaver's "An Early Spring" seems as though it might belong to that tradition, for what but death brings that attitude to the human body—eyes closed, hands folded across the chest, legs pressed together? She is naked, but we all will be before the mortician does his job. Or has he already done his work? She's pale, but wait—she doesn't have the marmoreal pallor of death. Blood, and not the embalmer's substitute, looks to be pumping yet through those veins. But she can't be sleeping; no one sleeps in that position.

Perhaps we're making the mistake that viewers of representational art so often make when they assume a work is "about" the people, objects, or scenes on the paper or canvas. On the other hand, we know when we look at Marden's "Cold Mountain" or Arp's "Mountain, Table, Anchors, Navel" that neither tells us as much about mountains as about the artist.

On that day, she was no more dead than those wildflowers outside the window—rendered in the looser brushstrokes we associate with the Impressionists—were in full bloom. Anyone familiar with Door County knows that a field will not bristle with points of pink, yellow, and lavender until the first weeks of summer.

At any rate, Francis Taub, the collector who bought "An Early Spring" and so many other Weavers, could not bear to look at the painting for long. He knew far more about oil deposits under the earth than about oil paint spread on a canvas, and he couldn't even be sure of what he felt when he gazed at that supine naked body, but he knew that his feelings disturbed him. "Early Spring" never hung on a wall in any of the Taub homes or offices.

T*he game was hearts, and no more than four men sat in at one time.* Anyone else gathered in Charlie Raven's shack could stand and watch the cards being played—but keep their damn mouths shut—or they could go outside and jig through one of the holes drilled in the ice of Weasel Lake. They could help themselves to a brandy or a beer—as long as they were as willing to replenish the supply as deplete it. They could tear off a strip of venison jerky, but they were not welcome to any of the chocolates— Charlie Raven had a sweet tooth, and the Russell Stover box was his private supply.

Henry stood alone at the window while the card game chattered on behind his back.

"Whoa! Is he going for it?"

"If he is, he ain't going far."

"Make him eat it. Make him eat that black bitch."

"Should we just get it over with and see if someone's got the stopper?"

Henry didn't belong there. He was younger than any other man by at least twenty years. He had a wife and a child and a house with a front and back door. His income was more or less regular. He liked to hunt and fish, but for him it was recreation, not a primary source of food. He had a name and a reputation in the county that stood for something besides poaching and hard drinking. And Henry could not keep up with these men at the card table. They played fast, they talked constantly, and they slapped their cards down as if they wanted to inflict harm.

But Max Sherry was a regular; Charlie Raven, Morgan Sherrill, and Barney Sykes were Max's friends, and Henry wanted to know if they, along with Ernie Glaser, the man who was supposed to have discovered Sonja, had also watched his wife while she posed for that artist. He wanted to know, but he didn't want to ask.

Since the day Max Sherry had told him about Sonja, Henry thought of little else, yet he couldn't make any of those thoughts move from his mind to his tongue. He hadn't confronted Sonja, and he hadn't asked any other man if he had ever had such a problem with his own wife, as improbable as that might be. He hadn't sought advice or consolation, though he could use both. He felt unmoored and unmanned, yet he put himself in the company of these directionless men who no doubt would, if they knew of his dilemma, mock his masculinity.

"Henry," Barney Sykes said, "we got any flags out there?" He assumed Henry was watching to see if any of the tip-up flags were up, indicating a fish on the line. For what other reason would Henry be staring out the window?

"No, but somebody out there is pulling in a shitload of bluegills."

"Georgie Bohn," Charlie Raven said as he shuffled the cards. "He loves those fucking bluegills. Fries 'em up like potato chips."

"And it's about as easy to make a meal out of potato chips," Barney said.

A chair scraped, and Henry heard Max's voice. "Fuck it. I'll go drill some new holes. We ain't got a hit so far with them in close."

"Stay away from Georgie," said Charlie, "unless you want bluegills tipping your flag."

"Henry," Max said, "you want to sit in here?"

"No, I'll give you a hand moving the lines."

The sunlight reflecting off the ice gave Henry a headache, but he tried not to squint. Ever since he fell from Buck and tore open his forehead, he had trouble with his right eye. If he pinched his facial muscles for long, his eye would begin to twitch so violently it threatened to shut itself, and that was all he needed—to have only one good eye to go with his one good ear. He wished he had a cap like Max's with a bill he could pull down low.

Henry and Max took turns drilling holes, exertion strenuous enough on that warm February day to allow both of them to break a sweat. They

unbuttoned their coats, and while Max put fresh bait on each line, Henry
lit a cigarette and kept his gaze fixed on the only available darkness—the
hole that peered into the lake's green-black depths.

"Don't much care for cards, do you?" Max said as he knelt on the ice
and reset the tip-up.

"Not really," Henry replied.

"Nor ice fishing?"

"I have trouble sitting still."

"Yeah, well, fishing and cards . . . they don't allow for much moving
around." Max stood and with the toe of his boot pushed a little slush back
into the water. "So what are you doing hanging out with us old farts?"

"I guess I wanted to find out if you'd ever mount an expedition to go
off and spy on my wife."

Max's laugh was as hard and cold as the ice underfoot. "We sure as
hell wouldn't do it when you're around, now, would we?"

"I suppose not."

"You ain't spoken to her about what she's been doing?"

"Not yet."

"Jesus, Henry. If it was my wife . . ."

"You'd what?" The question could have been belligerent, challeng-
ing, but coming from Henry's lips, it sounded like a plea for help.

"I'd let her know what time it is."

Max's choice of words struck Henry as so odd that he couldn't keep
from smiling, and that in turn seemed to anger Max.

"This is funny to you? Maybe you're one of those men who don't
give a shit what his wife does once she's out of his sight."

"It's not that—"

"Or maybe you never did believe me on this. Come over here and
stand beside me."

Henry did as he was told. Max pointed toward shore with one hand
and with the other pressed down on Henry's shoulder to get Henry to
hunch down and share Max's sight line. "See that stand of scrub oak just
back of Charlie's place?"

"I see them."

"Well, those leaves there are the same color as your wife's pussy hairs."

Had he wished, Max Sherry could probably have pushed Henry to his knees by only slightly increasing the pressure on Henry's shoulder. Instead, Max removed his hand and shoved Henry away.

"You sure as shit believe me now, don't you?" asked Max.

"Those men in there," Henry said, still staring in the direction of both the shack and the oak leaves, "how many of them have seen her?"

"Fuck if I know. I told you. Ernie's the one who found her, and I ain't too sure who he shared with."

"Charlie?"

"Why—would that bother you more because Charlie's part Indian?"

"Morgan?"

"Yeah, Morgan. He don't get too close though, because he's too fucking fat to sneak down the hill."

"Barney?"

"Okay, Barney. The others I don't know about. I swear to God. Ernie'd be the one to ask."

"You don't talk about this among yourselves?"

"We do some. Sure."

"And what do you talk about?"

"Your wife's a good-looking woman, Henry—what the hell do you suppose we talk about?"

Growing amid the deep green of those tall pines, the oak tree and its rust-colored leaves looked out of place, like something forgotten and left out in the weather. Henry kept his eyes trained, no matter how the right one twitched, on that tree. "Tell me, Max—you still have that pistol you showed me that day in the orchard? Because if you do, I'd be willing to buy it from you."

When he accompanied Max out onto the ice, Henry had no idea that he would make this request, yet once it was out of his mouth it altered not only the present moment but those preceding it as well. Yes, this was exactly the reason Henry had walked out of the shack with Max. Henry even felt as though some of that old power of being able to act on the instant was flowing back to him.

Max shook his head slowly and sadly over Henry's offer. "Henry. That's not the route you want to go. No sir."

"You don't want to part with it," said Henry, "that's okay. I can lay my hands on another."

"I'm sure you can."

"I'm not going to murder anyone, if that's what you're thinking. I'd just like to have it in my pocket. In case I need to show someone how serious I am. Like when you brought it to the orchard."

Squatting once again by the nearest hole in the ice, Max lifted his line slightly to test if the minnow was still on. Satisfied, he stood and shook the icy water from his fingers. "I'll make a deal with you," he said to Henry. "I'll *loan* it to you. But not today. You need to think on this business. And you need to talk to your woman, goddammit. You do that, and you still want to stick a barrel in that fucking artist's ear and scare the shit out of him, all right."

"So you don't have your pistol with you?" said Henry.

Max ignored Henry's question. "Today's Sunday. . . . You meet me next Wednesday at the Top Deck. Seven o'clock? I'll have it with me then, and if you still want to take a turn with it, it's all yours."

"Top Deck, seven o'clock. Wednesday."

"And in the meantime, find someone else to talk to about this. I sure as hell don't have any advice for you." Max rubbed his hands together for warmth. "Now, let's go inside and break the seal on Charlie's brandy."

As they walked back across the creaking ice, Max went back on his word. "When you're passing to Morgan," he told Henry, "hold back a high spade or high hearts. He's always looking to shoot the moon."

When Henry walked out of Charlie Raven's hours later, he paused for a moment beside his truck and stared up at the night sky. Maybe it was a good thing Max didn't have the gun with him. Henry might have taken it into Charlie's shack and shot the eyes out of every one of those old bastards.

Henry shuddered at the stupidity and savagery of his thoughts. Perhaps he should go back inside and tell Max to forget about the Wednesday meeting at the Top Deck. No, that would take time, and Henry was suddenly in a hurry. Earlier, in the double glare of ice and sun, he couldn't see clearly, but now, wrapped in darkness, his way was clear. He would talk to Sonja. That was why he had been so confused about what to do, trying to lay his hands on a pistol, hanging around these old mossbacks, when what he really wanted was to sit next to Sonja, take hold of her hand, and tell her about his dilemma. But he had to remind himself—he wasn't going to talk with her, he was going to lay down the law: She would stop posing for that artist. That was the first thing. Later, if she wanted to tell him her reasons for posing, maybe he'd listen. Maybe.

The house was dark, and though Sonja and June were probably sleeping, Henry burst in as if it were mealtime. He stamped the snow from his boots, but he was in too much of a hurry to take them off. Henry had his words and their order locked in tight, and he wanted to deliver them before they got away from him. He would keep his voice level and low and tell her—no argument about it—*Sonja, you've been posing for that artist. I don't know your reasons, and for now I don't care to hear them. You're going to stop, no ands, ifs, or buts.*

As he pounded up the stairs, he scolded himself. A gun—what the hell did he think, that he couldn't control his wife or handle that little bastard and his paintbrushes without taking up a weapon?

But Sonja was not asleep. She was not even in bed. She was sitting on a chair in the corner of the darkened room, and Henry was so startled to see her there that the thread on which he had strung his little speech snapped.

"What are you doing up?" he asked.

"Waiting for you."

"I told you I'd be home late."

"No, you didn't."

"You knew I'd be fishing and playing cards at Charlie's."

"I should not think you fell through the ice?"

"I haven't so far."

"So far."

"I'm a big boy. I can take care of myself."

"A big boy . . ."

Was she crying now? He hoped not—not before he had his say. "Look here, we're going to have a talk."

She was wearing one of Henry's flannel shirts over her nightgown, and she pulled it tighter around herself.

"I know what you've been up to," Henry said, "and it's got to stop."

She said nothing, but that wasn't unusual. Sometimes she could not think of the English word for what she wanted to say, and there was nothing to be done but give her time. Henry thought that as her years in America increased she should need less time to find the right word, but instead it seemed as though her silences had become more frequent and longer-lived. He was never sure how long he should wait, but now Henry felt his anger and frustration mount with each hushed second.

"What made you decide to pose for him, can you answer me that?"

She was looking in his direction, he could see that much.

"Did he flatter you? Tell you how beautiful you are? Did it make you feel important to have this famous artist painting you?"

If only there were more light in the room, enough for Henry to see Sonja's expression, then he might have been able to imagine what her reactions were and then address them before she could give them voice.

"Whose idea was it for you to undress? Did he suggest it or did you come up with that on your own?"

He was groping, stumbling—what happened to that clarity of purpose, that sense of certainty, that he felt when he entered the house?

"Was that it? Did he tell you how good-looking you are, and then by God you just had to show him he didn't know the half of it—you had to strip down and show him all your charms."

When she still didn't utter a word, Henry began to walk toward her, but slowly, as if floorboards might be missing in his path. Standing over her, he said, "Get up."

She didn't move.

"I said, get up!"

Sonja did not obey his command, but neither did she resist him when he grabbed her wrist and pulled her out of the chair. She allowed him to tow her across the bedroom, and only when they reached the doorway did she draw back.

"You think you're such a goddamn beauty?" Henry was close to shouting. "Is that what you think? Well, I'm going to show you just exactly who you are!"

When Sonja tried to grab the doorframe Henry jerked hard on her arm and her fingernails scraped across the wood. Once they were in the hall, the rag rug bunched and rippled under Henry's feet as if it too wanted to slow him.

At the end of the hall was a commode that had once been in the home of Henry's grandparents, but it was the mirror attached to this low chest of drawers toward which Henry hauled Sonja. As he drew closer, Henry slapped on the hall light and shoved Sonja in front of the glass. He stood behind her, held her in place with his hands on her shoulders, and forced her to confront her own image.

"Take a look," said Henry. "You think that face is a fucking work of art?"

That still wasn't what Henry wanted to say, but Sonja's tight-lipped impassivity unnerved him. He shook her hard, desperate for a response from her. "Are you looking? Are you getting an eyeful?"

Later in his life, when Henry thought back to this moment, he would not be able to recall June running out of her room to join her father and mother in front of the mirror. She appeared so suddenly it seemed as if she had, for the second time, sprung from her mother's body. Mother and daughter clung tightly to each other and stared into the mirror, their eyes widening with fear and defiance as they kept watch on Henry.

Henry saw now a resemblance between Sonja and June that had previously escaped him—something in the shape and set of the jaw—no, that wasn't it, not entirely. It wasn't physical. It was the ability—a gift? a curse?—to absent herself, to be present in body but not in mind or spirit. No, that couldn't be it either, they were there, all right, or else why would they be cowering in front of their husband and father. But they had both discovered a way to preserve a small portion of herself *for* herself, to keep it untouched by the moment. Henry envied them. He had nothing to protect himself from the shame he felt as he backed down the hall, moving slowly away from the two creatures he loved more than anyone or anything living under the sun or the stars.

Mother and daughter continued to hold each other close and keep their faces fixed on the mirror. Henry knew that meant he vanished from their sight sooner than if they had turned to watch him go.

After Max Sherry left, Henry House was the Top Deck's only customer, sitting alone at the bar with Max's sorry excuse for a pistol weighing down the pocket of his mackinaw. Henry had hoped Frankie Rawling would be the one mixing his drinks that night, but neither she nor Owen was in the establishment. Owen's sister, Agnes, was working behind the bar, and she told Henry that the owners were in Green Bay on business.

"Expecting them back tonight?" Henry asked.

Agnes, whose brashness made her closer in spirit to her sister-in-law than to her taciturn brother, said, "Yes, and they sure as hell better get here soon. I don't feature closing up this place and spending the night."

Henry knew that Agnes didn't drive, and he considered volunteering to take her home, but he was fairly certain she lived in Ellison Bay, the village farthest north on the peninsula. A light snow was falling, and though it wasn't likely to amount to much, it would wax up the already slick roads. He'd have one more drink, and if Owen and Frankie didn't return before he finished, he'd make the offer and hope Agnes refused.

He was down to nothing but the cherry and a final watery swallow of brandy when the Rawlings walked through the door.

Frankie and Owen both took off their coats and laid them on the bar, but Frankie immediately tossed her husband's back at him. "Huh-uh," she said. "You're taking Agnes home."

"She can sleep on the couch," said Owen.

Frankie merely jerked her head in the direction of the door. Owen thrust his arm into his coat sleeve with almost as much force as a punch, but that was as much argument as he allowed himself to make. "Come on," he grunted to his sister.

Before the headlights of Owen's departing car swept past the window, Frankie was fixing Henry another drink. She put it down in front of him, then locked the door and turned off the outside lights that announced the Top Deck was open for business. She sat down on the stool next to him and pulled one of his cigarettes from the pack.

Henry held out a match for her. "Have I ever seen you in a dress before?"

Frankie exhaled with a tired sigh. "Not unless you went to my mother's funeral. And that's going on ten years."

Henry didn't know much about women's clothing, but Frankie's dress, with its boxy shoulders and below the knee hemline, looked as though it went out of fashion in the forties. "Maybe you should wear one more often. That sure looks good on you."

One by one Frankie kicked off her high heels, sailing them halfway across the room. "What the hell. I can still button it." She tugged at her bodice, but there wasn't much play in the fabric. "But I had a supply of safety pins just in case."

"And what was the occasion that got you all dolled up? Agnes said something about business."

In reply, Frankie reached over, dipped her index finger into Henry's glass, and stirred. Then she put her finger in her mouth and sucked on it longer than it took to absorb the full flavor of the brandy. "How's the drink?" she asked. "Fixed to your liking?"

"You know it is. Perfect. Every time."

"Well, get yourself ready: It's soon going to be a new hand dropping in the cherry."

"How's that?"

"We're selling the place. Sold, is more like it. We signed the papers today. The Top Deck's new owners are a couple from Waukesha. He's always wanted to own a bar, and she's always wanted a place where she can show off her collection of carnival glass, whatever the hell that is."

"Jesus, Frankie. I didn't even know you were looking to sell. I don't know what to say."

She stabbed out the half-smoked cigarette. "You don't? How about congratulations? How about, I'm happy for you, Frankie? No more having to serve drunks and then clean up after them. No more listening to the sad fucking life stories of men whose lives wouldn't be so fucking sad if they'd get off their asses instead of sitting on a bar stool telling me their fucking life story. How about that—huh? Huh?" She punched Henry playfully on the arm.

Henry stared down at his drink where the ice cubes still gently rocked from Frankie's finger. The bar was almost dark, yet the ice and amber liquid shimmered as if a light somewhere in the room were trained on his glass, a phenomenon as inexplicable to Henry as the behavior of women increasingly was. "I'm sorry, Frankie," he muttered. "Congratulations. What will you and Owen do?"

Frankie was silent for a long moment before reaching over and grabbing Henry's face. She squeezed his cheeks, puckering his lips in the process, and then swiveled his head until his eyes met hers. "Now, what did I go and do?" she asked. "Did I hurt your feelings? Did you come here tonight to tell me *your* life story?"

Henry pushed Frankie's hand away, but even with his mouth unencumbered, he didn't speak.

"Come on. What's on your mind? Tell Frankie."

Henry had to direct his attention back to his brandy in order to ask the question: "What can you tell me about Ned Weaver? The artist? You know who I'm talking about?"

"He used to come in here all the time. I haven't seen him for a while."

"So you know him."

Frankie shrugged. "I know we probably sold this place for less than people are willing to shell out for one of his pictures."

Henry cleared his throat. "Did he ever paint your picture, Frankie?"

"He talked about it, but he never got around to it." She slapped herself on the thigh. "Maybe there's just too damn much of me to fit in the frame."

Henry crushed out his own cigarette. He started to count the butts in the ashtray, all his but one, but then stopped himself. "He's been painting Sonja."

"No kidding? Well, what of it. Your wife's got the kind of looks that painters like to paint."

"It's not just her face, Frankie. He's painting her naked. It's been going on for a long time. She's . . . I don't know. She's his regular model, I guess."

Frankie removed her hand from Henry's shoulder. "Is she getting paid?"

"I don't know."

"As far as I know, he usually pays the people who pose for him. And that's men and women both. He did a few pictures of old Pete Donley down there by his boat. The best money Pete ever made. Shit, Henry, would you rather she took in wash? Or worked as a maid in one of the hotels? Or go back to waiting tables for Axel?"

"At least she'd be doing it with her clothes on."

"Not if Axel had his way."

"Come on, Frankie. You know what I mean. If she's laying around naked in front of this fellow . . . Alone with him . . ."

Frankie took another of his cigarettes from the pack then put it back. "This is mighty strange talk coming from a man who's looking to fuck another man's wife."

"That's not what brought me here tonight, Frankie. I swear."

"Well, that's what you're here for now, Mr. House." She stepped down from her stool and walked around behind the bar. She unsnapped her nylons and rolled them off and then wriggled out of her girdle. She stepped out of her panties and laid all her underthings on the bar next to her coat. "When we signed the papers today, I thought, Now, what do I have to do before we clear out of here?" She came back to her stool, lifted her dress up to her hips, and sat down again, spreading her legs wide. "Now, drop your trousers and step up here so I can cross you off my list of unfinished business."

Henry hesitated, pondering questions of morality. Would the sin of fucking Frankie Rawling be diluted if, like an obedient boy, he was merely following an order? He'd had too much to drink too—did that further erode his volition until it was next to nothing? And what if a man's wife had strayed down her own path—what obligation did he have to walk the straight and narrow? Before he could come up with a single satisfactory answer, he found himself standing between Frankie's thighs and trying to push her dress and brassiere out of the way so he could get his hands on those big breasts.

Frankie unbuckled his belt, then began to fumble inside the sleeves of his mackinaw. "Come on, let's bare those broad shoulders. What do you think I bought my ticket for?"

Henry shrugged out of his coat and let it fall to the floor. There was a clunk from Max's gun in the pocket, and Henry had a funny thought: What if the gun went off and shot him in the ass? Better he should die on the spot than try to explain a wound like that.

Frankie was working on his shirt buttons. "This has got to go too, hon. And push up here a little higher. Uh-huh. That's right, that's right. Uh-*huh*."

Henry knew there was nothing, nothing his imagination could concoct that this woman would be unwilling to do, but almost immediately upon entering Frankie, he lost some of his enthusiasm for the act. Something was not right. Entering Sonja, it always seemed to Henry as though she surrounded him—Sonja, Sonja, everywhere!—yet inside Frankie he felt as though he were thrusting his cock into nothing but darkness. He pushed harder, close to violence in his attempt to touch something in her that almost certainly could not be touched.

And then, as suddenly as if the door of the Top Deck blew open and a cold wind ran up his spine, the realization struck him: The darkness was his. The place that couldn't be touched was in him. He wanted to be done fucking Frankie Rawling, but when he increased the speed as well as the force of his thrusts, he felt as though he might be slipping, as if Frankie's long-ago admonition—that he'd better hold on tight or she'd throw him off—were coming true. The stool rocked, Frankie yelped and dug her fingernails into his buttocks, and that was enough—with a final plunge Henry finished. He staggered back and almost tripped over his own coat.

"Jesus!" Frankie inhaled sharply to catch her breath. "Did you have something stored up there, Mr. House?"

Henry didn't answer. He buckled his trousers and then picked up his mackinaw, careful not to let the pistol slip from the pocket.

Frankie didn't bother going back behind the bar to put her underwear on and button herself up. She began to roll her stocking up her leg then quit and tossed it in the direction of her shoe. "The hell with it," she said, reaching for Henry's cigarettes.

"How long until the new owners take over?" Henry asked Frankie.

"I told them we'd be out by the middle of April. That should give them plenty of time to change things around if they like and still be ready for the tourists."

"You and Owen staying in the county?"

She took a step forward and kissed Henry on the corner of the mouth, the first kiss between them. "You sound like a man who's already worrying about a return engagement." Then Frankie stepped back, smoothing her dress over her body. "If it was up to Owen we'd stay. I'm for getting the hell out. Florida or Arizona, maybe."

"Someplace where you can lay out in the sun all year round, eh?"

"Well, somebody finally noticed." She held up the back of her hand for inspection, as if, even in the darkened tavern, she could gauge how well her tan was holding up. "Why not? Why not someplace where you don't have to put up with snow half the goddamn year?"

"Folks around here will miss you, Frankie."

"Let's not get too teary about this. I ain't gone yet. Besides, you'll sell too someday. All it takes is the right price."

"I don't know about that. The Houses have lived here close to a hundred years. Almost as long as Door's been a county."

"The right price, baby. That's all it'll take. Don't think you and yours aren't for sale too."

Her reference to his family stung, but that Frankie's remark might be intended to include Sonja too was a deeper hurt. To keep her from saying any more, Henry reached out and pinched the point of her dress collar between his thumb and index finger. With no more pressure than he'd use to tear a petal from a flower, he pulled Frankie close.

She gently pushed him away. "Sorry, baby. I'm shooing you out. I don't want you here when Owen comes back. My life's complicated enough right now."

Henry was pleased that he did not have to come up with an excuse to remove himself from the Top Deck. "Okay," he said, retreating slowly from Frankie, "you're still the owner."

Before Henry could unlock the door and let himself out, Frankie stopped him. "Hey—just for your information: You've got it over that artist in one way at least. He couldn't manage the business with the stool. He's just too damn short."

On the way home, Henry pulled over to the side of the road and stepped out of the truck. The snow had stopped, and he noticed a crescent moon blinking in and out of the wind-torn clouds. He brought the revolver out of his pocket and sighted on the moon's lower horn. He thumbed back the hammer and felt it catch reluctantly. A drifting scrap of cloud obscured his target, and Henry had to wait, his finger crooked on the cold trigger. The instant the moon returned, Henry fired. There. He'd fucked a woman not his wife, and he'd shot the moon, albeit with no more success than he'd had at the card table. The pistol's report echoed across the snowy fields and was answered by a distant bark. Let him yap, Henry thought. He seldom had an easy night's sleep anymore—why should he give a damn if some farmer's dog kept his owner awake?

True to Frankie Rawling's prediction, the day finally came when Henry House sold all the Door County property that was his to sell. Unlike the Rawlings, who, after agreeing to the terms of sale, returned temporarily to their home and business, Henry never went back. He signed the final papers in Manitowoc, Wisconsin, and when he left that squat brick building he got into his truck and drove inland, away from Lake Michigan. He never saw the lake again, much less crossed its waters into the county where his ancestors planted apple trees on a stony hillside almost a hundred years before.

*H*enry did not usually drive June to school, but that day he insisted, and less than fifteen minutes after they left, Phyllis drove up to the house. Sonja was on the porch shaking a rug, and she watched skeptically as her sister-in-law stepped out of her long white car and leaned across the roof. "I could sure use a cup of coffee," Phyllis said. "Do you have the pot on?"

"Henry's not here." Sonja felt she had to convey that information right away; whenever Phyllis phoned or—these occasions were rare—came to the house, it was to speak to her brother, although she always made sure she engaged Sonja in an interval of polite conversation. Sonja did not dislike her sister-in-law, but they had so little in common she often felt uncomfortable in Phyllis's company.

"That's okay," Phyllis said. "We can talk a little girl talk."

"Is your mother all right?"

"She's fine. I was down in Green Bay yesterday. She's driving the nurses up the wall, but that's nothing new."

Still wary, Sonja invited Phyllis into the house. When they entered the kitchen, Phyllis untied her scarf and shook loose her hair. She was not only pretty but stylish, yet for all her self-assured beauty, there was still something about her that made Sonja wonder about her sister-in-law's happiness.

"Mmm. What do I smell?" Phyllis asked.

"I baked cupcakes last night for June to take to school."

"A special occasion? Don't tell me we missed June's birthday?"

"No, no. Nothing special. Just a treat for the pupils. Would you like one? I have four extra."

"Oh God, not for me." Phyllis sat down at the table. "I ate like a pig in Florida. I must have gained ten pounds."

Phyllis and Russell had returned from Florida the first of April, and though the following two weeks had offered little more than rain and gray skies, Phyllis's tan still looked as dark as though she had just stepped indoors from sunbathing.

"How about you?" Phyllis asked. "Do you worry about your weight at all? I can't imagine you do."

"We don't own a scale." Sonja poured coffee for both of them, but she remained standing.

"Of course there are other ways of telling. I swear to God, Russ can feel an extra three pounds on me."

Sonja remained silent, and finally Phyllis said, "But you keep busy, don't you?"

"I keep busy. Yes."

Phyllis lit a cigarette and plucked a shred of tobacco from her lip. "Did Henry tell you what Russell's been up to?"

Sonja set an ashtray in front of her sister-in-law. "He didn't."

"He's buying a new sailboat. Another one, I said? But Russ just says after a couple years he finds he needs a bigger boat. So why don't you go ahead, I said to him, and make it a hell of a lot bigger this time. So we'll see. He's down in Sturgeon Bay today making the deal."

Sonja was not sure whether to congratulate Phyllis or extend her sympathy. "I'm sure it will be a nice boat."

Silence, this time lasting as long as ten ticks of the clock hanging over the stove, overtook them once again. Finally, Phyllis rose and joined Sonja by the kitchen sink, but then she seemed to have nothing to say. For a long moment, the two women stared out toward the barn as intently as if each had heard her name called from that direction.

Phyllis took a breath. "So." She exhaled. "Henry tells me we're going to have someone famous in the family."

The remark so puzzled Sonja that she leaned back as if she had to see the speaker whole to understand what she was saying.

"Do I have it wrong?" Phyllis asked. "I was sure Henry said you were posing for Ned Weaver."

Here it was, the reason for Phyllis's visit. Sonja looked frantically around the sink for a chore that needed to be done.

Phyllis put a hand on Sonja's wrist. "Honey, I'm not kidding. Do you know how well known your artist is? I mean, my God—you're going to be in *museums*. How many paintings of you has he done?"

"I . . . I'm not sure. Drawings too."

"Has he sold any?"

"If he has, he hasn't said."

"Do you know what he gets for an oil painting? Russ's dad looked into it, because his mother has a couple little watercolors that she bought at his gallery. She liked these so much Bernard thought about buying one of the big oils for her. He couldn't believe what they sold for. I mean, Bernard could afford it, but he'd never spend that kind of money for a painting. Never. But people do, plenty of them do."

"He never talks about such things."

"No? Why don't you ask him to give you one of the paintings or drawings he's done of you. He'd talk about it then."

"I don't think . . . Maybe he hasn't sold any of me. He once said he's not ready to release them into the world. Like one's child."

Phyllis turned on the tap and extinguished her cigarette. She opened the cupboard door under the sink and dropped the butt in the garbage. Straightening up, she looked sternly at Sonja. "Well, sweetheart, how do you think Henry will feel when those pictures *are* out there?"

Sonja gave back her sister-in-law's steady gaze. "I don't know how he'll feel. He hasn't told me."

"Honey. Come on."

Sonja picked up a washrag, and with the tip of her index finger inside the cloth began to scrub along the edge of the sink. "Did Henry ask you to talk to me?"

Phyllis laughed. "You're lucky he didn't ask Mom to intercede on his behalf. She'd probably have you down on the linoleum praying for your soul."

Sonja could never decide which version of the old woman was the more unpleasant, the one who formerly hid her cruelty in drink or the newer version who used the Bible for the same purpose.

"Seriously," said Phyllis, "you have to realize what you're doing when you expose your body to this man. Maybe you think this has to do only with what the eye sees, but it's your name too. Ned Weaver isn't just known as an artist; he has a real reputation up and down the county as a . . . as a . . . Well, I don't want to scald your ears. As a ladies' man. Let's leave it at that."

Sonja rubbed harder at the thin line of grime. It was not dark, like dirt, but close to white, the kind of stain snow or salt would leave, if such a thing were possible.

"He has a wife," Phyllis said. "Did you know that?"

"I know."

"Have you met her?"

Sonja shook her head.

Phyllis grabbed the dishrag from Sonja's hand. "Could you stop your damn scrubbing for just a minute! I'm trying to talk to you about something important."

Sonja started to reach for her washcloth, then stopped. She crossed her arms and stared wordlessly at her sister-in-law. Her tongue was no match for Phyllis's, but Sonja knew her silence had its own power.

"You know what I'm asking, don't you? Have you had relations with that man?"

"Is that what Henry sent you to find out?"

"I'm the one asking. Let's leave it at that."

"Others have posed for him. Men and women. I'm not the only one."

"But, honey, you're the only one who's married to my brother."

At this note of tenderness in Phyllis's voice, Sonja felt her eyes sting with the start of tears. Before they could spangle her sight and spill over, she found another task for herself. She crossed to the stove to make certain she had turned off the flame under the coffeepot. With her back to her sister-in-law, Sonja could speak again. "He looks at me. He looks and looks, and then he paints or draws what he sees. He doesn't show me the pictures, but I think it isn't me. No. He paints what is in his mind. But that doesn't matter. I am still myself. For the hour or two or three that I sit or stand or lie before him, I am me, just me. Breathing in and out. My heart beating. That's all. Clothed or naked, it doesn't matter. Just as it doesn't matter what he puts on the paper. It doesn't change that I am . . . myself."

This time the interval of silence stretched on so long Sonja wondered if she had won, although exactly what was at contest she wasn't sure. Finally, Phyllis said, "That sounds wonderful, honey, but don't you see—you're Henry's. You belong to him. How do you think he feels when another man—men—can just stare and stare at you in that way that's supposed to be only his?"

"I belong to him?" She wiped her hands on her apron as if that thought was a physical thing, and she had sullied herself in handling it. "I belong to myself. To me." Sonja didn't care for the way this sounded, but she didn't know any other way to express the idea.

"That sounds fine, but think about it. You're a couple. You need to stand together. Especially after . . . You need to help each other. But what you're doing . . . you're humiliating your husband. When the two of you walk down the street people will laugh at Henry behind his back. If they're not doing it already."

"Laughing . . ."

"That's right. Like a joke."

"I know what I've done, and I've done nothing wrong."

Phyllis leaned forward and squinted at Sonja as if a scrim had dropped between them. "Henry wouldn't agree with you on that subject, now, would he?"

"And he is the one to decide?"

"God *damn* it!" Phyllis threw her hands in the air and spun slowly across the kitchen. "I told Henry he needs to be the one to talk to you on this." She picked up her coffee cup, then just as quickly set it aside. "Look, I'm sure posing for a famous artist is flattering. You don't want to give it up. I understand. But can I just present this to you the way Henry sees it? You're alone with a man. You're naked. And even if there's nothing more to it than that, this man still gets to take in all of your charms for as long as he likes. I mean, does Henry even have that privilege anymore? He wouldn't come right out and say it, but he made it sound as though things aren't quite what they should be in the bedroom."

"Charms. That's exactly the word Henry used. Tell me, when you and your brother talk about 'my charms,' what part of me are you talking about?" Sonja retrieved the dishrag that Phyllis had tugged from her hand earlier, but now that Sonja had it in her possession once again she had no use for it. She put the cloth back down again, just as Phyllis had done with her coffee cup.

"It's just an expression, honey. You're naked in front of the man. I guess that means he's free to look at any part of you he damn well pleases."

The kitchen was not large, yet it seemed to Sonja that she and Phyllis had reached the point where they could say or do nothing to close the distance between them.

"Come with me. I want to show you something." She led Phyllis out of the kitchen and up the stairs. They walked down the hall to the bathroom, and Sonja then took Phyllis's hand and pulled her in until they both stood in front of the sink, both women's faces framed by the mirror. The day was sunny and the bathroom was bright, but Sonja still turned on the light.

"There you are," Sonja said. "Your pretty pretty face. Your charms."

At that, Phyllis tried to back away. "Oh, for Christ's sake, Sonja!"

Sonja gripped her sister-in-law's shoulders and held her in front of the mirror, just as Henry had held her. Phyllis's bones felt thin, birdlike, and it occurred to Sonja that perhaps this, Phyllis's delicate underpinning, was what Sonja had always noticed as her sister-in-law's fragility.

"Please," Sonja said. "Stay. I just want you to look, to look as long as you can. Don't dance away or say you must have a cigarette. *Look*."

A little tension went out of Phyllis's muscles, and Sonja relaxed her grasp but still kept her hands on her sister-in-law's shoulders.

"I don't know what you're trying to prove. . . ."

"Just keep looking."

"I'm not a vain woman, you know. In spite of what you might think, this is not an activity I enjoy."

"No? Perhaps then you'd like to concentrate on me looking at you. No, don't turn around to do this. In the mirror. Where I am looking at you too."

Phyllis tried to drop her gaze, but Sonja immediately put her hand on Phyllis's chin and lifted it back up.

"How long," Sonja asked, "how long do you think you could look at yourself? How long can you stand to have me look at you? You are not applying makeup. You're not searching for the eyelash caught in your eye. You're just *looking*."

Phyllis seemed to be cooperating fully now, so Sonja let go of her chin.

"Could you look at yourself for an hour? Two? Three? Of course not. Soon you'd grow tired of the shape of your jaw. Your tiny nose would sicken you. You'd want to turn away because you'd think of nothing but reasons why you're not worthy of such attention. You, a beautiful woman. Now, imagine that there is someone in the world who would look at you hour after hour, day after day. He would look at every inch of you and then look again. Because he thinks you're beautiful? Perhaps. But no matter what—because he believes you're worth looking at. All the world deserves this and you are simply one part of it. Do you know what a gift this is, just to be part of this living world that should be carefully examined? Almost all of us will pass out of this life without ever getting or receiving such attention."

The water in the toilet tank gurgled. The porcelain fixtures gave back as much of the morning light as they could. The warm smells of soap and shaving cream still hung in the air. The towel hanging on the shower curtain rod slowly, slowly gave up its moisture for the next bather.

Finally, in a voice little more than a whisper, Phyllis said, "I envy you."

Sonja leaned forward and pressed her cheek against her sister-in-law's, and as she did, both women's faces fit fully in the mirror's frame. "Should I ask him?" asked Sonja. "Should I ask him if he would like to meet you? To pose for him?"

Phyllis's laughter was as sudden as a cry of pain. "Are you kidding? Russ would kill me!"

The women fell silent again, and though Sonja would never dare say anything out loud, she wondered if they were both thinking the same thing: that no amount of laughter could conceal the fact that Phyllis's remark might be neither joke nor figure of speech.

In the house's other rooms, the hands of clocks swept seconds into the past and nudged minutes in the same direction, yet these two women stared motionlessly at their reflections. Eventually, Phyllis broke the spell. She stepped out of the frame and gazed at Sonja in the flesh. Then she embraced her brother's wife and whispered in her ear, "You pose for all of us."

Henry raised out of his crouch and peeked through the window just long enough to confirm that he was on the correct side of the cabin. He had seen a woman's naked back, and in less than a second he concluded that it was Sonja.

He had not looked long enough to take in any of the specific details—Sonja had, for example, four moles in a row across her upper back. And it was a back he saw—not a face—naked back and buttocks.

But Henry wasn't trying to talk himself out of anything. He was absolutely certain the naked woman was his wife, and if he raised his head to look through the window again it would not be to search for additional identifying marks but to see if the position of her body had changed. Did she have to remain in that awkward pose?

The hell of it was, Henry wasn't sure, once he got beyond those moles and the color of her eyes and a few other obvious features, if he could describe Sonja in the way that a man who had traversed every inch of her body should be able to do. How was her wrist different from any other woman's? That little hollow in the small of her back—was that deeper than most? If he had to, could he pick out Sonja by looking at nothing but her upper arm? It was freckled, wasn't it? How could it be that he wouldn't be able to recognize his wife's neck, no matter how long he had to examine it, yet he knew within an instant that this woman on the bed was Sonja?

A few years before, Henry traveled to Green Bay with Russell and Russell's father to watch the Packers play the Bears. It was Henry's first professional football game, and the size of the stadium astounded him. Russell must have known how impressed Henry was because, shortly after they sat down, Russell leaned over and said, "How would you like to have to find someone in this crowd?" Sonja, Henry thought; what *if he had to find Sonja here? And yet he believed he could do it. If he could move around or use a binoculars, if he had some means by which he could survey the thousands assembled there, he felt sure he could find her, and not because of the excellence of his eyesight. His confidence came from another source. Henry had a heart tuned to Sonja's frequency—whatever signal she sent out, he could receive.*

That was why it didn't matter that Henry couldn't describe the turn of Sonja's hip or tell how the curve of her ankle differed from any other, because he didn't need his senses to sense her. He hadn't identified Sonja on that less-than-one-second glimpse through the window; he already knew—his being vibrated to hers.

And it almost struck Henry as funny that on the same day he made this discovery about the nature of love, he planned to burst in on his wife with a gun in his hand.

Henry waited in the garden behind Ned Weaver's gallery, looking at the softball-size globes of spiky lavender that grew almost as high as his waist. He wished he knew the names of the flowers so that when Ned Weaver finally came out, Henry could point to these and say, "I was just admiring your ———." But aside from the few that even children recognized—daisies, lilacs, roses—Henry did not know the names of flowers. Blossoms and petals, stems and stalks, grew all over the county, but to him they were seldom anything but shapes and colors. His eyes knew what to do with them, but they didn't connect to anything in his mind. Flowers, they were just flowers.

He had left the pistol at home, wrapped in a bandana and placed in a coffee can on a shelf in the barn. Without it, Henry felt at a disadvantage, and he kept trying to think of things that might put him on equal footing with this artist. That right was on Henry's side was somehow not enough.

That was why he asked the young woman in the gallery to have Weaver meet him outside. Henry thought that out here his size would work in his favor. Away from those white walls and the drawings and paintings that hung on them, Weaver might see that Henry had some power and authority of his own that had to be reckoned with.

Not that Henry was thinking of this situation as one where physical strength would matter. Henry was holding that in reserve, his next-to-last resort; in the line of persuasion, it came just before waving a gun under Weaver's nose. This meeting would be talk, and that was why Henry wished he could put a name to this flower, so he could show this artist that he knew a thing or two himself. Maybe Weaver would come out eating an apple, and Henry could say, How do you like that McIntosh—tart enough for you? But it had begun to seem likely that Weaver simply wasn't coming out. Henry had been waiting almost fifteen minutes, and the artist had not shown his face.

Then, just as Henry was about to give up and leave, Weaver walked out of the gallery's back door. He was not eating an apple. A cigarette jutted from the corner of his mouth, and he was wiping his hands on a rag, which he jammed into the back pocket of his dungarees when he came within a few paces of Henry. He snapped his fingers and pointed at Henry. "Don't tell me—your rifle! You're looking to buy it back."

Henry shook his head, struck speechless once again because he did not have the right opening into the conversation. Finally, he stammered out his name. "I'm Henry House."

"Ned Weaver." They shook hands, and the strength of the small man's grip surprised Henry. But then he also noticed that under Weaver's T-shirt was a flat belly, and his arms looked as dark, hard, and knot-muscled as carved wood. "What can I do for you?"

"Sonja is . . . I'm Sonja's husband."

Weaver nodded. "Okay."

"You've been doing pictures of her."

He smiled at Henry. "Now, don't you suppose I know that?"

"But maybe you don't know she's married to me."

Weaver shrugged and turned his palms up.

"What I mean is, did you know she's a married woman? Did she tell you that?"

Weaver dropped his cigarette into the dirt and ground it out. "Let me see if I can't hurry things along here. These questions of yours—they fit precisely in the long tradition of ignorance about what happens in the studio. Like most people, you don't have a goddamn idea about what goes on, but you know that sometimes somebody's naked, and that's just enough to get your imagination running wild. You have as well a complete lack of understanding about the relationship between an artist and his model."

Henry raised no more than a grunt of objection, and Weaver put up his hand and went on talking.

"I'll present you with an analogy that might help you understand. What's your favorite fruit?"

Here was an opportunity for Henry to establish his own expertise. Unfortunately, before thinking, he answered simply, "Apple."

"Apples. All right. And I trust by that you mean apples are your favorite fruit to eat. But let's say you've been given an assignment. You're supposed to draw a picture of an apple. And you have an apple—no, a whole goddamn bowl of apples—in front of you to look at while you make your drawing. Now, even though you love to eat apples, you don't eat any of these, do you? You might even be hungry as hell, but you'll leave them alone. That's not what they're for, and that's not what you're for either. You're a drawing man, not an eating man."

"Jesus Christ," Henry said in wonder. "If you can paint half as well as you can talk, you must really be something. Can I see these pictures?"

"Nope," Weaver said. "Sorry."

"I'm talking about the pictures of my wife."

"But they're my paintings."

"Then I want you to stop making them. No more pictures of Sonja."

"Are you asking me or telling me?"

"Whichever."

Weaver laughed, a sound that in that sun-dappled garden came closer to the stony rustle of gravel underfoot than to the chatter of birds in the branches overhead. "Mr. House, let me tell you something about myself and my work. I go my own way. No one tells me what to do or not to do. I am not receptive to suggestions for alteration or revision, and I must have absolute freedom in my choice of subject and in my methods. Now, you may think you aren't intruding on my art. You believe you're simply trying to find out if I fucked your wife. But the fact of the matter is, you are interfering, and in an area in which I brook no interference. If God himself asked me what went on in my studio I'd tell him to mind his own fucking business."

It was the sort of speech a man might deliver and then spin on his heel and stalk off. Instead, Weaver surprised Henry by smiling and saying,

"You're right. I can sling the bullshit, can't I? Now, can you spare a ciga-rette? I've got to get something up my nose besides the smell of my wife's fucking flowers."

Henry brought out his Pall Malls and shook one out for each of them. Weaver struck a match before Henry could get his out of the cigarette pack's cellophane.

Now what? Henry knew he couldn't be the one to walk away. He had allowed Weaver to have both the first and last word, but here they were, smoking together; the argument—if there'd even been one—was over, wasn't it? Was Henry supposed to turn the talk to weather?

Weaver relieved Henry of the responsibility of speech. He put his arm through Henry's and began to walk him toward the gallery. "But I know what's bothering you," Weaver said. "You're thinking, it's not fair . . . the kind of access—*visual* access, mind you—this man has had to my wife. I understand your position completely. Now, I won't say any-thing that will inflame your jealousies and fears. You're no doubt letting your thoughts run away with you already."

Men didn't walk arm in arm like this, not unless they were father and son, yet Henry was reluctant to disengage himself from Weaver. The artist continued to talk, and Henry, with his bad ear, had to remain close or he wouldn't be able to hear.

"The history of artists and their models is absolutely riddled with myths and misunderstandings. Models have been regarded as everything from pets to sorceresses, and painters have been seen as Pygmalions or seducers. It's true that at times models were frequently enlisted from the ranks of prostitutes, but that was largely a matter of finding a group of available and willing females in suspicious, repressive times. The truth is, with few exceptions, the relationship is a professional one. And I have an idea of how I might illustrate that, and at the same time even out what probably seems to you to be the inequality between us."

Just before they reached the back door of the building, Henry heard a cry and looked back over his shoulder. A few gulls wheeled and hovered low in the sky just beyond the garden. Their presence shouldn't have been a surprise; Fox Harbor and the lake were less than two hundred yards away. And Henry had been hearing these birds all his life; you'd think he'd be inured to them. But their squeals often alarmed him, sounding, as they did, like something—a puppy, a cat, a child—in distress.

Weaver opened the door and motioned Henry up a flight of stairs. They ascended, and at the top Weaver opened another door, ushering Henry into one of the gallery's back rooms, a space largely devoted to storing and cataloging the paintings not yet on display or for sale.

Canvases, both framed and unframed, leaned against the walls, while empty wood and metal frames were stacked nearby. A large worktable was covered with rolled paper and cloth, mat boards, pieces of frames, a hammer and a jar of nails, a spool of wire, and coffee cans. A small desk held a typewriter and stacks of index cards.

"Harriet!" Weaver called out. "Are you still here?"

When no response came, Weaver said to Henry, "I don't think she's left for the day. Let me see if I can track her down."

Left alone, Henry immediately began to inspect the paintings, uncertain whether he hoped to come upon Sonja's image or not. He found pictures of the lake, of sailboats, of vases of flowers, of a bicycle leaning against what looked to be the porch of the nearby Loch Lomond Resort, but no humans, much less his wife. Henry was about to unroll one of the watercolors on the table when Weaver and a woman entered the room.

"Here she is, as promised! Mr. House, this is my wife, Harriet."

The smiling woman who extended her hand was, Henry guessed, in her fifties, slightly younger than her husband. Her features were small and delicate, yet she was also fleshy and buxom—in body she reminded Henry a little of Frankie Rawling. She wore a sleeveless summer dress adorned with tiny pink and green triangles and squares.

"I'm pleased to meet you, Mr. House." Her hand was small and damp.

"Likewise."

What had Weaver told her about him? She seemed uneasy in his presence, though the blush across her cheeks and at the base of her throat may have been caused by the heat. She tucked back a few strands of silver hair, and she kept putting her hands on her upper arms as though she was cold or embarrassed.

"I couldn't hear you," she said apologetically. "I was working in the garden out front."

"I was telling Harriet," Weaver said to Henry, "that you're still struggling with some of the fundamental questions of art."

She nodded enthusiastically, as though she knew not only what those questions were but also strongly approved of asking them.

"Do you work primarily in oils, Mr. House?"

An artist! She thought he was an artist! Well, why not. He and Weaver were dressed almost identically in T-shirts and dungarees, but Henry was wearing his workboots, the leather worn and scuffed almost to white, while Weaver was shod in torn, dirty sneakers. That someone might believe Henry and Weaver shared a profession flattered Henry.

"Henry is still searching," Weaver said, "for his medium."

Harriet looked expectantly at Henry.

"It's true," he said, although he was unsure of the truth he was acknowledging.

He didn't have to worry; Weaver was quick to cover for him. "Henry has been concentrating on landscapes, but he wants to see what can be done with the human form. Henry's had no professional training, so he's never had a life drawing class, for example."

Harriet continued to smile and stare at Henry, plainly waiting to learn why it was important that she meet this young man.

"I was explaining to Henry," Weaver continued, "the value and importance of an experienced professional model. So many young artists believe they need nothing more than someone who's willing to sit reasonably still."

"It can be quite exhausting," Harriet added.

"And the last thing you need is the distraction of a model bitching about being too hot or too cold, about being tired or stiff or bored."

Was Weaver trying to tell Henry something about Sonja's nature? Is that what this little meeting was for? Anger returned to replace Henry's bewilderment. The nerve of this little son of a bitch—first he takes Sonja away from Henry and installs her as his private model, and then he acts as though he knows her better than her own husband.

"I told Henry you used to sit for me. And on a few occasions for other artists, isn't that right?"

She nodded in assent, but wariness had now overtaken her features.

Weaver put his hands on his wife's shoulders. "I hope I didn't overstep my bounds, but I said you'd be willing to come out of retirement and sit for Mr. House."

"Oh, Ned . . ."

"From what he tells me, you are exactly what he needs. He's searching for a model embodying those rare, often incompatible, qualities of world-weariness and steadfastness. With, of course, her share of sensual beauty."

She looked at Henry for confirmation. He said nothing, but he knew that the way alliances were swiftly forming in this room, his silence put him on Weaver's side.

"This is something you'd be willing to do, isn't it, Harriet?" Weaver's voice assumed the tone adults use to soothe children to sleep, and though Weaver didn't say "for me," Henry believed those words were clearly implied.

Harriet glanced apprehensively from her husband to Henry and back again.

"He has to see the goods first, sweetheart," Weaver said, slipping the strap of her dress from her shoulder.

If his touch had been ice or fire, she could not have flinched any faster.

Weaver laughed. "Harriet. Let's not be ridiculous. This is for art. Since when have you been unwilling to do something for the sake of art?"

With the assurance of the long married who knows which way his mate will turn, Weaver stepped behind his wife just as she took a backward step. He gripped her bare arms and maneuvered her to face Henry head-on. Henry had held Sonja just like this when he made her look at herself in their mirror. Could Harriet see her reflection in his eyes?

Henry had not moved, but she shook her head quickly as if to warn him away from any action. "Please," she said, "he's only testing us."

Weaver was barely visible behind his wife when he spoke. "Jesus Christ—the two of you! So you're uncomfortable—what the hell does that matter! What if this . . . this collaboration between you led to a great painting—shit, even a *good* one? You'd be sorry as hell if you let a little embarrassment prevent that, wouldn't you?"

"Wait . . ." She was pleading with Henry, not her husband. "He might lose interest." Her arms hung limply at her sides, and she stared straight ahead without expression. Had Weaver somehow put her in a trance? Then Henry realized what Weaver was doing. He was unbuttoning his wife's dress.

Henry had to say something. "Look, this is all a mistake. . . ."

"A mistake?" Weaver said. "You think this is a mistake?" With that, he pushed his wife's dress forward so that it fell from her shoulders. It would have dropped all the way to the floor, but the material caught and gathered at her waist.

"Can you tell yet—will she serve your purposes?" From behind his wife, Weaver peered out at Henry. "Does she have the requisite attributes? I want you to look closely, but blur your eyes a little too. You have your own vision, I'm sure, but you have to be aware of all the possibilities your model offers as well."

Slowly, delicately, Weaver slid the satiny straps of his wife's brassiere from her shoulders, and only then did she make a move to cover herself. She did not, however, put her hands over her breasts; she clapped her arms over her stomach, and when she did, her husband reached around and swiftly pulled down the cups of her brassiere.

She winced and let out a tiny mew of pain, as if her heavy breasts did not merely tumble free from their restraint but threatened to tear away from her flesh. She could not cover herself immediately—her own garments caught her arms at her sides—and though Henry tried to focus on Harriet Weaver's face, he saw enough—large nipples and aureoles so palely pink they might have vanished were the surrounding flesh not so milky white. A second later, Harriet Weaver got her hands up over her breasts, an action that she somehow performed not frantically but with a kind of dignity, even while her eyes were welling with tears.

"Well, how about it? Are we there yet?" Weaver asked Henry. "Is your sense of justice satisfied?"

Because Harriet Weaver's expression was so tightly drawn, Henry felt as though he could suddenly see what she looked like before the years added their layers and lines. And yet it did not seem as though time was falling away as he stared at her; instead, it accelerated, and he saw through to her skull, to the structure of chin, cheekbone, and brow that was responsible for her good looks and that would be left behind when her flesh fell away.

"Ma'am, if you give me the word, I'll get ahold of the son of a bitch and break both of his arms before he can do another thing to embarrass both of us."

Perhaps if Henry had made a different threat, Harriet Weaver might not have responded as she did. She suddenly seemed more frightened of Henry than of the man mistreating her. "Please please . . . don't do anything," she said. "Don't you understand? He and I—we're together. In spite of everything, we're together." That this plea came from a woman leaning toward Henry with her hands over her breasts gave it an urgency he had to heed.

He began to back up, but he wasn't sure he was moving toward an exit.

Weaver held up a hand to stop Henry. "Just a minute. There's more." He reached down and pulled the hem of his wife's dress above her knees. "Or maybe you don't need any more?"

Henry looked to Harriet again, and once more she shook her head, perhaps because she could no longer trust her voice.

At that sign from Mrs. Weaver, Henry said, "Mister, you are a piece of work," and walked from the room.

If Henry could have been sure that that was laughter behind his back, he would have turned around and given Weaver the beating of his life. Nothing enraged Henry like being laughed at. But with his impaired hearing, Henry wasn't sure he could pull out laughter from the dominant sound of what he was sure was weeping.

Any attempt to determine if the painting "The Doctor's Daughter" was inspired by this episode of calculated humiliation is problematical, at best. First of all, it's next to impossible to know whether the portrait was done before or after that event because Weaver, for what seemed to him perfectly good reasons, seldom bothered to date his work. Although Weaver was capable of completing a work quite quickly, it was also possible that he might tinker with an oil painting for as long as a decade. A single watercolor could have been preceded over the years by an almost identical series. Beneath a fully realized image might be an underpainting that began as nothing more than spontaneous brushstrokes. Even when a year appears below Weaver's signature it's likely that was only something he added to satisfy a curator, gallery owner, or prospective buyer.

What evidence is in the portrait itself that suggests Weaver painted it after baring his wife's breasts to Henry House? Harriet looks to be about the right age, and since it's one of the few works she posed for after she turned forty, there might be some logic in assuming that that event caused Weaver to see once again his wife's potential as a model. Her hair is worn in the same fashion she wore that day, but then that Gibson girl style was hers for close to twenty years.

Yes, her shoulders are bare, but since the bottom of the canvas goes no lower than the top of her sternum it's impossible to know if her breasts are uncovered. She might be wearing an evening gown or a strapless swimming suit. The background—what could be an approaching storm if such clouds were not swirls of dark blues and grays but reds and burgundies—offers no clue. Plainly, those are not the walls of the gallery or its back room behind her.

What about her body language and expression? She looks less like someone who doesn't want to be seen and more like someone who doesn't want to be photographed—her head is turned slightly to the side and her

178 · Larry Watson

hand is raised as if to block the camera's view. Her palm, clearly creased with an *M*, is as detailed as anything in the painting. Embarrassment could have brought the color to her cheek, but so could exasperation— *oh, don't take my picture!*—or the heat of a summer day.

Finally—and isn't this the strongest argument for concluding that something other than the incident in the gallery served as the impetus behind "The Doctor's Daughter"?—the artist's vantage point is in *front* of Harriet, just where Henry House stood that day. Who would ever believe that Ned Weaver could imagine his way into that man's shoes?

Sonja knew that asking for favors meant that one had to be prepared to grant favors in return. To that end, she put on the lace-trimmed slip that she seldom wore and her good navy-blue jersey dress. She applied a darker shade of lipstick and a light smear of rouge. Between her breasts, behind her ears, and on her wrists she dabbed the Chantilly perfume that Phyllis had given her for her birthday.

This was Sonja's plan. Today she would ask Mr. Ned Weaver if he would be willing to paint a portrait of John, and this painting she would present to Henry as a Christmas gift. Or, if Weaver could not complete the painting in time, she would give it to Henry for his birthday. And once Henry saw his son's image brought back from that netherworld that eventually not even memory could reach and made into art, Henry would understand why Sonja posed for that artist. Henry would set aside his jealousies and let go of his worry over what the townsfolk might whisper about them—how small and unimportant, after all, was reputation compared to art with its power to make marvelous what otherwise was the ordinariness of life!

But Ned Weaver did not make art for nothing. Sonja knew what he would want in payment. She would have to allow him to fuck her. And that was the word she used, in her mind, to describe the arrangement she would have to agree to. The ugly word would keep her from pretending that affection or desire or pity—yes, she could pity that arrogant little man—was behind her action. For a favor he could fuck her. More than once? He would want to fuck her many times. Well, that would be something they could arrange.

She had come close, very close, to such a bargain once before, but then she had negotiated only with herself. It had been more than a year ago, summer, and July's heat had pressed down on the county for a week, yet on that day he would not open a window in the studio or turn on a fan. Sonja lay on the bed, naked save for the sweat that covered her from head to foot like another layer of skin. Weaver was behind her, crouched on the floor, his face no more than an inch from her back, so close she could tell exactly where he was by the cool of his breath.

He was examining her carefully, he said, because he needed to know exactly the texture of her skin, every mole, every blemish, the origin of every contour and shadow. He was painting *her,* he told her time and time again, not an approximation of her. She was unlike any other woman, and in order to capture her uniqueness on canvas, first he had to take that in through his eyes. Had she allowed it, he surely would have used his fingertips as well.

Down her spine he slowly traveled and stopped at the hollow of her back. Did he blow on her? Did he sigh? She remembered the chill she felt, and the sensation—so restricted yet so specific—made her feel as though the parts of her body were disconnected. Or did that sense come from the knowledge of what Weaver was doing? Since he could only see a few inches of her at any time, did that diminish the existence of the rest of her? Was she most fully alive where *he* breathed, where *his* eye rested?

In addition to this sensation, she felt something else, equally strange and new. For the first time, she seriously considered giving herself to him. Was her resolve melting in the heat? Did she suddenly desire him? No. If she made this gift to him it would be to repay him, not for putting an image of her on paper and canvas but for this moment, for paying her this kind of attention.

She made this agreement with herself: If he touched her with anything more solid than air, she would roll onto her back and reach for him. And she would not deceive herself about her motive. She would not merely be paying him back. She would be satisfying her curiosity as well. She would know what it was like to be made love to by a man who had looked at her so closely he knew not only how many moles were lined up across the top of her back but the circumference of each tiny dark circle.

After another moment, however, Weaver pushed himself up from the floor and walked a few paces away. "You know why I need to know exactly what you look like?"

Because she was posed, Sonja did not turn around, but she knew he was back at his easel. "Why?"

"I'm trying to memorize you, my dear. I'm trying to burn every inch of you into my brain, so I can continue to paint you when you're gone."

Gone? Gone? Where did he think she would go, and how could he presume to know her future? But he was right, because a part of her *had* departed, flown from that room though all the windows were closed. And what part of her left never to return? The part that would willingly allow between her legs a man not her husband.

Today, however, would be nothing like that. This would be business. Henry already thought her a whore, so why not collect a whore's payment?

Sonja had the photograph of John in her hand, and she was almost out the door when she had second thoughts. John, she was going to ask for a portrait of John. . . . It was one more way she would seem to be favoring him. On the kitchen table were the pictures that June had recently drawn and colored in school, and penciled on the back of one sheet was a note from the art teacher. *June shows real talent!* Sonja would ask for something for both her children. . . . She scooped up June's artwork, and because the air of this October day was thick with a mist threatening to coalesce into rain, she put the drawings and the photograph in a paper sack to protect them.

Sonja entered the studio carrying a wrinkled grocery bag, and by the way she cradled the bag carefully in her arms, Weaver figured that its contents must be both fragile and valuable. She took off her coat, and Weaver noticed that she was wearing a dress he had never seen before. The amount of makeup she wore was also unusual for her. Once she saw him, however, she quickly set aside the bag, along with her reason for bringing it, and rushed over to him. "You are ill?" she asked.

So, he thought, I look that bad. "I was," he said. "I'm doing much better. Thank you for inquiring."

For the previous two days he had been vomiting and shitting uncontrollably—"going off like a Roman candle at both ends" was the phrase his brother once used. Weaver was reasonably certain of the cause. On Friday night, he and Harriet had driven down to Green Bay with the Beckers to try a new Italian restaurant. Weaver was the only one who ate chicken, and he was the only one who woke during the night and scurried to the bathroom. On one of his many visits there he passed out on the floor and came to with Harriet shaking him and asking if she should call an ambulance. He scoffed at her concern, assuring her it was only food poisoning and cursing again the chicken cacciatore.

Food poisoning. Yes, he was sure that was what he had. And yet . . . Even now, as he was recovering—that morning he'd been able to keep down a cup of tea and he could smoke once again without reeling—it felt as though a trace of poison lingered in his body, something he could live with but that would never leave him. It wouldn't kill him, yet it had somehow brought his death a day closer.

He tried to dismiss these thoughts as typical of a man soon to turn sixty, a man who was slowly pickling his liver, who spent the first five minutes of every day coughing in an attempt to clear his lungs, who sometimes found himself breathless after doing nothing more than walking up the hill from his house to his studio.

In an attempt to deflect Sonja's concerned and pitying gaze, Weaver pointed to the bag. "What do you have there?"

She continued to stare at him. Weaver knew he still sounded like a sick man. Long after he had nothing more to bring up, he had continued to retch, and he had scraped his throat so raw that in the end he was spitting blood and bile into the toilet bowl.

"The bag," he rasped again. "What's in the bag?"

She looked at it as though she had forgotten she brought it. "Oh, that. It's nothing. It's—I thought I might ask . . . No. Nothing."

"Go ahead. What did you want to ask?"

"I thought perhaps . . . when our session is over . . . I could ask a favor or two?"

Ah, the irony! It seemed as though the opportunity he had waited over a year for had finally arrived, yet it came on a day when he felt awful. But this had to be the moment—if he said yes to her request how could she continue to deny him what he wanted?

"We'll put the session off for a while. What's the favor you want to ask?"

"If you're too ill—"

"Let me decide what I'm too ill for. Now, let's see what's in the bag."

She went to it eagerly and carried it to one of his worktables where, on the gouged, paint-scabbed surface, she lovingly laid out five crayon-colored drawings. "My daughter's. In school they say she is . . . that she has a gift."

Weaver took a step back to look over the entire series: two pictures of children on a playground, one of a truck at the bottom of a hill, one of a horse, and one drawing of a deer standing in a pond. Weaver completed his inspection in less than ten seconds, but he pretended that more time was needed to assess properly the child's art.

"Tell me again what the teacher said."

"That she has a gift."

"And who is this teacher? Is there any reason we should think she is at all qualified to judge talent?"

"Mrs. Knoll. She teaches—"

"I know who she is." Gladys Knoll taught art in the Door County schools when his daughters were enrolled. If either Emma or Betsy had shown any artistic aptitude he would have pulled her out of school rather than subject her to Gladys Knoll's crabbed, ignorant instruction. "What's your daughter's name?"

"June."

"And how old is June?"

"Eight."

Weaver swiftly stacked four of the pictures on top of one another and dismissively set them aside. The picture of the deer, however, he pulled forward and then tapped it so hard it seemed as though he was testing to find out if its surface would crack.

"This one," he said. "You see how the deer is looking backward? How his hind end seems closer to us than his head? That's foreshortening. Perspective. That can't be taught. At least not by Gladys Knoll. And not to an eight-year-old."

Sonja looked at him as if she hadn't heard him clearly. Was his voice so bad he couldn't make himself understood?

"Talent," Weaver said. "I'm saying your daughter has talent."

Sonja tried in vain to suppress her smile.

"But many people have talent," Weaver said. "More than talent is required."

"She could be an artist?"

Had she still not heard him? Weaver gave up. He stacked the picture of the deer on top of the other drawings. "What I say she's capable of won't make a damn bit of difference in the long or short run. It'll all depend on——what's her name again?"

"June."

"On June. She'll have what it takes or she won't."

Sonja kept looking at him, her eyes shining, it seemed to Weaver, with both gratitude and expectancy. Now, pounce *now,* he thought, yet at the same instant his gut gurgled and cramped and he had to lean on the table for support.

For the first time, her hand reached toward him, but he had to step back. That was not how he wanted her to reach for him.

"What else? You said favors, didn't you? Plural?"

She stared at him without speaking. Was she growing fainthearted? She had to make her other request; so far no indebtedness had accumulated on the basis of what she had asked for.

"Come on," Weaver urged. "Let's hear it. Don't go timid now. You came here to ask for something."

Wordlessly she reached into the bag. She brought out a small black-and-white snapshot, and she placed it on the worktable as slowly and deliberately as a poker player turning over his hole card. In the photograph was a small fair-haired boy, perhaps three years of age, seated precariously on the top step of a wooden porch. He held a cone-shaped party hat, but his solemn expression was hardly that of a celebrant. A disembodied hand hovered near him to make sure he didn't topple from his perch.

"My son," Sonja said.

"Uh-huh." Weaver waited for more.

"He is . . . deceased."

"Yes, you mentioned that. Very sad. He looks like a sweet child."

"I would like . . . Would you paint him? A picture of him?"

When Weaver didn't respond immediately, Sonja quickly added, "I have other photographs. If you need to see him . . . different."

"You would like me to paint a portrait of your son."

She nodded eagerly, but she must have heard the lack of enthusiasm in his voice.

As tenderly as he could, Weaver said, "I generally do not accept commissions."

That was a significant understatement. As a young man, Weaver had studied at Chicago's Art Institute, but he dropped out of the program when he could no longer abide spending his time doing the exercises his instructors asked him to do. And the early years of his career would not have been so difficult if he had been willing to accept other assignments—portraits, magazine covers, book illustrations—but though Weaver had no assurance that he would succeed going his own way, he refused to consider any other.

"I would . . . reward you," Sonja said.

"Would you."

At that, she stepped close to him, and, though her body was at the sideways angle generally not conducive to this activity, she bent down and kissed him below the ear. At least Weaver believed it was a kiss; it was hard to differentiate between the warmth of her breath and the papery dryness of her lips. When he did not react, she reached across his body, took his hand, and brought it to her breast. She continued to nuzzle at his

neck, and though her actions had all the spontaneity and passion of someone following steps written out in an instruction manual, Weaver closed
his eyes and allowed himself to luxuriate in the moment.

But only for a moment. Weaver took his hand away and slid from her
embrace. When Sonja grabbed his hand again and tried to return it to her
breast, he quickly reversed her grip so that he was now holding her wrist.
He pulled her hand to his lips and softly kissed her sweating palm, the kind
of kiss one bestows upon a child leaving home.

Still holding her wrist, he said, "Let me show you something," and
pulled her toward his easel.

Since early morning he had been working on an oil that he had begun
the previous winter—skaters on the ice of Fox Harbor. The perspective
was of someone looking down from high above, and the human figures
looked scattered and small compared to the gray immensity of frozen lake
and sky.

Weaver pointed to the skater closest to the left edge of the canvas.
"See there?" he said to Sonja. "What if you had come into the studio
today and told me I could fuck you to my heart's content if only I'd dab a
little red into the picture? What if you said you'd get down on your knees
and suck my cock right now while I was putting a tiny brushstroke of
scarlet over in that corner? Do you know what my response would be,
what it would have to be?"

He had released Sonja's wrist, but she did not move away. She kept
staring at the canvas.

"I would have to refuse the offer." The huskiness had returned to his
voice, but he went on speaking. "If my life depended on it, I would refuse.
I don't delude myself. I know who and what I am. I'm a selfish prick. I've
been an unfaithful husband and an indifferent father. I've neglected friends
and family, and I don't give a good goddamn about the problems of my
fellow citizens. But I've never compromised on my art. Do you know what
that means?"

She struggled to produce a small, mirthless smile. "That you will not
paint a picture of my son."

"That's right. And it means you will not have to give up your body as a bribe. I'm sorry. What was the word you used? *Reward*. And my God, what a reward it would have been. What a hell of a reward . . ."

Sonja pulled at her sleeves and smoothed the front of her dress exactly as she would have done if she had just put her clothes back on after lovemaking. Then, as if she remembered where she was and her true reason for being there, her fingers went to the dress's zipper. "Would you like to continue with yesterday's pose?"

He had been painting her at the window where she stood naked, leaning on the sill and gazing contemplatively at the woods. In his mind, he shifted while he worked from one informing narrative to another. In one, she had just risen from her lover's bed, and she was looking out at all the licit world beyond. In another, she waited for that lover to arrive, thinking that if not that day then soon it would be their last together. He had shared neither story with her, yet without prompting she had assumed an expression that worked for either version.

"Not yet," Weaver said. "I'm not finished with my demonstration."

With that, he picked up a round number two sable brush and dipped it in the red he had mixed that morning. He used the lightest of strokes—he likened it to a tongue flick—and in exactly that part of the canvas he had referred to earlier, he gave one of the skaters a red scarf.

He put the brush down. "Do you understand?"

"I understand."

"I *planned* to put a bit of red in the picture, but it can only be there because it comes from inside me."

"I said I understand. You intended that all along." She had unzipped her dress and started to pull it from one shoulder. "I should go to the window again?"

Even though her tears had not spilled over but merely glossed her eyes, it was enough to alter the look that Weaver wanted for the painting in progress.

"I think we'll skip today's session," Weaver said, then quickly added, "but I'll pay you for two hours."

"You are still not feeling well?" She ventured another quick wipe at her eyes with the base of her thumb.

Weaver's guts still cramped from time to time, but they squeezed down on nothing but air and his morning tea. If he swallowed any more regret, however, he'd have a lump in his stomach that he might never digest.

"Let's just say I don't feel like working."

Sonja put her daughter's colored drawings back into the bag, but the photograph of her son she placed in her purse. She closed the clasp and was on her way to the door when Weaver stopped her.

"Wait. You said you had two favors to ask, and I'm not sure I understand what you wanted for your daughter."

She shook her head. "It doesn't matter."

"No, come on. What did you want?"

"If I bring my daughter to you someday, would you . . . would you help her?"

Weaver wondered if that was truly what she wanted to ask, or if she was making up something to help her reach the door. "Help her how?"

"A word of advice. Encouragement. Anything."

"I'm not a teacher. I don't have the patience or the temperament."

She nodded as if that was exactly what she expected to hear.

"I'm sorry. I struck out on both your requests." To Weaver's own ears his apology had a tinny ring; how must it have sounded to Sonja? But she merely shrugged, and then she was out the door.

Even seconds after the fact, Weaver had difficulty believing what he had done, and he went to the window as if only sight could confirm the deed. Yes, there she went, down the aisle formed by the untrimmed lilac bushes, their leaves so shriveled and dry this late in the year that Weaver expected them to fall simply from the movement of air she created in hurrying past. "You think your daughter might want to be an artist?" Weaver said to the window glass. "Stop her before it's too late."

It was not the painting of skaters or the portrait of Sonja at the window that Weaver returned to after she left. Instead he pulled from the shelf a sketchbook. He decided to begin work on a painting he had done the pencil study for decades before, a view looking through open French doors, across an empty balcony, and out to the sea beyond. The final work would allude to Bonnard but would have none of that painter's blobby imprecision of color. Weaver remembered well the day he conceived of the painting. . . .

As soon as the girls were old enough to understand what it meant to visit a foreign country, he and Harriet took them to France. They rented a small apartment in Brittany, and Weaver rode back and forth to Paris on the train to meet with gallery owners and a few artist friends. Harriet wanted to be free to accompany Weaver on these trips, so they brought with them from the States an au pair. She was Becky Morse, a sixteen-year-old neighbor girl. Emma and Betsy loved Becky, and she was a capable, dependable sitter.

Late one afternoon, after a day at the beach with the girls, Becky came out onto the balcony, where Weaver sat sketching and drinking a glass of white wine. Becky approached on all fours, both girls on her back, and all of them alternately giggling, whinnying, and trying to make the clip-clopping sound of a horse's hooves. When Weaver turned toward the girls, he noticed how the fabric of Becky's bathing suit sagged with the weight of her still-new and perfect breasts, and before he could look away, he saw clear down to the tips of her mauvey-pink nipples. He drew in his breath sharply, but he realized almost immediately that there was as much despair as desire in his gasp. She was little more than a child herself, given to the care of his own children. She was the daughter of a friend, and Weaver had pledged to Brian Morse that his daughter would be looked after and protected. And to Becky, Weaver was a stand-in for a father—aging, foolish, trustworthy. The only reason for which she would ever get down on her hands and knees before him was to carry his own daughters to him. Or away. He told Becky to take the girls back into the apartment; he was trying to work.

Weaver was not much interested in analyzing the psychological states that lay behind his or any other artist's drawings or paintings. The work was what was important, and whether it was born of ecstasy or boredom or joy or despair mattered not at all. And that he began to work on this painting on a day when he had learned—again—that some breasts could not be touched, why, what possible effect could that have on the finished product? By the time he finished it, all his thoughts would be preoccupied with color and shadow and no longer on his unmet desires.

Harriet Weaver had been in Green Bay all day looking at carpet samples, and when she returned at dusk to a house that smelled like pumpkins, her first thought was, *Emma's home. She's brought the kids home for Halloween, and Ned's carving jack-o'-lanterns for his grandsons just as he once did for his daughters.* Before she reached the kitchen, however, Harriet amended that thought. Except for the room she was walking toward, the house was dark and silent, and it could be neither if the boys were there. All right, they hadn't arrived yet, but they were coming, and Ned was preparing the pumpkins for them.

Nothing in the kitchen initially told her she was wrong. Ned was sitting at the table hollowing out the first pumpkin while the second waited on the counter. The seeds and stringy, smelly pulp were piled on a newspaper. In addition to his tools, an X-Acto knife and two kitchen knives, Ned had near at hand his cigarettes and a water tumbler.

The fact that he was working with scant light—only the flickering fluorescent tube over the sink was on—made Harriet uneasy, but she decided to proceed on the basis of the optimism that had entered her with the first whiff of pumpkin.

"Should you carve one for Emma too?" Harriet asked. "You know how she loves Halloween."

The chill of autumn's early dark had settled in the house, but Ned sat shirtless and barefoot at the table. He turned a dark, blear eye on her, and even before he spoke Harriet knew it was not water in the glass and that children would not soon walk through the door.

"What the hell are you talking about?"

"I just thought . . . Never mind." She picked up the tumbler and sniffed, less to confirm her suspicions and more to replace the aroma of pumpkin with an odor more in keeping with the spirit of the household. She took a cautious sip. Well, she had been mistaken. Vodka, not gin.

When she put the glass back on the table, Ned grabbed it and slid it out of her reach.

Harriet pulled one of his cigarettes from the pack and lit it. This time he made no protest of possession.

"Who are the jack-o'-lanterns for?"

Weaver kept scraping at the inner wall of the pumpkin. After so many years of marriage, Harriet knew Ned's varieties of drunkenness the way some women knew the flavors and uses of cooking spices. So this was to be a bout of silence, just the thing to salt these frosty nights of late October.

"Or perhaps," she suggested, "you're planning on entering them in the Pumpkin Patch Festival." The few establishments in their village that stayed open throughout the year kept trying ideas to lure off-season tourists. This year residents and merchants were encouraged to decorate their homes and businesses to celebrate harvest and Halloween.

Ned said nothing in reply but fitted the stem and lid on the hollowed-out pumpkin.

"Though, really—don't you think an artist of your standing has an advantage over the rest of the citizenry?"

Ned leaned back from the table, assessing the pumpkin as though its features were already plain and it could smile, grimace, or scowl back at him. "This is for a little girl."

"Someone we know? Or just any little girl?"

"I made her mother cry."

As he said this, Ned himself seemed close to tears. Had she made another mistake? Was this the maudlin rather than the morose drunk? "And how did you do that?"

"I told her I wouldn't paint a picture of her son."

"Were you perhaps a little blunt in turning down her request?"

He laughed sardonically. "It broke my fucking heart to tell her!"

"She offered to pay you?"

He picked up a knife and dragged his thumb across the blade. "She would have paid. Any price I asked she would've paid."

"But she didn't understand you don't accept commissions?"

"Something like that."

"Hardly an occasion for tears." Over the years they had had some violent quarrels, but Ned had never threatened her physically. Nevertheless, she wished he'd put the knife down. The sentimentality was so unlike him, perhaps another darker emotional excess was lurking in him as well. "What am I not understanding here, Ned? Why do you feel as though you owe this woman something?"

He looked up at her, and before a sound came out, his mouth twisted down as though his words had a bitter taste. "The boy is dead."

Harriet couldn't help it; she stepped back from this announcement. "Oh, Ned."

"No, no. A photograph. She brought in a goddamn snapshot of the kid. Her little birthday boy. Her little fucking prince."

"Do I know this woman?" Harriet asked.

Ned shook his head.

"Do you have a relationship with her?"

As soon as she asked, she knew he was not likely to answer. She pushed ahead anyway. "Are you in love with her?"

He said nothing, but Harriet couldn't help herself. Into the maw of his silence, she threw one more question. "Does she have something to do with Mr. House?"

"Jesus Christ, Harriet. Why won't you let that go? I apologized."

"And I accepted your apology. As I always do. But you'll understand if I can't put an incident like that behind me so easily. It takes a little time to get over being exposed and humiliated. And since you exceeded even your capacity for cruelty on that occasion I have to wonder if there wasn't more involved than your desire to show another man your wife's breasts. Not that that in itself is understandable."

Ned put down the knife and picked up the glass of vodka. After a long swallow and a pause to let its heat subside, his equanimity returned. "I told you before. It was a slow day. I thought I could enlist you and Mr. House to relieve the boredom. To provide a little of the excitement I crave now and then. I misjudged. Now leave it the hell alone!"

"I'll let it go, Ned. But only because I know I'm not going to hear the truth from you."

Ned ignored her and turned his attention again to the pumpkins. He looked from one to the other as though he was trying to make a decision. When he finished his appraisal, he stood and, as if one of the jack-o'-lanterns had just insulted him, he slapped it hard with the back of his hand. Like a guillotined head, it tumbled from the table and rolled across the floor. In the aftermath of the blow, most of the pumpkin's wet innards slopped onto the floor.

"I'm through here," Ned said. "You can make a pumpkin pie out of this shit if you like."

After Harriet had fortified herself with her own glass of vodka, she began to clean up Ned's mess. She set both jack-o'-lanterns on the cupboard next to the sink. One of the pumpkins, Ned had carved into a face that was half man and half wolf. He had transformed a bulge in the pumpkin into a snout, and the mouth leered with the exceptionally long teeth of a canine, but its eyes were sadly human. The other pumpkin, the one that had been slapped to the floor, had a face that Ned probably believed was comic, but its close-set eyes and gap-toothed grin gave it a giddily maniacal look. Although Harriet admired Ned's artistry, she wondered how he thought they could possibly be given to a child. They were the stuff of nightmares.

She spread yesterday's *Chicago Tribune* on the cupboard and put the Wolfman on the sports page and proceeded to chop it into small pieces with a meat cleaver. She repeated the process with the gruesome clown, then wrapped all the blocks and wedges of pumpkin in paper and took the remains out to the garbage.

Not until she was hurrying back to the house did she question her behavior. Why had she turned the face of each jack-o'-lantern away before hacking into it? Their eyes were nothing but holes carved in a gourd, yet she couldn't lift the cleaver while they were aimed in her direction.

She didn't want to, she didn't want to, she didn't want to, but Daddy told June she had to go trick-or-treating with Betty Engerson and her other friends. He said what he said every Halloween, that since there weren't many kids like in cities, the people out here gave out extra candy. He told her again about the house on Pinery Road where he got a silver dollar when he was a boy. June didn't argue with him—maybe down in Green Bay or Milwaukee they really did give out only one piece of penny candy—but she didn't think the treats she and her friends got were so grand. She couldn't remember ever getting a full-size candy bar, and most people handed out things they made themselves—little cookies or popcorn balls or caramel apples or pennies tied up in tissue paper.

And June couldn't say the real reason she didn't want to go. She was afraid that if she wasn't there, her father might hurt her mother again the way he did that night when June found them in the hallway. She didn't know why Daddy had made her mother look in the mirror, but June could tell Mommy was scared. And June was too, and she didn't want to be afraid of Daddy, so she made herself think it wasn't Daddy, it was the mirror, it was a magic mirror like in *Snow White* or *Alice in Wonderland*, and if Mommy stared at it too long she would faint or vanish or fall into a spell and she wouldn't be herself anymore. June knew there was no such thing as magic, she knew that, but she also knew that bad things could happen in the world—like with John, and that was on a day she wasn't home. If she had to go trick-or-treating she'd leave the other kids the first chance she got and run back to her house.

She dressed as a hobo. Again. It wasn't really a costume at all. The only thing that made her look like a bum was the old felt hat tied on her head, and the burnt cork Daddy smeared on her face to make it look as though she needed a shave. Otherwise, she just wore some of her dad's old clothes, and Mommy made her put those on because they were big, and June could be bundled up underneath. This was another of those cold Halloweens—a little snow had fallen during the day, and little drifts had formed in the dirt alongside the road.

Once June began running with her friends from house to house in Fox Harbor, however, she sometimes forgot about home, and even when she remembered, she told herself that trick-or-treaters would be going there too, and how could something bad happen when children knocked on the door every few minutes? And her father was right—somebody gave her a real Hershey bar.

Then they went down to Lake Road, and at the first house a man with a beard made them reach into a jack-o'-lantern for their treat, but he hadn't let the pumpkin dry after he hollowed it out, and when June reached in, her hand touched the side and it was slimy, and she thought she'd found ways to keep from ever thinking of John in the ground again, but the slick inner wall of the pumpkin brought back the grave and its sides and the way the sliced dirt looked tan and dry near the top but dark and muddy the deeper down the coffin went, and June backed away from the house and she told Betty she didn't feel good and she ran for home. The snow was waving and rolling across the road like a snake, a roller snake—what she called rattlesnakes before she knew their real name— but these were white so they were ghosts, the roads of Door County were haunted this Halloween by ghost snakes but she could run right through them so they didn't frighten her.

And when she got home it was strange because nothing was strange. Daddy was in the kitchen doing something with his fishing reel and tangled line, and Mommy sat on the end of the couch sewing the lining in her winter coat. Wait, wait—something was strange. June stood inside the front door breathing hard, and even before Mommy said hello or Daddy asked her if she got a good haul, she heard . . . nothing. And June knew that all the time she was gone no one in this house had spoken, and suddenly it was not so important for her to stay close. Whether June was there or not, nothing went on between her mother and father. Nothing.

Hardly any trick-or-treaters came that night. June should have known. Their house had a long, steep driveway, and the kids wouldn't want to waste their time walking all the way up there to knock on a single door. Only Betty Engerson came, and that was because her mother drove her there to see if June was all right. June knew no one else was coming, so she gave Betty a whole handful of caramels.

"Why did you quit trick-or-treating?" Betty asked.

"I just didn't feel good."

"Did you have the diarhee?"

"No." June hated the way Betty's family talked about some things.

"A sick headache?"

"No."

"Do you have a temperature?"

"I wasn't really sick. My mom is, and I thought I'd better stay with her."

"What's wrong with her?"

"She has . . . a disease."

"Can't your dad take care of her?" While they talked, Betty unwrapped three caramels, and now she put them all in her mouth at once.

"He might not hear her. Because of his bad ear." June reached into the bowl and grabbed more caramels. She gave these to Betty, hoping she would shove these into her mouth too and so be unable to ask any more questions.

"Is it like polio? Your mom's disease?" A thin stream of tan spittle bubbled out of the corner of Betty's mouth.

"It's a little like that. But different."

Betty nodded, wiped her mouth, and shifted the wad of caramel to the other cheek. "I'll see you on the bus tomorrow."

But then Betty dropped the extra pieces of candy back in the bowl, and June wondered if from now on Judy Tilghman would be Betty's best friend.

Daniel Chen, whom June met and married when they were in college together at the University of Minnesota, eventually became a professor of film studies at Western Minnesota State University, and he often told his classes that *Meet Me in St. Louis* was a "perfect" movie—not the greatest, not the most profound, moving, innovative, or complex film, but of its kind, without flaw. He found it endlessly interesting, and whenever he came across it on television, he watched it.

June, however, had to leave the room during the movie's Halloween sequence. It was not only that Tootie's hobo costume was similar to June's, but Margaret O'Brien's near-hysteria after the trolley car incident also reminded June of that cold night when something seemed to gust inside of her as well as in the trees as she ran home to make sure her father had not murdered her mother. Daniel teased her about this sensitivity, but June said, "I OD'd on Halloween candy when I was a kid, okay?"

During the period when she was in thrall to the Abstract Expressionists, June attempted a painting that she thought of as Halloween-inspired. Onto a large canvas she painted great Motherwell swaths of black paint—reminiscent to her of burnt cork—and these she lined with narrow, dripping orange strips. Daniel professed to find something arresting in the work, but June dismissed it by saying it looked like something high school students might have wiped their brushes on when they were doing the decorations for the Halloween dance.

Weaver *professed not to believe in inspiration—the work itself* could be counted on to provide more work—yet occasionally an idea for something new came to him in such a way that it seemed it could only have issued from the gods. When this happened, subject, setting, medium, perspective, and tone all came together at once, and Weaver knew enough not to question the gift.

This occurred on an evening in early November, at the end of one of those gray flannel days when it seemed as though dusk fell shortly after noon. Weaver was nursing a bourbon and idly flipping through a book on Degas. Generally he didn't like to look at reproductions because they couldn't offer a sufficient sense of technique, which was what most interested Weaver in the work of other artists, but since this collection was a present from his daughter Emma, he felt an obligation at least to page through it. His other daughter Betsy—Betsy, who understood him as well as anyone—had long ago caught on to the futility of giving him anything related to art—would you give golf balls to a professional golfer?—but Emma, sweet, slow Emma, had never learned.

How long had Weaver looked at "After the Bath" before inspiration— fuck it, no other word would do!—struck? In one instant he was thinking, yes, he'd stood for a long time in the Courtauld Gallery noting how Degas had used lines of blue to approximate her pallor, and in the next second he was trying to remember when he had last worked in pastels, and then, by God, there it was! He slammed the book shut, and it was all he could do to keep from calling her then and there and begging Sonja to come over. Was it any wonder Weaver felt he needed her near at hand every hour of every day?

Harriet was sitting at the kitchen table drinking tea when they came in the back door.

"Don't get up," Weaver said to her. "We're on our way upstairs."

The woman who came in with him stayed by the back door as if she were unwilling to venture far into Harriet's territory without permission.

Weaver spoke to his wife's bewilderment. "Working, Harriet. We're going to be working. If you need to use the bathroom, you'll have to use the one on this floor."

Harriet turned to the woman by the door. "You'll have to excuse my husband. As you perhaps have noticed, when he's eager to get to work he forgets everything, including his manners. I'm Mrs. Weaver—Harriet."

"I'm Sonja House. How do you do?"

"Have we met before, Miss—Mrs. House? You look very familiar to me."

Harriet knew very well from where she recognized Sonja House. For more than a year this young woman had walked past the house on her way to Ned's cabin. And Harriet, in her secret forays into the studio, had seen Sonja's face and body rendered in ink, charcoal, watercolor, and oil. Ned had never shown her a single one of those works, and for that reason, Harriet found a way to make them her own. The best of them, at least those to which she had the strongest response, she removed from the studio—easy enough to do since Ned had always been careless and uninterested when it came to storing, much less cataloging, his work. Those tasks had always fallen to Harriet, Ed Lear, or Gloria, his gallery manager. If Ned missed any of the paintings or drawings she took from the trunk or the locker in the studio, he never said anything to her. Besides, it wasn't as though this work was gone for good; it was all in the attic, Harriet's own private collection, compensation for the thankless job of being Ned Weaver's wife. Certainly Sonja House was familiar to Harriet.

And just as Harriet was wondering how complicated these introductions could become if she were to say, I've met your husband, Mrs. House, and had my breasts exposed to him, Ned said, "All right, Harriet. We can get acquainted some other time."

Harriet stood, tightening the belt of her robe. "Can I at least offer you something, Mrs. House? Coffee?"

"No, thank you."

Weaver set down his easel in order to grab Sonja's arm. "Upstairs. Come on." To his wife he said, "You can play the hostess some other time too."

He picked up the easel again, tucked it under his arm, and repeated his command to Sonja. "Straight ahead. Go."

Before they left the kitchen, Harriet called out, "Mrs. House, do you have a daughter?"

Sonja stopped abruptly on the threshold. "I have a daughter, yes. How did you know?"

"Oh, Ned must have mentioned it. Or perhaps because I have two daughters myself I'm able to recognize something in other women. Did your daughter have a nice Halloween?"

Sonja turned to face Harriet Weaver. "Like most children, she ate too much candy. Are you angry that I'm here?"

Ned was about to insert himself into this dialogue, but even he must have been able to see that something was now playing itself out between these two women that he could not be a part of.

"Angry? No, Mrs. House, I'm not angry, and I'll tell you why. I believe in my husband's greatness, and I would be a shallow, selfish person indeed if I allowed my tiny domestic concerns to interfere with the production of great art. We probably both know something about the sacrifices that have to be made at the altar of Ned Weaver. Now, for reasons he probably hasn't shared with you either, my husband wants you upstairs. You should go with him."

Ned clapped his hands slowly. "Very impressive, Harriet. But it sounded too damn good to be spontaneous. Have you been rehearsing that little speech?"

"For decades, Ned. For decades."

Weaver set up his easel and pastels outside the bathroom door and gave Sonja her instructions. She was to undress and prepare for her bath exactly as she would if she were unobserved. When she climbed into the tub, she could either wash herself or lie back and relax, whichever activity appealed to her at the moment. When she was finished, she should dry herself and get dressed once again. At no time should she look back at the door, open a few inches to allow Weaver to watch from the hallway. She should not think of herself as posed at any time, yet she should also be prepared to freeze in any position, no matter if that meant she was putting a washcloth in her ear or standing on one leg as she stepped in or out of her underwear.

And why, after such a careful setup, didn't it work? Weaver couldn't find any combination of line or color that made the room seem anything but washed out, and he had hoped to make it shimmer with morning light streaming through the window and reflecting off the water. Were the white walls, the white sink and tub, the problem? As Sonja shed her clothes, her flesh, her exquisite flesh, seemed to turn paler and to lose some dimension. Weaver knew November's light was wan, but shouldn't that only serve to accentuate her warmth?

Or was the problem Weaver's vantage point? He positioned himself in the hall because he wanted to make the picture seem, like those in Degas's series, as though the woman were being watched at her unselfconscious ease. Or perhaps Degas's technique was blocking Weaver. He couldn't apply a line or stroke without questioning it, so aware was he of the way Degas's hand had moved over the paper.

And somehow Harriet seemed an obstacle as well, and Weaver couldn't figure out why. He was upstairs, she was downstairs—how could she possibly interfere? Yet each time Weaver saw Sonja in a pose that he might want to reproduce, it seemed as though he could hear Harriet pointing out something about Sonja's anatomy—*look, when she raises her arms to tie up her hair, her breasts lift and you can see that one is larger. There, as she steps into the tub, notice her buttocks tense as the muscles anticipate the water being too hot or too cold.* Had that brief exchange between the two women allowed Harriet to take possession of Sonja in a way he could not? Ridiculous—and to stake his claim Weaver darkened the room he had already created on paper and made a vaguely phallic shape, a shadow characteristic of the day not beginning but ending, hover over the bathtub.

Harriet looked up Henry House in the Door County directory, and when she heard the water running in the bathtub, she placed the call. A man's voice answered, and Harriet said, "Mr. House? Henry House?"

"Yes. That's me."

"Mr. House, this is Harriet Weaver calling." As soon as she gave her name, Harriet realized that she had picked up the telephone with no clear idea of what she hoped to accomplish with the call. Perhaps she had a vague notion of taking Henry House up on his earlier offer. Mr. House, I've changed my mind: *Would you please come over here and beat the hell out of my husband?*

"Who?"

She was tempted to say, You've seen my breasts—remember? Did they—did I—make so slight an impression? "My husband is Ned Weaver. The artist? We met . . ."

"Okay, I know who you are."

"Mr. House, did you know that your wife is here?"

Henry's silence was so protracted that Harriet finally added, "Here, at our house."

"I know your husband's been painting her. Against my wishes. Not that what I say makes a damn bit of difference."

"I think the circumstances are slightly different today, Mr. House. She's not out in the studio. She and my husband are *here*, in the house. Upstairs." When Henry House said nothing, Harriet added, "I believe she's taking a bath."

"Yeah," Henry said. "I saw. I mean, I didn't see her going into the bathroom, but I saw the two of them walking into your house."

Henry House's voice sounded slow and thick, and initially Harriet wondered if her call had woken him, but could it be unconcern that dulled his voice? Could he have been drinking? Could he have found a drug to help him cease to care? If he had, she envied him.

"You saw?" she said.

"That's right. I've been keeping my eye on your little cabin for some time now. Or I follow Sonja just to be sure it's your place she's going to. We don't live so far apart. You're on the lake and we're on the hill on the other side of Fox Harbor. I just came in when you called."

"Mr. House . . . you *follow* your wife? And you just watch . . . her and my husband?"

"Ma'am, I don't know what else to do. I've told Sonja and your husband both that I don't approve of what's going on, but you can see how far that's got me. Now, I don't know what you were hoping to accomplish with this phone call, but if you're looking to get a rise out of me, you might as well hang up. Getting mad hasn't worked. Begging hasn't worked. I'm about at the end of it. Half the time I'm crazy trying to think what I *can* do, and the rest of the time I scare the living hell out of myself with thoughts of what I *might* do."

Of course Harriet couldn't—wouldn't—ask anything of this man. She had wanted to do something to prove, perhaps to herself above all, that she wasn't powerless, but this phone call couldn't do that.

"I'm so sorry, Mr. House."

"Henry. Don't you think we've come far enough we can call each other by our first names?" For the first time in the conversation his voice seemed to lift and brighten. "Besides, what the hell do you have to be sorry about?"

"Ned's my husband. . . ."

"So? He's just doing what he does. He ain't going to stop. Sonja's another story. She's a wife. A mother. If either of us has an apology to make, I'm the one."

Harriet stretched the telephone cord as far as it would go. She was trying to look out the kitchen window, back toward Ned's studio and beyond, to the hill where the woods had thinned to make way for winter.

The bare gray trees reminded her of bones. Was that where Sonja House's husband set up his watch on the cabin? How close had he come to the house? Harriet often left her curtains open, and in summer when she sunned herself on the patio she sometimes tugged her swimsuit down to her waist—had Henry House seen her before the day Ned exposed her? She suddenly felt as though the Houses, husband and wife, were an invasionary force, limiting her freedom both inside and outside her walls.

"Perhaps what I called to tell you, Mr. House—Henry—is that Ned inevitably tires of his models and mistresses. He moves on as reliably as a migrating bird. I've learned to be patient, and if you can do the same, your wife will eventually come back to you."

"Patience?" His laugh was tired and rusty from lack of use. "I ran out of that long ago."

Ned Weaver came downstairs when the phone was still warm from Harriet's ear. He scraped a chair back from the table and sat down heavily. Harriet watched him, but if she had continued staring out the window she would still have known not only that her husband was present but that his mood was dark.

"What's wrong?" she asked quietly.

Ned lit a cigarette. His tossed match missed the ashtray. "How the hell do I know? It's just not working, that's all."

"What isn't?" She spoke so softly she could barely hear herself. If he understood her that meant they were attuned to each other as only those who were ideally mated to one another were. She deliberately did not include love as part of this formulation; love was as likely to hinder as enhance communication between a man and a woman.

He heard. "The picture. The pose. The pastels. The whole fucking idea."

"Degas?"

"I'm beginning to think he's the problem."

Harriet walked over behind Ned's chair and began to knead his neck, upper back, and shoulders. After massaging him just this way for so many years she felt she could discern with her fingers the difference between muscles cramped from overwork and those knotted with frustration and anger.

"If Degas is the problem," she said, digging hard with her thumbs into the ridges on either side of his spine, "then you have to push him out of the way."

Ned dropped his head and leaned forward so she could work her way down his back. "Easier said."

"Well, where would he be?"

Ned laughed into his chest. "On his knees, looking through the keyhole."

"And where were you?"

"I tried something like that. I set up shop in the hall."

Harriet heard water running again upstairs. "Don't you think that's the difficulty? You need to be in there. Degas never showed the faces of his bathers, did he? That's the work of an artist who feels nothing for his subject. And that's not you and this young woman, is it? So go up there and try again. Set up your easel in the bathroom. Sit on the toilet—no, don't laugh. I'm not joking. Try it and see if that isn't the difference."

If Ned hadn't risen at that moment Harriet would have taken hold of his narrow shoulders and helped him to his feet.

Soon the water stopped. The pipes cooled and clanked, and in the basement the water tank hissed with the effort of heating water for the next bather. That would be her, Harriet thought, and climbing into the bathtub after Sonja House had been there would surely feel strange, but then life with Ned Weaver created many anomalies of ownership and possession. Harriet also planned to make her own the pastels that her husband produced during what she already thought of as the bathroom session. She felt she had earned that work.

Sonja had run the bathwater so hot it divided her body perfectly—red below the waterline and pale pink above. Was that why he had left his post in the hall (she saw his reflection in the mirror)—because by doing nothing more than turning one tap more than another she had altered the look of her body? Perhaps his plan for today did not include drawing or painting a woman striped like a beach ball.

He would no doubt come back soon and request something else of her. He might want her to lie naked on the cold tile floor, or perhaps he had gone to fetch ice cubes and when he returned he would order her to replace the hot water with cold, so he could make her lie in frigid water as he told her another artist had once done because he wanted his model to look as blue as if she had drowned. Ah, well, in the meantime she would enjoy her bath while it was hers alone.

These were rich people, yet their bathtub was not longer or deeper than the one in her home. Was that because Mr. Ned Weaver was a short man? And was Mrs. Weaver too afraid of her husband to say, no, I want a tub I can stretch out in? Or had the Weavers, like Henry and Sonja, simply bought a house already built and then shaped their lives to all its borders?

But the temperature and amount of hot water was certainly superior to the House's. Sonja reached forward to cool the bath slightly, and as she touched the tap, it happened. What was it—the sight of her body divided by water and, as with any image of above and below, she reflexively thought of above and below the earth? Was it the feel of being confined to a strange container? Or was she wrong to look for cause at all—John could come back to her at any time, and he needed no summons or invitation.

Perhaps it was a good thing that Mr. Weaver had refused to paint a picture of her son. A portrait by a famous artist would probably have to be displayed, and then John would not be her son so much as a Ned Weaver creation. He would remain forever the age he was in the painting, and Sonja had tried all along to imagine her son changing—growing taller, losing his baby fat and baby teeth, keeping his hands still at his sides instead of reaching for something to fondle or stroke. She knew that sometimes she was not fair to June, in the way she watched her daughter for the alterations that age brought and then tried to picture what those changes would have meant for her boy. But thinking of him aging was one of the few methods she had to keep from dwelling on what was never to change. Or to think of what changes could occur only in the grave. Or, worst of all, to cease thinking of him altogether.

Water that ran belowground was cold, cold, cold, and Sonja turned off the tap and pulled the plug. The spiral of draining water reminded her of a rose's closed petals.

Someone knocked on the door, and before Sonja could answer, Ned Weaver was in the room.

"Put the plug back in," he said. "We're not finished here."

How many times, during their years of marriage, had Henry said to Sonja, when she asked about the spelling or meaning of a word, "Look it up"? He hadn't meant to be harsh or unhelpful. He was merely repeating the lesson he learned from his sophomore English teacher, Mrs. Stamper, who similarly refused to define or spell words for her students. "If I tell you," she said, "you'll forget. But if you look it up for yourself, you'll remember."

Yet not until Henry hung up the telephone following his conversation with Harriet Weaver did he realize they did not have a dictionary in the house, or at least none he could find. He went out to his truck and drove to the public library in Sturgeon Bay, thirteen miles away.

Webster's New Collegiate Dictionary was a red-bound volume so tattered that lengths of string trailed from its cover, but Henry chose it exactly because of its signs of wear. It must have been pulled from the shelf often because of its reliability. He turned the thin pages carefully until he came to the M's, and there he found, as the fifth definition for the word *mistress,* "a woman who habitually fornicates with a man not her husband."

Henry had been sure this was the sense with which Harriet Weaver used the word, but he thought, with so much at stake, he should seek verification. He was equally certain of the meanings of *fornicate* and *adultery,* but he looked up those words as well.

In his mind he drew lines from word to word, and as they connected they combined and together pointed Henry in the direction he had thought all along he would have to go. Now, however, his impulses were validated, corroborated by the words on paper, and not by the Bible or some other manual or guidebook on right behavior but by the impersonal, unbiased, independent authority of the dictionary.

Henry could not decide—should he knock on the door or try the knob and hope to walk right in? If he knocked, he would be giving them warning, and they might have time not only to stop what they were doing but to agree not to answer the door at all. Yet if he turned the knob and found it locked—wouldn't that little rattle raise an even more urgent alarm?

He finally settled on a knock, but with the butt of the gun, a sound to freeze their hearts with fear. They would have to open up.

When he raised the gun to bang on the cabin door, he caught the faint, acrid smell of cordite, though it had been hours since he'd fired the gun.

Shortly after they were married, Henry had asked Sonja—dared her, would be more like it—to walk across the county with him. The distance was only ten miles, from the waters of Green Bay in the west to the great blue expanse of Lake Michigan in the east, and Sonja was confident she could walk that far. Three things made the trek much more difficult than she had imagined. The heat—they set out on a mild sunny morning in August, and by the time they finally arrived back home in the afternoon the thermometer on their porch read ninety-five degrees. Sonja did not care for the taste of beer, but she drank a bottle in a tavern in the town of Adamsport on the other side of the peninsula. Second, she hadn't considered the effect the hills would have. Later in the day it was as hard to walk down as it had been to climb up. She had to shorten her stride when they descended or she would feel the shock all the way up her spine. Finally, when she accepted Henry's challenge to walk across the county, she hadn't realized that of course they would have to walk back as well. She couldn't protest, because he would only tease her—how did she think they would get back home! But that night and every night for the following week Henry massaged her legs with witch hazel, his long powerful fingers working the liniment deep into her muscles.

Now there was no chance that Henry would offer that kind of relief. Sonja could not even allow him to see she was sore, much less to reveal the reason why.

The previous day Weaver had kept her in the same pose for hours. He had her kneel on the bed with her back straight, her head up, and her arms at her sides. Her only relief came when he repositioned her and his easel to accommodate the shifting angle of the light. At the end of the session, she was stiff, but she had no idea that this morning simply descending the stairs would be so difficult. And when June had trouble with her snow boots, and Sonja knelt down to help, the pain in her thighs intensified until it felt as though the muscles had been set on fire.

It was the second time in as many days that she thought of part of her body burning. Yesterday, when she allowed her back to bend and her head to droop for a second, she caught sight of her pubic thatch, blazing in a shaft of light so that individual hairs looked like wires heated to glowing, and today Ned Weaver would want to light that same fire again. Before their session ended, he had marked her position on that itchy green blanket with chalk. If she did not want to be completely crippled tomorrow, she would have to insist on more frequent breaks.

Just then Henry came out of the kitchen, those strong fingers that moments ago Sonja had been dreaming about wrapped around a coffee cup.

"First snow, huh?" Since his voice was cheerful, Sonja knew he was speaking to June. "I remember when I was a kid how I looked forward to tracking up the first snow of the season." Perhaps he was not so removed from the pleasures of his childhood. He had left the house before dawn, and returned with the leather of his boots soaked through.

June said, "Huh-uh! It snowed on Halloween!"

"Just a dusting. We can't count that. Has to be at least an inch, and we got that and then some last night." He glanced out the window next to the door. "And it looks as though it might not be done yet."

"Stay out of the snow before you get on the bus," Sonja cautioned June. "No snow angels until *after* school."

Henry held the door open for his daughter while Sonja pulled June's muffler up to cover her chin. Sonja kissed her and Henry patted her back as she walked out of the house. Together they watched her walk down the driveway, lifting her feet higher than the new snow's height required.

Once the door was closed, Sonja said, "She needs new boots."

"Can it wait until Christmas?"

Although the Christmases of her own childhood were austere, Sonja disapproved of using gifts to provide the necessities of life. "We'll see." She resolved to use her own money for June's new boots.

Henry followed Sonja into the kitchen, where she began to clear the breakfast dishes. Finally he cleared his throat and the statement she had been waiting for came forth. "I'm thinking of buying the old Pepperdell orchard."

"Another orchard." She did not attach a question mark to these words. "Where is this one?"

"Not far. You maybe didn't know it was there. It's up behind your artist's place."

"My artist . . ."

"Well? I'm only saying what's so."

She knew he would probably like nothing better than to draw her into argument, so she held her tongue. She continued to do her chores, and each time she paused and glanced in Henry's direction, she caught him watching her, staring so intently he seemed in doubt of her identity.

Finally he asked, "Do you want a ride over there today?"

"Over there?"

"To your artist's. You're not going to tell me you aren't planning to go?"

Sonja unplugged the percolator and disassembled it. She dumped the grounds on an open newspaper and then put the bundle in the garbage. He was right; she was scheduled to be at Weaver's studio today, and he'd asked her to come as close to nine o'clock as she could.

"Are you wondering how I know you're going over there?" Henry asked.

She lifted the coffeepot. "There's a little left. Do you want it or should I pour it out?"

"Your dress," Henry said. "On the days you go over there you wear a dress."

Sonja shook her head, but she could say nothing to correct him. The truth was, she wore a dress only on the days when she knew she would disrobe, and only then because either of the two dresses she might wear had buttons up the front and were easy to take off and put on. The blue dress, which she'd worn only once, zipped up the back. But hadn't he noticed the many times she left the house for a modeling session in different attire?

"So, as long as we're traveling in the same direction, I could drop you off." He held out his cup, and she poured the remaining coffee into it.

"The same direction?" Sonja trusted neither his smile nor his offer.

"I told you. The Pepperdell orchard. I'm driving over to give it another look."

"Thank you. No. I'll walk."

"Suit yourself." He swirled the coffee in his cup, staring at it as though even his morning coffee should be regarded with suspicion.

On the floor under the table lay a scattering of crumbs from June's breakfast toast. They were lined up like insects following their leader. Sonja was on her way to the closet for the broom and dustpan when Henry grabbed her wrist.

The memory of the night when he dragged her out of their bedroom and into the hall must have leaped into Henry's mind at the same instant as Sonja's because he released her immediately.

"Please," he said. "Not today."

Now she realized why his expression today looked so strange. Although his face was split by the smile that Sonja always thought he turned on as effortlessly as a light switch, his eyes glistened the way they did in the days following John's death.

"I must," she said.

"You must, huh. Like a job, you mean?"

She wished she could say, Very well, today I will not go. Instead I will stay at home, and you will buy another orchard, and every problem of our lives will be solved. On those trees apples as large as pumpkins will grow, and the fruit will be as sweet as candy and one apple will yield a gallon of cider. Oh, why not let the apples from the Pepperdell orchard be all that and more—let them be magic apples and a single bite enough to erase any memory of loss or forethought of grief to come!

"Like a job. Just so."

Henry nodded as though this was the answer he expected. "Okay, go. But do me this one favor, will you? Tell me you're not doing it just for the money. Give me that much respect."

That was odd. She would have thought he'd make the opposite re-quest. "All right. It's so. I don't pose for the money only."

At that, Henry bent low and with one arm made a sweeping motion toward the door as if to say she was free now to leave and with his bless-ing.

The crumbs under the table would have to wait. Sonja jerked open the closet door. Hanging there was the refutation of her belief that we should not make gifts of necessities. The Christmas after John died Henry gave her this coat, made in Germany of soft red wool, hooded and adorned with buttons of elk horn. Of course, she had needed a coat, but hardly one as expensive as this—she had seen it displayed in the window of the Treasure Shoppe in Fox Harbor. But she had no time now to discuss philosophies of gift giving. She pulled out the coat with such speed the hanger clattered and spun off the rod, and she was out the door before further words of argument or, for that matter, of farewell, could pass be-tween them. All the possibilities of Henry's anger were not what hurried Sonja on her way. She was afraid that Henry would ask another question, one she feared she could not answer. Why did she do it, if not for the money alone?

Henry led Buck out of the barn and into the icy dark of—what was it, late night or early morning? The horse obviously did not retain a memory of snow from season to season because his first steps in this year's first snow were, as in all other years, higher and more cautious than usual. Henry would not have been surprised to see Buck lift a hoof and then shake it, just as a cat quivers its paw after stepping in snow. A few fat wet flakes still fell, and when they hit Buck's back he twitched in defense as though summer insects furnished his only memory of something lighting on him from the sky. Henry wanted Buck to move faster, but that wasn't about to happen until the horse accustomed himself to the strange substance underfoot and the muscle-stiffening effects of the cold. Finally, by the time they reached the apple trees, Buck settled into a gait that matched his owner's sense of urgency. Henry's resolve, meanwhile, flickered like the flashlight beam that lighted their way.

Horse and owner were heading toward the hollow at the northeast end of the orchard, near that large brush pile still waiting to be burned. Henry had dug the hole there not only because he believed the soil was less rocky but also because he figured the frost line was deeper. He was right on both counts, but a hole of those dimensions had still taken two days to dig. As he came closer now he saw that the new snow had turned his mound of fresh dirt white while the hole itself remained dark to its depths.

Henry positioned Buck right at the edge of the grave, though it meant he had to back the horse up and lean hard on his flank, a procedure not unlike parking a car.

Henry's reasoning, the thoughts that brought horse and owner to this site well before dawn, was both primitive and complicated: First of all, Henry believed that if something were to happen to him, he could not be certain Buck would be cared for. His dog, Sandy, yes. Even June could take responsibility for Sandy, if it came to that. But Buck couldn't be fed table scraps or sleep under the porch; he needed the kind of attention that required special knowledge of horses. And Buck had reached the age when he needed more attention, not less. No, Buck had been Henry's charge for over twenty years—the horse was, in fact, the first life other than his own that Henry was responsible for; it wasn't right that Henry trust now that someone else feed and stall the animal, much less brush and exercise him and throw down his throat those kidney pills he needed daily.

But Henry also believed that if he and Sonja were to survive to see the darkness at the other end of this day, then maybe, maybe what he was about to do would bring her back to his side and keep her there forever. Among the losses of the past couple years, Henry counted the power to distinguish half-crazed notions from sensible ones, desperate strategies from the practical, but with this plan he didn't care. So many obstacles had come between Sonja and him, perhaps eliminating one might make a difference.

Henry did not shine the flashlight on Buck's head to pinpoint where
the bullet should go. Instead, Henry ran his finger down along the velvet
of the horse's ear until he came to the depression behind which was the
horse's brain, and then Henry quickly substituted the pistol barrel for his
index finger. Henry stood at Buck's side because he was sure once he
pulled the trigger he'd have to give the horse a shove to make certain
Buck fell sideways into the hole. For that reason, Henry didn't face Buck
and aim the bullet at the tip of his white blaze.

The action of Max's pistol was balky and unpredictable, and when
Henry thumbed the hammer back it didn't catch but fell on the cartridge
and in the same instant that the gun fired Henry thought, Oh no, it's not
enough; I need something of a larger caliber for this job.

It was enough.

Buck did not fall sideways, not exactly. His legs crumpled under him
immediately, as if this were the very second in his twenty-six years of life
when the heavy cask of his body finally became too much for his spavined
joints to bear. And into the grave he went, although rather than topple in
sideways he slid, his weight collapsing the freshly dug edge he had stood
upon, and for an instant Henry feared that he might follow Buck into the
hole.

Into the gun's echo came a great exhalation from Buck's lungs, a rush
of air a little like a dog's whoof, and this sound seemed to coincide with
the thump of his fall, and to Henry's imperfect hearing the wind that was
breathing now in the apple boughs might have begun with these vibra-
tions.

Henry had left his shovel stuck in the freshly dug dirt, and now he
used it to refill the hole that he had worked so hard to dig. Although he
threw shovelful after shovelful *down,* since he couldn't see where each
load of dark loam landed, it felt as though he could have been flinging dirt
into the night itself. He didn't shine the flashlight in the hole until he was
certain Buck was completely covered, and then Henry looked in only for
a second. He quickly turned the light off again and continued shoveling.
When he finally set out for home he further saved on the flashlight's bat-

teries and made his way back not by light but by darkness, following the footsteps that he and Buck had melted in the snow.

One of the many myths concerning human tears is that they readily freeze on the cheek in cold weather, and more than one unobservant writer has included such a detail in his story or poem. In truth, temperatures must fall to a rare extreme for such a phenomenon to occur. The relative warmth of flesh and the salt content of tears are enough to keep them flowing until they are stanched at the source.

Sonja stepped in the footprints June had made walking down the driveway. The shorter strides not only helped Sonja keep her footing—there, she could see June slipped there—but they were also a better match for Sonja's sore legs. She kept listening for the growl of the truck's engine—Henry coming after her to haul her back home or at least continue the argument, but when she reached the road with no sign of him, she decided that for today anyway his interest in the new orchard dominated his thoughts.

What had he expected her to say? Oh yes, by all means, let's go deeper in debt to buy an old neglected orchard that is likely a season or two from yielding a useful harvest. Was his mind so hemmed in from living all his life on this rocky peninsula that he could imagine no other way to bring money into their home but to grow more apples?

This first snow had picked up moisture as it swept in over the lake, so by the time the flakes fell on the county they were as wet and gluey as plaster. Even a grass stem or weed stalk could carry its own tiny freight of snow, while the great hardwoods that had shed their leaves barely a month before now looked as though they had found a new way to blossom, crowned with snow flowers in imitation of the apple and cherry trees of May. Not a tire track or footstep blackened the road leading to Weaver's, and as Sonja came closer, in order to linger a few moments longer in the morning's beauty, she took steps even shorter than June's going down the driveway.

Not for money alone . . . Sonja had no artistic talents or skills to capture or save such scenes as this one, and she could no more stop the wind from blowing or the sun from melting the snow from the trees than she could keep her own looks from wearing away with time. But she could enter a partnership with Ned Weaver so that when she stood before him and permitted him to use her image she made her own contribution to the celebration of the world's beauty. And preserved a measure of her humility as well. What Weaver made was the beautiful thing; it was not she. No, Henry, it was not for money alone . . . but money would buy the boots that would keep her daughter's feet warm and dry as she walked out in the loveliness that was the season's first snow.

Someone knocked, and Sonja's first impulse—she didn't know where it came from—was to say, Don't answer it, but Weaver merely cursed—"God *damn* it!"—put the handle of his brush between his teeth, stood, and walked to the door. He would want her to hold the pose, but Sonja used the interruption to drop back on her haunches. Then, and she knew this would upset him even further, but she didn't care—the knock on the door frightened her—she pulled out the blanket she had been kneeling on, the blanket on which he had chalked the outline of her pose, and covered herself. She held it tightly to her body though its rough wool chafed her skin.

Weaver opened the door, and when Sonja saw it was Henry she wanted to ask, June? Has something happened to June? Then she saw the pistol, but still she thought of June. Dagny will care for her until a permanent home can be found. Henry's sister will not take her in—Russell would not want a child in their home—but perhaps the Engersons will adopt June, and she can continue going to school with Betty, and the pain June will feel over losing not only her baby brother but also her mother and possibly her father will lessen over time because June will have Betty as a sister, and all the Engersons, that family of arm touchers and loud talkers, will help June overcome the feeling that she has been singled out for sorrow.

Sonja stepped off the bed, still clutching the blanket tightly to her although only her mother could have gazed at Sonja's naked body more than these two men had. "Please, Henry," Sonja said. "Please. Don't." And though these words might have been construed as a plea for her own life, Sonja's thoughts were still for another. She didn't want Henry to do something that would further degrade him from the decent man he once was. But was this a selfish thought? Perhaps Sonja did not want to consider that she could marry—to say nothing of love—a man who would do what Henry was about to do with that gun.

"Well, well," Henry said. "Isn't this a pretty picture."

For an instant Sonja thought that he was talking about the painting Weaver was working on, and that wasn't fair. Weaver never let her see any of the pictures of her before they were finished. But no, that couldn't be. Henry wouldn't be able to see the easel from where he stood.

Weaver took the brush from between his teeth, and, as if he felt nothing but frustration over this interruption to his work, flung it at the wall. Enough paint was left on the bristles to leave a smear where the brush struck. Sonja tried to determine the color of this blotch, but it simply showed as dark. Logic told her it must have been a shade of green, and Weaver was painting the blanket when Henry knocked. But then why should she assume he was depicting the blanket, the whitewashed walls, the blue-striped sagging mattress, or her chilled pink-mottled flesh as they really were? She had learned that even those paintings of his that looked like photographs were always a mix of what was and what was in his mind.

The gun—Weaver had to have seen it too. He was backing up as people do in the face of danger, yet he began to laugh, and not the strained, nervous laughter born of tension. He threw his head back and barked out a laugh as spontaneous and free as sunlight would be if it suddenly found its way through the clouds and into this room.

If Sonja loved anything about Weaver it was his laugh, but she wished she could clap her hand over his mouth. Nothing was as sure to enrage Henry as being mocked.

"I'm probably going to be sorry I asked," Henry said, "but what the hell do you think is so goddamn funny?"

Weaver waved his hand at Henry's question and continued to step back. "Years ago a friend of mine told me I'd likely meet my end at the hands of a jealous husband."

"Your friend was trying to warn you. You should've listened."

Weaver shrugged. "I thought it would at least be over a woman I managed to fuck." He picked up his cigarettes from his paint tray and shook one to his lips. "But since I got away with plenty, maybe this is how things even out."

Sonja saw now that Weaver had not been backing up in fear; he had moved there to block Henry's view of the painting on the easel.

"Mister," Henry said, "if you're trying to tell me something, you better say it plain."

Weaver shook his head sadly. "I can't say it any plainer. Besides"—he pointed at the gun—"nobody can tell you anything. You've made that clear."

Did Weaver want to die? Sonja couldn't understand what was happening in this room. Did men have some sort of code—if someone wanted to kill you then you had to act as though you didn't care? This was supposed to be about her, yet neither man acknowledged her presence.

"Henry," she said softly, "we should not be here. We should go home. . . ."

He turned to her with the expression he might have worn if she had proposed something indecent. "Home? With you?"

She nodded emphatically and then cut her eyes in Weaver's direction, but only for an instant. She returned her gaze to Henry to see if they might share a recognition as husbands and wives do: Look at this situation we're in—will we laugh about this someday? In our old age will we shake our heads over how crazy we once were?

Henry's eyes gave nothing back to her, and in the ensuing seconds Sonja felt something change in the room, a change that could not be more drastic if the very roof over their heads suddenly lifted away. She knew at that moment what she had to do, no matter what the consequences.

She let the blanket fall to the floor, and she walked naked to the old chest of drawers where her clothes were neatly piled. She began to dress, all the while facing Henry. "Did you come here to shoot me?" she asked him. "If that is what you mean to do, you should do it quickly because I am soon going to walk out the door." Just before she put on her brassiere she had a moment's hesitation—should she tell these men that if they wished to look at her breasts again in this life they should look now because they would never have another chance? And should she kiss each man before she walked out the door—Henry's last kiss from her and Weaver's last and first? No, she had never taunted either man, and she would not begin now. She hooked her brassiere and adjusted its cups but kept watching Henry. The hand holding the pistol was now hanging at his side.

"I just wanted things back the way they used to be," Henry said.

"And you thought you could get that with your gun?" she asked. "I would laugh if I wasn't so frightened."

"In my meager experience," said Weaver, "no one ever gets things back the way they used to be." He blew a stream of smoke toward the ceiling. "Because they never were the way they used to be."

Henry whipped the pistol up to eye level, aiming it directly at Weaver. "You! I don't want to hear a goddamn thing from you!"

"Easy." Weaver turned his head to the side and brought his hands up before his face, but he did this in a casual way that announced he knew he had no powers that enabled him to block bullets.

"From me, Henry?" Sonja asked as she hurriedly pulled on her dress and stepped into her shoes. "Do you want to hear something from me? Because if you do, you must ask for it quickly before I leave. And I am leaving. Alone. You were right: We can't go home together. Never again."

Henry kept the pistol leveled at Weaver, but the threat in his voice was aimed at Sonja. "You stay right where you are."

And she knew he meant her. Nevertheless, she grabbed her coat from the nail and without pausing to button it against November's cold, she headed for the door. She passed so close to Henry he could reach out and grab her. That way, if he were determined to stop her, shooting her would not be his only recourse. But he did nothing to impede her, and then for the second time that morning Sonja was opening a door with the expectation that her husband might come after her with the intent to alter not only her movement but also her mind.

The snow on the other side of the threshold must have come from Henry's boots—did he pause, even today, to stamp his feet before he entered, or had he stood there so long the snow melted off in clumps? She did not pull the door shut behind her, so the sound she had to keep listening for was not the rusty latch but a gunshot. But that could not be right—wouldn't she feel the bullet slam into her back before she heard it? Oh, what a target she must make, her red coat the brightest color amid all those shades of gray and white!

Five, ten, she was fifteen feet past the door and down the walk and still no shouts or gunshots to make her stop. And then she had the strangest thought: They did not need to have her there, in the room with them, not when they could have her picture. That was what allowed her to go free—the naked Sonja on the canvas remained a hostage so the red-coated Sonja could walk off through the snow.

Sonja had just reached the road when she heard one gunshot and then another. The first, she assumed, killed Ned Weaver, while the second Henry would have used to take his own life.

Weaver blew a lungful of smoke at the end of his cigarette and watched the ember glow bright orange. "My friend," he said to Henry House, "I believe you've driven her off for good."

"Shut up. Just shut the hell up." He kept the gun pointed in Weaver's general direction, but Henry's head was turned toward the open door so he could watch Sonja hurry away from the cabin.

"The thing is, I'll be able to get another model. I've never had any trouble in that regard. But frankly, I don't like your chances of finding another woman, certainly not one of her caliber."

Henry took an angry step in Weaver's direction, raising the pistol overhead as if in his fury he had forgotten it had any purpose deadlier than its use as a club. "Goddammit! Can you shut your fucking mouth for just one fucking minute?"

Weaver was surprised at his own behavior. There was an excellent possibility that Henry House would shoot him, yet Weaver couldn't keep from goading the man. Did Weaver have a death wish? He doubted it, but he had never been patient or tolerant of suspense. If his death was coming today, he'd just as soon it arrived quickly.

Nevertheless, Weaver now waited a moment, long enough for Henry's clenched expression to relax somewhat. "You know, if you shoot me, you'll make my wife a very happy woman."

"I don't doubt that. I'm sure she's put up with a lot of your shit over the years."

"Maybe I should have said you'll make her a *rich* happy woman."

Puzzlement flickered in Henry's eyes, and at least for the moment, Weaver's execution was delayed. "An artist's work almost always appreciates right after his death. But like this? Hell, prices will go through the roof. 'Painter murdered by jealous husband.' My God, they won't be able to resist. I wish I could be around to see it."

"Like *that* painting?" Henry pointed the pistol in the direction of the easel.

Weaver stood to the side to examine his work. "That? The unfinished painting he was working on at the time of his demise? Oh yeah. They won't be able to get their fucking checkbooks out fast enough." He dropped his cigarette and crushed it out on the wooden floor. "Are you sure you and Harriet haven't gone into partnership?"

As he looked at the painting of Sonja kneeling naked on the bed, Henry cocked his head to one side just like a patron in a gallery. But then he swiftly brought the gun up to eye level, pulled back the hammer, and fired at the canvas.

Weaver might have expected Henry House to aim at his wife's image, but the bullet blinked a hole through the window in the painting. In the echoing aftermath of the pistol's hollow *crack,* a crow began to caw in the woods behind the cabin. Just as Weaver turned to see if the bird had been startled into flight as well, Henry shot out a pane of glass in the real window.

What was House doing—conducting his own strange experiment into the nature of art and reality? Weaver couldn't speculate for long. His fear was fully awake now and trying to take over his entire being. Each time Henry House pulled the trigger it would become easier to pull it again.

"Hey!" Weaver said. "Let's not get carried away here." He chose the phrase for its note of understatement, yet something cringing in his voice betrayed his rising panic.

House, meanwhile, looked as though finally firing the gun had calmed him. Purposefully, he crossed the room and picked up the blanket his wife had used to cover herself. He dragged it back and tossed it under the painting. He surveyed the room before asking Weaver, "You got turpentine around here, don't you?"

So, Weaver thought, it wasn't enough for House to blow a hole through the painting; now he wanted to wash the paint away. Nevertheless, Weaver simply pointed to the bench where his brushes rested in coffee cans and mason jars—right next to the turpentine and varnish.

Keeping the gun aimed casually at Weaver, Henry House backed over to the bench, unscrewed the cap on the tin of turpentine, and, letting it trickle all the way across the floor, carried it back to the easel. He poured the remainder of the can on the blanket. The oily, piney odor of turpentine stung Weaver's nostrils.

House flung the empty can toward the window he had shot out. He missed, and the tin clanged against the iron bed frame.

"Carried away?" House said to Weaver. "You'll get carried away from here a dead man if you don't get the hell out now." With that, he brought out a box of kitchen matches from his coat pocket.

Weaver knew what he was supposed to do. He was an artist, and this was his life's work being threatened. He should throw himself on that blanket, even if it meant he would be lying down on his own funeral pyre. But Weaver was never much for doing what he was supposed to do.

"This is your show," Weaver said, and, snapping Henry House a quick salute, headed for the door.

Weaver was halfway between the cabin and the house when he heard the studio door slam shut. Because the sound might have meant House was coming after him, Weaver broke into a run and did not stop until he was inside his home. He bolted the lock, and only then did he permit himself a look back.

Each of the cabin's windows framed a fiery dance so perfectly that it looked, just for an instant, as though someone had hung the cabin's drab exterior walls with paintings of orange flames.

Weaver kicked slowly through the wet, charred remains of his studio, looking for signs of color. The fire's ability to turn everything to a shade of gray to black fascinated him. In some instances—the red Folgers coffee can for example—the fire covered the object with black, and in others, the blaze found a way—the iron bed frame, most conspicuously—to bring out the blackness waiting in the material. Fire had the talents of an artist, an alchemist, and a conjurer, and Weaver was quite willing to pay obeisance where it was due.

Fire, however, did not have the power of a god. Yes, it could devour every drawing or painting Weaver had stored in the cabin, it could destroy his brushes and pencils, it could reduce to ash every book and sketch pad in the bookcase—but every time Weaver found a streak, smear, blotch, or shadow of color, he felt it was a victory of sorts. There, for example, was a crimped, blackened paint tube, its label burned off, but when Weaver stepped on it, cadmium red squirted out, its oil separating immediately from the water of the sooty puddle it lay in. That little ooze of color—as without form as a child's toy might be if its plastic melted in the blaze—was enough to reassure Weaver and make him feel as though the forces of composition and selection would find a way to triumph over the anarchy of fire, water, and air.

Even as the cabin burned, Weaver had watched for changes in the flames' colors. He thought, for instance, when the fire found his cache of canvases in the rafters or when the heat melted the lock on the old steamer trunk and the paintings hidden there curled up and then disintegrated, he might see a tiny flare of the flesh tone or lake blue he had worked so hard to mix just right.

He saw none, of course, but then nothing about this entire experience proceeded according to expectation. Weaver would not have thought that he could watch his cabin and all his equipment, along with a lifetime of souvenirs, burn to the ground and feel nothing but a mild consternation over the time it would take to replace his materials and find new studio space. He would not have thought he could contemplate the loss of so much of his work, including all the Sonja pictures, and feel—was this possible?—something akin to relief. The quick pencil sketches and rapid watercolors, the cross-hatched pen-and-ink drawings and the large oils, some of which took months to finish—all, all blazing into ash. Yet Weaver thought, there, now no evidence would survive to prove that once he was so deeply in thrall to a woman that he was reduced to eyes and hands in her presence and neither pair could come as close to her as she had come to his heart. Weaver was free—nothing bound him to a technique or subject of the past. If he wanted, he could start anew. Maybe he'd show his critics a thing or two and become an Abstract Impressionist. Maybe he'd do nothing but watercolors of the sand and the sky for the rest of his life.

And when the sheriff phoned Weaver with word of an arrest made in a Sturgeon Bay tavern, Weaver would not have thought the news could bring him so little satisfaction. Certainly he wanted Henry House behind bars, yet learning that he was there gave Weaver no special pleasure, another surprise since he was usually delighted when misfortune came to anyone who dared oppose, offend, or displease him. And no critic's pen had ever threatened him the way Henry House's gun and match had.

For a moment, Weaver gave up on his search for color amid the ashes and picked up a piece of charred wood that the fire had shaved and sharpened to pencil size. He squeezed one end, and when it did not crumble in his fingers, he began to plan his first post-fire drawing. On paper as white as he could find, he'd sketch the remains of his studio, and he'd use this bit of char to make every line, even if the final result looked like nothing more than a sheet of smudges.

While his hand was fairly trembling to start drawing, Harriet called out to him from halfway up the walk. "Ned, can you come inside for a moment? I'd like to show you something."

He stuck his pencil substitute into the pocket of his peacoat, dropped his cigarette butt into one of the few fire hose puddles that didn't have a skin of ice on it, and, walking through what had once been a wall, followed his wife down to the house.

Once he was inside, Harriet Weaver took her husband's hand and led him up both flights of stairs until they stood outside the door to the attic. "Now close your eyes," Harriet said, "and don't open them until you're inside."

She opened the door, and Weaver breathed in that musty, woody odor that always brought back his childhood—the attic in his parent's house had served as his first studio. And perhaps in the days since the fire Harriet had already begun converting their attic into a workspace for Weaver. The area was heated, airy, and natural light came through the windows at each end. Additional construction would be required before it was an entirely satisfactory studio, but in the interim Weaver could work in the basement. No, he'd be better off buying or renting a small house somewhere in the county, a place where Harriet would have to do more than climb a few steps to see what he was up to. And once he found a suitable place he'd reveal its location to no one.

He heard her pull the chain that turned on the light. "You can open them now," she said.

Harriet had been busy, all right. In a semicircle she had arranged boxes, trunks, an old rocking chair, its back and seat in need of recaning, a small dresser, even the girls' rusty wagon; and leaning against or resting upon these objects were many of the drawings and paintings that Weaver thought had gone up in flames. The bulb still swayed on its cord, and in and out of the light appeared the painting of Sonja huddled in the dunes near Whitefish Bay, Sonja lying on the studio bed looking as though she were in her coffin, Sonja with her arms draped over the tree branch, Sonja braiding her hair, Sonja in the snow, on the beach, among the wildflowers . . . Sonja, Sonja, Sonja. They were not all there—that would have been impossible, but enough, enough. . . .

Weaver turned to his wife. When she lay in the hospital bed with their firstborn child in her arms, Harriet had not looked any prouder than she did at this moment.

Of all the questions he wanted to ask, Weaver could only stammer out the simplest: "How . . . ?"

Harriet shrugged as if to minimize her accomplishment. "I didn't do it all at once, if that's what you're wondering. Never more than one or two at a time. I tried to keep track of the finished works, and once you'd set them aside for a month or two, I thought it was safe to bring them up here. I've numbered and dated them, though I know those are only approximations—"

"You thought it was *safe*?"

"Oh, you know what I mean. I could take a work out of the studio without your missing it."

"No, you're right. I didn't miss them."

"You haven't seen them all. Look on the other side."

Dutifully, Weaver walked around Harriet's display. Sonja with her arms in a pile of fallen leaves. Sonja gazing out at the whitecaps, her hair blown back. Sonja on the office chair. "I guess we're lucky the crazy bastard didn't torch the house too."

"I don't know that *lucky* is a word I'd use to describe any part of this."

Sonja's long neck, her strong jaw, Sonja's hips and thighs, her breasts squeezed between her crossed arms . . . Weaver had to walk away before Harriet noticed his eyes welling up.

From the south window, he couldn't see any of the rubble, but the effects of the fire were plain. Extending a good twenty yards from the cabin, the snow-covered lawn was blackened by soot and ash.

She would almost certainly think these tears had their source in gratitude, and why shouldn't she? Hadn't she saved from the flames the work that meant the most to him, the work that had consumed him—as though he himself had been burning? Wouldn't Harriet, wouldn't anyone, believe that Weaver would have gladly tossed into the fire every other work—the watercolors of the lake, the pen-and-ink drawings of the hawk that hunted the grassy field north of the cabin, the oil painting of the old Ford pickup abandoned at the edge of Blay's woods—that survived from that period if he could only save the Sonja pictures?

How could Weaver make anyone understand that when he looked at a work as quick, simple, and understated as that chalk drawing of Sonja's naked back that what he felt was not gratitude or relief or exultation but pain—pain was in every brushstroke, every palette-knife scrape, every pencil line, and when he walked through Harriet's crude little gallery, he had to think, it's not over, it's not over, it's not over, it's not over.

Once he was certain he wore an expression that would not be misinterpreted, Weaver turned back to his wife.

"I'll tell you what," he blithely said. "Since you went to all that trouble over these pictures, I'm going to make a present of them to you. They're yours, and you can do anything you like with them. You can sell them, you can let them sit up here and gather dust. You can build your own goddamn bonfire and chuck them in if you like. I don't care. I have only one stipulation: If you decide to keep any or all of them, don't hang one where I can see it. Because if you do, I swear to God, I'll destroy it myself."

Harriet's speechlessness could not have been more profound if Weaver had struck her. While she was searching for her tongue, Weaver pushed past his wife, and as he did he swatted at the electric cord, setting the bare bulb swinging wildly. As he descended from the attic, the steps themselves seemed to appear and disappear with the swaying light.

He looked back only once. At the top of the stairs, shadows flickered across Harriet's face and all the faces of Sonja arrayed under the rafters. As far as Weaver was concerned, darkness could take them all.

Harriet Weaver could no doubt have made more money by selling the Sonja pictures one at a time, thus allowing each sale to generate suspense and interest in the next. However, once she decided to release the pictures, she entertained only one offer. Through Ed Lear, Harriet learned of a prospective buyer, the Texas oil millionaire Francis Taub, and she invited him to Wisconsin to see the works.

Harriet had led her husband up the stairs, but this time she waited below while Lear and Taub went up to the attic. The two men saw the pictures arranged exactly as Ned Weaver had. Within an hour, they descended, and Taub was prepared to make an offer for the entire series. The amount he paid has never been made public, but James McCord, Ned and Harriet's grandson, in a 1998 *Atlantic* essay in which he attempted to assess his grandfather's place in twentieth-century American art, estimated that one year after Ned Weaver's death his grandmother received $4 million for twenty-seven pictures of Sonja House.

T*wo days after his release from the state penitentiary in Waupun,* Henry signed the papers to turn the last of his Door County property over to a man from Illinois who planned to build a miniature golf course on the small parcel of land that had been the site of the House family's roadside fruit-and-cider stand. Once that transaction was completed, Henry could leave the state with nothing to compel him to return.

Henry also walked out of prison a single man. Sonja had filed for divorce during his first year behind bars, and though not a court in the land would have refused her anything she asked for by way of a settlement, Sonja wanted nothing but the termination of the marriage. Through his sister and Nils Singstad, Henry heard that Sonja vacated their house soon after his arrest and that she and June moved to Minneapolis.

And Minneapolis was where Henry intended to spend his first night out of Wisconsin. He checked into a motel on the city's western edge, and once he was in his room he opened the telephone directory to the H's. There were seven Houses listed but only one Sonja. She lived on Kenilworth Avenue and obviously in an apartment, since the number 3 followed the address. Finding her was so much easier than Henry expected that he was forced to the early realization that he didn't know what he could say to her. It was a pattern familiar to Henry's entire life, and prison had not rid him of the faith that he had only to plan step one and then the subsequent steps would take care of themselves. But just as he had once walked through a door with a gun in his hand and no sure notion of what would follow, so he sat in front of the telephone in the Tip-Top Motel with no idea of how he might represent himself to his ex-wife.

He had not yet unpacked his suitcase, so he grabbed it from the bed and went back out to his truck. Within an hour of stopping in Minneapolis, Henry was on the road again. He drove through the night and into the following day, and he did not stop for more than gas and coffee until he arrived at the dusty western town where he would live out his remaining years. Henry chose Gladstone, Montana—or did it choose him?—because it seemed a place as unlike his native land as he could find. Whereas the verdant hills of Door County were narrowly straddled by the waters of Lake Michigan, Gladstone was surrounded by miles and miles of windflattened prairie, dry, gritty country in which no color existed that could not be found in a sparrow's plumage.

Henry found work with the Gladstone Parks and Recreation Department. He raked and limed the base paths at the baseball and softball diamonds and chalked the yard lines at the football field. He waxed the floor of the basketball court at the World War Memorial Building, and he pushed a broom across it at halftime. He flooded the rectangle that was the town's skating rink and swept the ice. He mowed the block-long city park and weeded the flower beds along its margin. For these duties and others, Henry House was paid minimum wage, and he accepted it without complaint.

Henry took at least one meal a day, usually supper, at Teed's Frontier Café, and he soon began to keep company with Ann Teed, a pretty, plump widow four years older than Henry. Henry did not keep secret the fact that he was a divorced man who had once been imprisoned for arson, but Henry's explanation of the circumstances of the crime—that he burned down the cabin of a man who had been sleeping with his wife—satisfied Ann. No one in the community was surprised when Henry House and Ann Teed were married.

True to his vow, Henry did not return to Wisconsin, but a part of his past life, in the form of a recurring dream, followed him to Montana. On those troubled nights, it was apple harvest again, and Henry had to fill odd-size containers with fruit, the problem being that those dream apples were already on the ground, skittering and rolling in every direction like marbles on an uneven sidewalk. When Henry was able to get his hands on one, he found it had shrunk to the size of a pea. No matter how many of those apples he dropped into a bag, box, or basket, he knew he would never be finished with this harvest.

But though this dream stayed with Henry until the end of his days, many of the details of his life in Door County gradually retreated to a country whose borders his memory could not cross. He could no longer remember which of his orchards were devoted to Jonathans and which to Cortlands. He couldn't recall the name of the nursing home where his mother lived to the age of ninety or the price he paid for his first house. He couldn't find his way to the Grouse River where he hunted ducks in the fall or to little Elm Lake where he fished for crappies and bluegills as a boy. He couldn't bring back the faces of his children, and that he knew Sonja's image from those paintings that had worked their way into the country's cultural consciousness Henry did not count as testimony to his own powers of memory because that was not his Sonja but Ned Weaver's.

At Henry House's death at the age of seventy-eight, his wife had his body cremated, and she scattered his ashes on the Montana prairie outside of Gladstone. After all, he seldom talked about his life in Wisconsin, and he answered so many questions about that time and place by saying "I don't remember" that Ann Teed House had no reason to believe there was any other place on the planet where his remains belonged. And she certainly could not have known, given the many ways his memory failed him in his final years, that right up to his last hour he still remembered, indeed sometimes chanted to himself like the prayer to a god only he served, a telephone number that he never dialed: Fremont 5-2232, Fremont 5-2232, Fremont 5-2232 . . .

The controversy that to this day swirls around Ned Weaver's death began with the conflicting reports of the three eyewitnesses.

Roger Spragg and Calvin Patent were having lunch at King's Café, and their table was right by the west window, giving them a perfect view of the little egg-shaped bay that shared a name with the town of Fox Harbor. They first noticed Ned Weaver on the concrete pier and figured he must have walked down there from his gallery up the hill.

While the two men watched, Ned Weaver climbed off the end of the pier and began to walk out onto the frozen bay. The month was March, and the county had enjoyed a spell of unseasonably warm weather. Spragg and Patent, lifelong ice fishermen, knew that once the ice became mushy and honeycombed with air pockets, it was no longer safe to walk on. Moreover, they were certain that Ned Weaver shared their knowledge of the conditions. Spragg did yard work for the Weavers, and he knew Ned Weaver to be an observant man who was conversant with the lake's behavior no matter what the season. And certainly from the windows of his gallery Ned Weaver would have been able to note that for at least a week no fisherman had drilled a hole and dropped a line through the ice of Fox Harbor.

For these reasons, Spragg and Patent were certain that Ned Weaver had stepped out on the ice knowing full well that at some point it would give way beneath him and he would drown.

Which is exactly what happened. Well before Weaver reached the midpoint of the bay, he began to stumble as first one foot and then, a few yards farther on, the other went through the ice. He pulled himself upright each time, however, and kept moving awkwardly forward. But then he teetered as though he were trying to balance on a narrow curbstone, and when he toppled over onto his side, water surged up on each side of him with such suddenness it seemed as if the lake had been waiting to receive Ned Weaver. The lake gave him back eight days later, when his body washed up on the rocks at Cooley's Landing, almost two miles north of Fox Harbor.

No testimony regarding Ned Weaver's mood or character—his wife swore he had not been despondent, and she, his daughters, and his friends all said he was the least suicidal of men—could move Patent and Spragg from their certain judgment of what had happened. The man who walked out on that ice wished to die.

No suicide note was found, but many people took as additional evidence that Ned Weaver took his own life the fact that a mere four months earlier a fire had destroyed his studio, along with many of his drawings and paintings. And yes, Harriet Weaver was forced to admit, he had not been able to resume working since that catastrophe.

On the day of Ned Weaver's death, Margaret Carnahan was shaking rugs outside the main lodge at Loch Lomond Resort, directly across the bay from the pier. Mrs. Carnahan and her husband lived rent-free at the lodge during the off-season, and in return they worked to ready the resort for the tourists. Because of the warm weather, Mrs. Carnahan had been doing chores outside throughout the morning. Her observations of Ned Weaver did not jibe with those of Patent and Spragg; to her, Weaver did not appear to be a man searching for the right spot to end his life. On the contrary, he seemed to be walking purposefully across the ice, intent on reaching the other side of the bay. Margaret not only thought he was headed in her direction, she also believed he waved to her as he made his determined way across the slush.

At the time she witnessed Ned Weaver's death, Margaret Carnahan was thirty-two years old. A tall, slender, wide-shouldered woman, she was, on that warm day, working outside without a hat or scarf, and her oaky-blond hair blew free in the freshening breeze. If one were sitting across the table from Margaret Carnahan one would never confuse her with Sonja House. Margaret's close-set eyes, her small mouth, her delicate jaw—really, there is no facial resemblance at all. But from a distance, from, say, across a frozen bay on a day when the sun slants toward springtime yet the light still has a glacial shimmer, why yes, yes, one might mistake one woman for the other.

Sonja House's cancer began in her right breast. Whether this was the breast that Ned Weaver once saw as slightly smaller than the other, or whether he ever represented this difference in his art, is unknowable. One would need access not only to every work in the Sonja series but also to every pose—and then to see how they might have distorted her body's actual proportions. Even that may not have been enough. The truth, finally, resided in the artist's eye and mind.

Sonja was fifty-five years old—still a lovely woman—and living in Minneapolis at the time of the initial diagnosis. She and June moved to the Twin Cities in January 1956, and they shared an apartment on Kenilworth Avenue until June married Daniel Chen and accompanied him to Keene, Minnesota. Shortly after mother and daughter arrived in Minneapolis, Sonja, with the help of her uncle, found work in a gift shop specializing in products imported from Scandinavia—everything from Icelandic sweaters to Swedish lingonberry jam. One day, two tall square-headed gentlemen came into the store and asked in Norwegian for a brand of vodka bottled in Finland. Sonja tried to tell them that the store did not sell liquor of any kind, but the men became belligerent, insisting they would not leave until they received their vodka. Only when Sonja, alone in the shop that day, was about to tell the men they would have to leave or she would call the police, did they break into laughter and reveal their identities—they were Anders and Viktor Skordahl, the brothers she had not seen since she left Norway as a child.

The men were partners in a prosperous farm implement business and in the country for an agricultural convention, and when Sonja said good-bye to them two days later, it was with the promise that she would visit her brothers and their families in Norway. Even after Sonja discovered the lump in her breast, she carried on with her plans for the journey, believing she might never have another opportunity to visit her homeland.

But the closest she came to traveling across the Atlantic was in a dream in which she floated on the sea in a boat no larger than a child's rubber raft. The ocean was calm, so when small waves set her craft gently bobbing she knew it was not from a rising wind but from someone in another boat paddling toward her. She believed it was Henry, but since she could see nothing but sun-struck sea and sky in any direction, she could not be sure. When she woke from her morphine sleep, she was lying on a bed that June and Daniel had moved into their living room. The cancer had spread so rapidly after its discovery that Sonja was soon unable to care for herself, and her daughter and son-in-law took her into their home to live out her final days.

Although June was a practicing artist and a part-time art teacher at her husband's university, she had never asked her mother to pose. Nor had June ever revealed that Sonja was the woman in Ned Weaver's paintings. Since Sonja herself had never made a public announcement of it, June felt she had to respect her mother's wish for privacy.

Yet after all those years of restraint, as June sat by the bedside while her mother drifted inexorably toward death, June was moved to pick up her sketch pad.

She had not drawn in months, but despite the period of inactivity, her pencil soon moved in the practiced ways, reproducing the hollow cheek and the sunken eye of Sonja House in her drugged sleep. June had been sketching for almost an hour—trying especially to capture the way approaching death was erasing the tension from her mother's face—when Sonja woke and looked questioningly at her daughter.

"I'm drawing you, Mom," June said. "Could you move your head this way just a bit?"

Sonja smiled faintly and did as her daughter asked.

Forever after, June regretted making that request because it meant that the last sounds her mother had to hear in life were the words of someone asking something of her.

And it was so unnecessary, since at that point June was no longer sketching her mother as she really was but as she needed to be for the artist to make a satisfactory composition of line and shadow.

Orchard

LARRY WATSON

A Reader's Guide

To print out copies of this or

other Random House Reader's Guides,

visit us at www.atrandom.com/rgg

Questions for Discussion

1. The author compares the novel's form to an Impressionist painting. Where do you think this idea comes from? Does the form work?

2. How might *Orchard*'s nonchronological form be justified? How would the novel change if it were structured differently?

3. Much is made of possession and ownership in this novel; we see shifts in power among almost all of the characters. Discuss some of the manifestations or variations of this theme.

4. Why do you think Harriet Weaver stays with her husband? Do you understand her motivations? What would you do in her position?

5. Throughout *Orchard*, paintings are portrayed in vivid detail. How do these descriptions function in the novel?

6. It is clear that several of Watson's characters undergo emotionally draining experiences. How do these characters change over the course of the novel?

7. What does *Orchard* say about the responsibility of the artist? Ned Weaver has a very definite view on the matter. Are readers likely to share his opinion?

8. What inspires Sonja to pose for Weaver? Do you think her reasons change? Does she harbor any regrets about her decision?

9. Is it enough to say that Henry House is jealous that his wife is posing for Ned Weaver, or are his feelings more complex?

10. What are some of the different attitudes toward art in the novel? Toward artists?

11. Would you pose for an artist?

12. How is a muse different from a model?